MW00577438

ALL *Hallows' Eve*
COLLECTION

A TIMELESS Romance ANTHOLOGY

ALL Hallows' Eve COLLECTION

Sarah M. Eden
Annette Lyon
Heather B. Moore
Lisa Mangum
Jordan McCollum
Elana Johnson

Mirror Press

Copyright © 2015 by Mirror Press, LLC
Paperback edition
All rights reserved

No part of this book may be reproduced in any form whatsoever without prior written permission of the publisher, except in the case of brief passages embodied in critical reviews and articles. This is a work of fiction. The characters, names, incidents, places, and dialogue are products of the authors' imaginations and are not to be construed as real.

Interior Design by Rachael Anderson
Edited by Cassidy Wadsworth, Julie Ogborn, Jennie Stevens, and Lisa Shepherd

Cover design by Mirror Press, LLC
ShutterStock Image #143705743

Published by Mirror Press, LLC
http://timelessromanceanthologies.blogspot.com
E-book edition released August 2015
Paperback edition released October 2015

ISBN-10:1941145590
ISBN-13: 978-1-941145-59-3

TABLE OF CONTENTS

Historical Romance Novellas:

Contemporary Romance Novellas:

OTHER TIMELESS ROMANCE ANTHOLOGIES

Winter Collection
Spring Vacation Collection
Summer Wedding Collection
Autumn Collection
European Collection
Love Letter Collection
Old West Collection
Summer in New York Collection
Silver Bells Collection
All Regency Collection
Annette Lyon Collection
Under the Mistletoe Collection
Sarah M. Eden British Isles Collection
Mail Order Bride Collection
Road Trip Collection

Of Ghosts and Gardens

by Sarah M. Eden

Other Works by Sarah M. Eden

Seeking Persephone
Courting Miss Lancaster
The Kiss of a Stranger
Friends and Foes
An Unlikely Match
Drops of Gold
Glimmer of Hope
As You Are
Longing for Home
Hope Springs
For Elise

One

To be Welsh was to believe in the wondrous, and Enid Pryce was inarguably Welsh. Her family, like so many others, included a great many Englishmen and Scotsmen and even the occasional Irishmen if one looked hard enough. And her family, like so many others, chose not to look overly hard. After all, they need only point to their garden, haunted by a famous, long-dead Welshman, to prove how very strong a claim they had to their nationality.

Enid first made the acquaintance of the ghost of Dafydd Gam at four years old when he caught her pilfering flowers from the garden. The one-time opponent of the 15th-century Welsh rebellion had spoken to her next when she was six and gathering a collection of autumn leaves, something which, she discovered, required his permission.

"You must not take what is not yours." That was all he ever said to anyone, and only ever in response to someone attempting to make off with a bit of the garden.

She wasn't firmly decided on whether or not Dafydd Gam's place in history ought to be viewed as that of a traitor or a hero, a topic of some debate amongst those for whom the contradictory conduct of a man during the course of two wars fought four hundred years earlier was still incredibly relevant—which, if she was being honest, likely included most of Wales—but she knew one thing about him for certain: he was a very particular gardener.

Now a grown young lady of nineteen, Enid had been dragged quite against her will to Bath, along with a great many other young ladies whose families hadn't the means to grant them a proper Season, to mingle with an endless supply of penniless soldiers, younger sons, and widowers looking for someone to raise their horde of unruly children. Hardly a recipe for matrimonial success and happiness.

After a tiring summer—they'd extended their stay beyond the usual time frame in the hope of catching the trickle out of London—Enid returned home a happy failure and, upon arriving, went directly to the garden, intent upon immersing herself in the scent of late summer roses. She also secretly hoped Dafydd Gam would make an appearance. His presence would be a much-needed bit of evidence that she was home again.

"Dafydd," she called out as she walked the familiar paths. "I've come to pilfer your garden. You'd best come scold me for it."

Not even the wind picked up in response. Dafydd Gam had always been too stubborn for something as simple as answering a summons.

I'll have to steal something. She wasn't sure what was most likely to bring down spectral wrath upon her head. Roses usually worked, but the bower looked so nice, and she'd not seen a decent rosebush in all the months she'd been in Bath. It would be a shame to desecrate these. Autumn had not yet rendered the leaves gold. Plucking leaves outside of autumn really didn't make a great deal of sense.

Spring wildflowers would have been a nice option. Had it been spring. And had wildflowers been permitted to grow there. One year an extremely late frost had killed all of the wildflowers in the garden, which everyone of sense had agreed was a message from Dafydd Gam that he found wildflowers objectionable.

Perhaps if she plucked a few stems of rosemary . . . No. That wouldn't work. The ghost didn't generally object to the picking of herbs, owing, no doubt, to herbs being quite useful and, therefore, the picking of them not being particularly wasteful.

Another circuit of the frustratingly ghost-free garden produced no grand schemes. She might have picked any number of things, but Dafydd Gam had grown very stubborn. He no longer appeared every time she made off with something. Summoning him often felt like a puzzle she was required to solve. But after months of Society and balls and uncomfortably fashionable gowns, followed by dire predictions of her miserable future as a speedily aging spinster, Enid was too weary for riddles.

"I don't know what to steal," she announced in ringing tones. "I am perfectly willing to make off with any number of things; you simply have to tell me which."

The voice that answered, though decidedly male, was not Dafydd Gam's. "I am not intimately acquainted with the laws governing Brecknockshire, but I am relatively certain thievery is as much a crime here as it is in the rest of the kingdom."

Enid turned toward the unfamiliar voice. His tone and timbre, though pleasant, hadn't prepared her for the picture he presented. He was not the sort to send entire ballrooms full of women swooning en masse, perhaps, but he suited Enid's tastes quite perfectly. Dark hair to contrast her golden, eyes of a very light blue, tall, and of an active build. His smile hitched up a touch higher on one side than the other, something that sent her heart into a rather absurd rhythm.

And this handsome stranger thought she was a thief who talked to herself in gardens. It was, technically, the truth, but still a terribly unpromising way to make a gentleman's acquaintance.

"One must not take what is not one's own." She paraphrased Daffyd Gam's signature declaration. "But as this is my garden, stealing from it wouldn't truly be stealing."

His brow pulled low in thought. "Why would you be stealing from a garden?"

"To summon the ghost who lives here."

With that, his eyes opened wide, and his smile blossomed fully. "It appears I am in the right place, then."

"You have been searching for a ghost in a garden?"

"I have been searching for the particular ghost in this particular garden." He spoke with utter sincerity. "I should very much like to make his acquaintance."

"You believe he's real, then?" She'd mentioned her family specter to a few people she'd met during her Season and was always met with doubt, both about the ghost and about her mental state.

"I have no reason not to believe it," the stranger replied.

"In that case, sir, welcome to Wales."

Two

Welcome to Wales. Those had become Burke Kennard's three favorite words over the past half-decade. Wales was not his home, but it had come to feel as though it were.

The young lady he'd come across in the garden was watching him expectantly. He wasn't at all sure what the connection was between her intention to pilfer something from her gardens and the ghost who was purported to frequent its paths, but he'd always been of a curious nature and looked forward to learning all he could.

"I hadn't wished to disturb your solitude, miss," he offered by way of apology. "I simply wanted to ascertain if this was the garden I was looking for before foisting my presence upon those in the house."

"Come, then." She motioned him toward the garden's entrance. "I'll foist your presence upon them."

She moved with an unhurried but confident stride. He'd found the women of Wales generally fit that mold. They possessed all the assurance of Society ladies without the pretentiousness. Burke rather liked the combination.

"I promise not to make a nuisance of myself," he said. "I simply wish to ask some questions about your ghost."

She smiled at him, her head turned in his direction, her chin very nearly touching her shoulder. It was an adorably coy look, one to which he was not at all immune. "There is nothing this household enjoys discussing more than our ghost. You could talk all the day long and into next week, and no one would be the least put out with you."

"It has been my experience that the Welsh always enjoy speaking of their history and legends." He held the garden gate open as she passed through it.

She pulled her shawl a touch tighter around herself. "There are two things we never run short on here: tales and rain." Her eyes darted toward the leaden skies. "I'd wager you'll be subject to both before long."

"I've spent a great deal of time in this area of the country. Not even a Welsh downpour frightens me any longer."

She paused on the back terrace and eyed him with a touch of skepticism. "Do ghosts frighten you?"

"Not so far."

That brought a contemplative look to her face. That was another difference between the women he encountered here versus those in Society: they didn't feel the need to hide their thoughts and emotions the way ladies did in London.

"Have you encountered many ghosts?" She seemed to doubt it.

"I have visited Wales upwards of eight times a year this past half-decade."

That was answer enough for her. She gave a quick, firm

nod, then indicated he ought to open the terrace doors. He happily obliged. There was something infectiously energetic about her.

Only a moment later she led him into a sitting room occupied by a gentleman and lady whom Burke was relatively certain were his guide's parents. They looked up, he from a book and she from a bit of sewing, and immediately focused their attention on him.

"What is this, Enid?" the young lady's father demanded. "Have you picked up a stray again?"

A stray? Again?

"No, Father. I found him in the garden."

Enid's mother set aside her sewing. "Dearest, simply because a gentleman happens to be in the garden does not mean you can keep him. You must not take—"

"—what is not yours." Apparently that was a familiar turn of phrase in this family, as his guide—Enid—finished it without prompting. "I hadn't intended to keep him, only introduce him. Father. Mother. This is—" Her brow pulled deep as she turned to look at him once more. "Who are you, anyway?"

"You've brought him in and don't even know his name?" Enid's father clicked his tongue in disapproval. "He really is a stray, and I have told you we won't permit any more—"

"He wishes to ask about our ghost, Father."

All objections ceased on the instant. "Does he, now?" Enid's father rose and crossed to where Burke stood, his hand held out for shaking. "You're most welcome, stranger."

"Burke Kennard," he said, shaking the man's hand.

"Griffin Pryce." He nodded toward the women, both now seated nearby. "This is my wife and daughter. Now"— he indicated Burke should sit—"what is your interest in our ghost?"

This was proving remarkably easy. "I have spent a decade making an academic study of the 15th-century Welsh

Revolt—I am considered one of the leading experts in the kingdom—and am compiling all I can learn into a book for future scholars."

"And you wish to ask Dafydd Gam for information about the Last War for Independence?" Mr. Pryce said. Many in Wales preferred that title for the uprising of nearly four hundred years earlier.

Burke thought it best to answer judiciously. "While I would be interested in his thoughts, I am more keen on knowing your experiences with him. How long has he been appearing in your garden? Do you know what brought him to this particular corner of Brecknockshire?"

"Gam was a Brecknockshire man, you realize," Mr. Pryce said.

"Yes, I know he was born in this county, but not in this particular corner of it."

The entire family puffed up, with Mrs. Pryce speaking for them all. "This is a lovely corner of the county. Why shouldn't a famous ghost take up residence here?"

If Burke wasn't careful, he might have a new Welsh uprising on his hands. "I was not attempting to demean your very beautiful area of the world, nor to cast doubts on anyone's desire to spend eternity haunting its environs. I only wished to discover if the particulars of Dafydd Gam's journey here were known or the reasons why he wandered so far afield from the place of his death to settle so near his home and yet not at his home. It is not doubt that compels me to ask, but curiosity."

He was, after all, collecting folklore and legends to include in his study of the Welsh Revolt, and tales of ghosts fell firmly within that sphere.

"Tradition holds that Dafydd Gam, in his current form, was, indeed, on his way to Penywaun when he was pulled here by the smell of leeks and the sight of daffodils." Mr. Pryce held his chin at a proud angle. "We grow them here to this day."

This tale fit so perfectly the type Burke most wanted to collect. A legendary Welshman, in the county of his birth and ancestry, choosing his haunting grounds based on the presence of leeks, the symbol of St. David, patron saint of Wales, and daffodils, a symbol of Wales itself. "And that is why he remains?"

"That, and, we believe he likes our family. The Pryces have always been very welcoming and careful to obey the rule he insists upon."

Oh, this grew better and better. "He has a rule?" Burke looked from face to face. Their eagerness to share matched his own excitement to learn.

All three Pryces met one another's eye before reciting, in unison, "You must not take what is not yours."

"How do you know that is your ghost's rule?" Burke asked.

Miss Pryce—Enid—smiled broadly, seeming to keep back a laugh by sheer force of will. "Because he told us so."

He froze on the spot as his brain spun those five words about. "Do you mean—Am I to understand that you have *personally* seen your ghost? That you have spoken with him?"

Mr. Pryce did not seem at all impressed with Burke's intelligence in that moment. "How else would we know he was real?"

How else? Were they truly so convinced that all people saw ghosts at regular intervals that their declaration ought not to have been surprising? "I have spoken at length with a great many of your countrymen who believe utterly and entirely that ghosts roam the corridors of their homes or walk the length of their grounds, but have only the accounts of previous occupants on which to base their belief. You are the first to have claimed a personal acquaintance with one."

"Clearly, you've not yet visited Radnorshire." Mr. Pryce hazarded the guess without the slightest hint of doubt.

"I've been there many times. Is there a frequently seen ghost in Radnorshire?" He'd want to look into it if there was.

"There is, indeed." Mr. Pryce's mouth made a perfect, upside-down U. "A frightful ghost, from what I understand, but not nearly so important a figure as our Dafydd Gam." His brows jutted down in a surprisingly well-executed V. Just how many letters could the man's face form? "We should build a memorial explaining how significant our ghost is. I believe he would appreciate that."

"Only if we etch somewhere on it, 'You must not take what is not yours,'" Enid said. "I doubt he would accept the offering otherwise."

"He is very fond of that rule, then?" This was proving far more intriguing than Burke had anticipated.

"Very fond," Enid answered.

"Why is that, do you think?" Burke posed the question to all of them at once.

"Perhaps you'd care to ask him yourself." Enid's suggestion sounded equal parts sincere and teasing.

What was her position on the reality of their ghost?

"An excellent idea," Mr. Pryce said. "If you've no urgent business, Mr. Kennard, we'd be honored to have you here as our guest on the hope that Dafydd Gam will prove generous and show himself to you."

"I would like that very much." Very much, indeed.

Three

"Mother, I refuse to use my feminine wiles on a man simply because he accepts the reality of ghosts. That is hardly a basis for pursuing a courtship."

Mother offered Enid a look of dry doubt. "You know perfectly well that if you had any feminine wiles, we wouldn't be in this predicament."

Predicament, of course, meaning Enid's fast-approaching spinsterhood. An unattached lady did not, after all, reach the horridly old age of nineteen without coming to a very real sense of her impending doom. In quiet moments when no one was looking, Enid indulged in an inordinate amount of eye rolling over the entire thing. She didn't feel old. But what Society declared to be true, Society believed. And Society had declared her decrepitly aged.

"I wish Trev were here," Enid sighed. "He would convince you to abandon the schemes I can practically hear swirling about in your mind."

"This is your opportunity, Enid. I will not allow it to be wasted."

Enid pulled on her gloves, knowing full well that her objections wouldn't be heard. "Would you like me to tie Mr. Kennard to the stone bench whilst you fetch the vicar?"

Mother didn't smile or laugh or swat playfully at the jest. She actually appeared to be pondering the idea.

"'You mustn't take what is not yours,'" she reminded her well-intentioned but ill-planning mother. "Mr. Kennard doesn't belong to us."

"But he could, Enid. With a bit of effort, he could."

This was not going well. "What if I don't want him?"

"Then you will be the next ghost to call our garden home." Enough of a laugh touched Mother's tone to take any real threat from the declaration. "At least be willing to consider the possibility, dearest."

"I will." *For all the good it will do.* Any gentleman whom she had found the least bit intriguing had beat a hasty retreat after only the briefest acquaintance. She couldn't imagine this one would prove any more interested than the others.

Still, he had proven himself a good conversationalist, and he was inarguably handsome. An afternoon in the garden with him wouldn't be the worst thing that had happened to her lately.

Mr. Kennard poked his head into the sitting room. "Your father has declared that the rain will hold off for the next hour. If we are to go speak with your garden ghost, we had best do so now."

"Ghosts likely aren't troubled by the rain," Enid pointed out, not bothering to hide her amusement.

"But I'd wager your slippers *are.*"

She pointed her foot forward, revealing the tip of her ankle boots.

"Very sensible footwear." He clearly approved.

"The Welsh are nothing if not sensible." Her serious expression didn't remain in place long under the influence of his doubtful gaze. She smiled. So did he. Enid had always had a weakness for a gorgeous smile.

"We'd best go see if Dafydd Gam will grace us with his presence," she said.

Mr. Kennard offered his arm, which she gladly accepted. She caught sight of her mother's hopeful expression. Perhaps a hasty retreat was best. Enid did her utmost to speed their departure without actually dragging her companion down the corridor.

She saw the confusion in his face in the instant before he assumed the perfectly contented look that gentlemen were taught to wear in a lady's company. His manner of dress and address had already convinced her he belonged to the gentry at the very least, but from which of England's families did he hail? And from which corner of the kingdom? She knew he wasn't Scottish. He most certainly wasn't Welsh.

"You have grown very contemplative, Miss Pryce. I hope you are not displeased with our outing."

"I am not at all displeased. I enjoy searching for Dafydd Gam. In fact, I was undertaking precisely that errand when you arrived this afternoon."

"Ah." The noise was one of understanding, but he still appeared confused. "What was it, then, if I may ask, that had you looking so ponderous a moment ago?"

Enid never had mastered the art of feigning sheepishness. Any person who spent more than a few minutes in her company quickly realized she was overly talkative and prone to speak her mind, so there seemed little point pretending to be anything other than herself. "I was pondering you, sir."

His eyes pulled wide, and she swore his mouth even hung the tiniest bit open. Her laughing response was as unavoidable as it was unforgivable.

13

"Am I such a mystery?"

Was he attempting a jest? She couldn't be entirely certain. Still, that seemed the most likely interpretation. "A scholar with the speech and bearing of a gentleman, who rides about the countryside searching for ghosts? What could possibly be mysterious in that?"

Oh, that smile of his! Not only was it quite, quite handsome but a far preferable response than the expressions of horrified disapproval her boldness usually elicited.

They stepped out into the still-damp gardens. The heavy sky cast doubt on Father's prediction of an hour of dryness.

Mr. Kennard's gaze had turned to the sky as well. "I am not at all confident the heavens are smiling upon our endeavor, Miss Pryce."

How easy he was to speak with. Too many of the gentlemen she'd known in Bath had been unbearably pompous. She found herself wishing she knew more about him, that she could count him as an acquaintance rather than merely a step above a stranger.

"From which part of the country do you hail?" she asked.

If he was surprised by the abruptness of her inquiry, he didn't allow it to show. "My family resides in Cheshire, though I currently call Cambridge home."

"Has your family been in Cheshire long?"

He nodded, something in the gesture almost heavy. "As my father is fond of saying, 'Since time immemorial.' Most of the Kennards are convinced Cheshire would simply cease to exist if not for our residency there."

"And, yet, here you are in Wales. Have you inquired after the continued existence of Cheshire while you're away? One would hate for its demise to go insufficiently mourned."

His shoulders shook with a silent laugh. "I am certain my grandfather would have announced on the floor of Lords if something had happened to the family seat."

The floor of Lords? Does he hail from the aristocracy,

then? The possibility set her mind spinning. The Pryces had only the barest claim on the gentry. Was she truly walking about in her garden with the grandson of a lord?

"Mind the puddle, Miss Pryce." He indicated a few paces ahead where a puddle spread nearly the entire width of the path.

She slipped her hand from his arm and tiptoed around the edge of the water. "What does your family think of your interest in Wales?"

Mr. Kennard managed to navigate the puddle as well. "My father is very much like his sire. He disapproves of anything not considered a common pursuit for a gentleman of leisure. He has no comprehension of the misery I would feel spending my days at cards or billiards. Even a bruising ride can only do so much to break the monotony."

She could appreciate his struggle but doubted he realized hers. "Imagine how that boredom is compounded when one's choices are limited to either needlepoint or gazing serenely out of windows."

"Under such dire circumstances, one would, no doubt, flee to the gardens and threaten to steal things."

He remembered that part, then.

They reached the innermost circle of the garden where a statue of Hermes stood guard over the expanse.

"I have to steal things," she said.

"And why is that?"

She turned up the collar of her spencer jacket against the quickly stiffening wind. "Because doing so is the one thing that regularly summons Dafydd Gam."

"Stealing things from the garden?"

Enid nodded. "We aren't at all certain why he dislikes our pilfering so much. And, admittedly, it doesn't always bring him around."

"Oh." He pulled the single syllable out long. "That is the reason for his rule about taking things that aren't one's own."

"Precisely." Enid glanced around. "What shall we steal?"

"What is most likely to earn his ire?"

"Daffodils." She didn't even have to ponder the answer. "But they aren't in season just now. I'm afraid anything else is not at all guaranteed to be effective."

Mr. Kennard took whatever disappointment he felt in stride. He held his arm out to her once more. "I am in no hurry. Let us enjoy the momentary good weather and simply wait to see what happens."

He didn't have to issue the invitation twice.

B urke had spent a great many afternoons in conversation with Welsh men and women, but he couldn't say he'd truly enjoyed any of those visits as much as he was enjoying this one. Miss Pryce was a delight in every sense. She was witty and energetic. She didn't shy away at expressing her opinion. She was pretty without allowing that, and that alone, to define her.

It was, of course, a great deal to decide about a person based on a single thirty-minute discussion, but she made no attempts at artifice. He would wager he knew her better than some people he'd spoken with dozens of times.

"What is this, Enid?" A decidedly Welsh, inarguably male voice floated across the otherwise deserted garden. "Have you finally found someone as daft as you are, who'll sit here under threatening skies on the thin promise of an appearance by a man dead these four centuries?"

Far from offended, Miss Pryce grinned broadly and hopped up from the bench they were occupying. "Trev!" She rushed toward this newcomer, a gentleman likely very near to Burke's age, and was greeted with an enthusiastic embrace.

Burke felt a surprising stab of jealousy at having lost her companionship so easily and so completely to "Trev." *I am becoming a nonsensical gudgeon.*

"Is this another of your strays, Enid?"

Burke eagerly hoped to hear about Miss Pryce's strays. He would wager it was a diverting tale.

"I do hope this family means to eventually allow me to live that down." Miss Pryce was all offense and wounded pride, though it was clearly nothing more than an act.

Burke stood.

"Trevor Pryce." Miss Pryce's brother, it seemed. He made the expected, small bow of greeting.

Burke returned it. "Burke Kennard."

He had once contemplated giving a false surname whilst going about his studies. Seeing recognition dawn in the young Mr. Pryce's eyes made him wonder once again if he'd been wrong to abandon the idea.

"Mouldsworth's Kennards?"

That brought Enid's surprised gaze to her brother once more. "The Marquess of Mouldsworth?"

And thus it would begin. All of the pretense and posturing. Why must he forever be Mouldsworth's grandson and never simply Burke?

Mr. Pryce grinned at his sister. "Did you not realize you were sitting on a grimy bench with the grandson of a marquess?"

"I can't say I did."

"Would it have made a difference?" Burke asked quietly.

Miss Pryce seemed to genuinely contemplate the question. "I would imagine the grandson of a marquess is in the habit of carrying an extra square of linen on his person. If

I'd known your full identity, I might have asked you to wipe the bench off a bit. My maid will be furious when she sees the state of my spencer."

Quick as that, the weight that had settled in his stomach disappeared. Miss Pryce was like a fresh breeze on a stifling summer day.

Mr. Pryce brushed something from his nose. Miss Pryce wiped at her forehead. Burke had only a moment to ponder the action before he, himself, was hit squarely on the cheek with a drop of rain.

"Do grandsons of marquesses melt in the rain?" Miss Pryce asked.

Her brother answered. "We're about to find out. Unless Mr. Kennard can outrun a cloudburst."

As it turned out, none of them could. They were all three soaked to the skin by the time they rushed through the terrace doors at the back of the Pryces' home.

"Were you simply passing through, Mr. Kennard, or were you to stay for a time?" young Mr. Pryce asked.

"Your parents offered me their hospitality. I believe my belongings were taken to a spare bedchamber."

"Come along, then." Mr. Pryce slapped him on the shoulder. "You have dry clothing awaiting you somewhere in this old pile of rocks."

"Let us hope there is also an accommodating fire somewhere as well." He walked up the stairs beside his new friend. "If I weren't entirely enamored of Wales, your tendency toward drowning rainfall might put me off the place entirely."

Mr. Pryce sent him a sidelong look. "I suppose it never rains in Cheshire."

Burke puffed out his chest. "I, sir, reside in Cambridge."

He received a look of feigned horror in return. "A Cambridge man? This is an Oxford family, I will have you know."

Only as they reached the first floor landing did he take

note of the sound of soggy footfall behind them. He'd forgotten Miss Pryce entirely. There she stood, only a few paces behind them, clutching the collar of her spencer, wet hair plastered to her face, shivering. What sort of gentleman was he to have so quickly turned his thoughts away from a lady in distress?

Except she didn't appear to be in distress. She didn't seem overly bothered by her misery. Her eyes danced above a perfectly contented smile. "I am creating something of a pond here on the landing. Perhaps we could retake our journey toward dry clothing and accommodating fires."

"Is your sister always this practical?" Burke asked.

Mr. Pryce laughed. "Practical? Enid is as daft as St. Abner's Day."

Miss Pryce shook her head. "There is no such day."

"Which makes it particularly daft, does it not?"

She pursed her lips and raised an eyebrow. "Brothers are, without argument, the very worst sort of siblings."

"You said 'brothers,' though I believe the correct word is 'sisters'."

The Pryce siblings were proving enormously diverting.

"I have two sisters and two brothers," Burke said, "and I have to agree with—"

His companions watched him with matching grins and eager anticipation. Heavens, if his own family was this enjoyable to spend an afternoon with, he might make the trip to Cheshire more often.

"—neither of you," he finally finished. "It is, in fact, *older* siblings who are the worst sort."

Miss Pryce turned a triumphant gaze on her brother. "I still win."

Mr. Pryce made a bow of acceptance. "In deference to your victory, I will allow you to slip past us so you can rush to your bedchamber before you catch your death of cold."

"You would mourn me, would you?" Miss Pryce stepped past them both.

"I suppose." It was a very brotherly response.

She was soon a great many paces ahead, and Burke and Mr. Pryce were once again making their walk toward warmth. "Your sister is quite unlike most young ladies in society, Mr. Pryce."

"Call me Trevor, please."

He nodded his agreement and made an offer of his own. "Burke."

"Yes, Enid is unique." Though he'd teased his sister mercilessly, Trevor's fondness in that moment could not be mistaken. "She has only just returned from a Season in Bath, and I am beyond relieved to see that it did not fundamentally change her. Society has a way of convincing young ladies to conform to the same bland mold."

"In my experience, a *London* Season is most likely to create conformity in a young lady. A *Bath* Season is most likely to create uncertainty."

Trevor stopped once more. "Uncertainty?"

Not wishing to overly alarm Trevor, Burke kept his response quick and unconcerned. "Too many of the gentlemen who spend the Season in Bath do so because there is little to recommend them. That leaves the young ladies who flock there, often for reasons of economy, with very few desirable choices and a higher likelihood of what their families, Society, and, too often, they themselves deem 'failure.' I have seen it plant seeds of doubt in even the most confident of ladies."

Trevor's brow drew as his gaze turned toward a closed bedchamber door just a step beyond where they stood. "You don't suppose Enid thinks ill of herself for having returned unattached. Though she's my sister and I enjoy ruffling her feathers a bit, I'd hate to think she was unhappy or, worse still, that she'd feel she needed to change herself."

"I have only known Miss Pryce for a few hours," Burke reminded him, "so I am no authority. I have, however, seen

Bath twist too many hearts to not feel I needed to warn you of the possibility."

Trevor nodded. "Thank you. I will be vigilant."

Did Miss Pryce realize how very fortunate she was to have a family who cared so very much? Burke had only ever dreamed of that.

* * *

"If Trev does not stop looking at me as though he fears my untimely demise is imminent, I will have no choice but to brain him with his own walking stick, if he has one, that is."

Burke didn't even try to hide his amusement. "If he has one *what*? A brain to have bashed or a walking stick to bash it with?"

She lifted a shoulder. "I have my doubts about both."

The rains had still not let up, though the family had long since finished dinner. Miss Pryce stood near the tall windows in the drawing room, looking out over the dark expanse as though she was contemplating dashing out into the night to escape her brother. Burke felt a little guilty about that, but only a very little.

"Perhaps he fears you took a chill this afternoon," he suggested.

She dismissed that immediately. "We are Welsh. We have spent our entire lives wet, and we've not died of it yet."

Burke turned to look more directly at her. "How long has it been since you and your brother were in company with one another?"

"Three months. He refused to go to Bath. I was not permitted to refuse."

She really hadn't enjoyed her Season, it seemed. "Would you have preferred London?"

"I would have preferred Wales." She flashed him a smile that would have melted even the most cynical of gentlemen.

Perhaps it was fortunate she hadn't made her bows in Town. Between her wit and vivacity and that smile, the *ton* would have been brought to its knees.

"What of you, Mr. Grandson of a Marquess? Do you prefer London to Bath?"

How was it she could fashion him such a ridiculous moniker—focused as it was on an aspect of his identity he usually preferred be left unacknowledged—and, rather than ruffle his feathers, make him laugh?

"If you must call me something other than Mr. Kennard, I would far prefer Burke to Mr. Grandson of a Marquess."

She folded her hands where they hung in front of her, the posture one of theatrical innocence. "But think of the scandal, sir. Using Christian names would be unthinkable. What would my mother say?"

"Besides 'Fetch the vicar'?" At Enid's sudden but subtle stiffening, he added, "Does not every mother of an eligible daughter have those three words fresh on the tip of her tongue?"

His companion relaxed by degrees. "Mine certainly does, for all the good it has done her."

"Perhaps your brother will give her reason to make use of it."

They both looked over at Trevor, seated across a chessboard from his father. Burke had never before seen anyone laugh whilst playing chess, but Trevor had done so regularly throughout the evening.

"He spends far too much time at Oxford to ever strike up a courtship."

"He's a scholar, then?"

Enid nodded. "He hides it well, does he not?"

Burke could not recall the last time he'd so thoroughly enjoyed another person's company. She was a delight.

"I hope we will have a chance to return to the gardens tomorrow," he said.

"Father believes it will rain all day, which is generally a good predictor of dry weather." She stepped away from the window but glanced at him as she did. He hoped she meant the gesture as one of invitation to take a walk about the room with her, as that was how he intended to interpret it. "But even if the heavens cooperate, I cannot guarantee Dafydd Gam will. He is terribly temperamental."

"And I do not wish to trespass upon your family's hospitality longer than I must."

She didn't immediately answer, though he could see thought after thought flit across her lovely face. "We would none of us mind if you extended your stay." She spoke more quietly than was usual for her, but her sincerity could not be doubted.

"What if you discover, after knowing me for more than six hours, that you do not particularly care for my company?"

She daintily waved her hand, dismissing his objection. "We will simply toss you out and lock the door."

Heavens, he couldn't imagine anything he would enjoy more than spending another day—or several—in her company. "I accept your challenge, Miss Pryce."

Her dancing brown eyes turned toward him once more. "Did I issue a challenge?"

"Indeed, and I intend to make quite certain that you still particularly care for my company after knowing me better."

They completed another circuit of the drawing room. The candles were flickering low. Mrs. Pryce had nodded off in an armchair near the low-burning fire. Trevor still grinned over his game of chess, though his father seemed quite serious. Enid smiled at Burke's side.

This home was peaceful, and its occupants were happy and loving. For his part, Burke hoped the fabled ghost took his merry time making himself known, for then Burke would have a ready excuse to remain.

Five

Enid had only ever seen such a large percentage of the local population gathered in one place when marking a birth, marriage, or death. Not one of those things had transpired, yet there they all were, leaning against the iron fence surrounding the Pryce family garden, watching Burke intently.

"Are they also hoping to catch a glimpse of your ghost?" Burke asked. She likely shouldn't think of him by his Christian name, but she'd allowed herself the silent indulgence the night before and found it had already become an unbreakable habit.

"Ghosts are hardly reason for excitement. An Englishman traipsing about in the mud, however . . ." She let the sentence dangle.

"I am making a spectacle of myself?" Unlike every other gentleman she knew, excepting her father and brother, he did not seem overly concerned about appearing less than perfect. She liked that about him. "Perhaps if I sang a verse or two of 'Ar Hyd y Nos,' they would find me less of an oddity."

"In the original Welsh?" she pressed.

"Of course."

Her heart flipped about inside. He knew Welsh folk songs *in Welsh*. He likely even spoke the language a bit. She'd been mocked in Bath for the Welsh turn in her voice, not having been trained to sound more English, as so many of the wealthiest Welsh families insisted their children be. Trev had admitted to much the same treatment at Harrow and Oxford. Enid had simply assumed the English weren't overly fond of the Welsh. But Burke was. So much so, in fact, that his life's work involved studying Wales's history and people and culture.

An idea suddenly entered her mind, and, true to form, she spoke it immediately. "Good heavens. What dunderheads we are being. You have come to Wales to gather folklore and tales, and here you are surrounded by an entire town of Welshmen, and you've not spoken to a single one of them."

She could see the moment her idea became clear to him. "Would they talk to me, do you think? Even with my Englishness on full display?"

The grandson of a nobleman and, yet, he was humble, unsure of his reception amongst a group of people who would likely go entirely unnoticed by most in his position. Was it possible to continue liking him more with each passing moment?

"They might be wary at first," she acknowledged. "But as soon as they realize how sincerely you wish to learn from them and how deeply you value them as Welshmen, they will spill every story they know into your ears."

"Would you be willing to make the introductions?" Heavens, but he looked nervous. "Your endorsement would, no doubt, ease any concerns they might have."

She offered him her hand, a gesture she knew would earn her the censure of all the judgmental matrons in Bath but which, she found, perfectly suited the moment. He slipped his hand in hers and allowed himself to be led toward the crowd.

"Neighbors," she greeted them. "This is Mr. Burke Kennard, an Englishman."

The expected ripple of curiosity mingled with disapproval made its way around the fence.

"He is here in Wales because he finds us far better company than his countrymen."

She heard Burke stifle a laugh. How rare it was to find someone outside of her family who shared her sense of the ridiculous.

"Further, he wishes to learn more of our culture and history. He is here, most particularly, to make the acquaintance of Dafydd Gam."

Nods of approval bobbed in all directions.

"And, while Dafydd Gam is being his usual difficult self, I am hopeful that we can find tales enough to share with our visitor so his love of this land will grow all the more."

"Have you told him of Arwel the Uneven?" Leave it to the butcher to think of that tale first.

"I have not," Enid said. "Perhaps you'd care to share."

The butcher leaned against the iron fence. "Arwel did not start out uneven, having been born with all his limbs and essential bits. But when one earns one's keep felling trees, one ought not to be loose-gripped with the ax."

Burke was mesmerized, just as Enid knew he would be. She'd grown up with a father who loved a good tale and a brother who craved knowledge the way most gentlemen craved brandy. Three months amongst the gentlemen of the *ton* had left her despairing of ever meeting one who shared her family's odd taste in diversions. Yet here he was, a fascinating gentleman who had quite literally walked into her life.

As one tale led to another, Burke grew entirely at ease with the gathering, at one point slipping through the garden gate to sit among them, jotting notes on a stack of small-cut squares of paper he pulled from his jacket pocket. He repeatedly encouraged them to share more.

Old Mrs. Gowans was called upon to share a song but shied at the suggestion.

"I know it only in Welsh. The English don't care for our language."

Burke's gentle smile immediately began working its magic, and Mrs. Gowans hemmed and hawed a bit. But when he, as he'd jokingly suggested earlier, began singing to her in Welsh, the dear old woman simply melted. She joined in, and soon the entire gathering took up the familiar tune.

Enid watched in amazement. He was magical. Wonderful. "I want him to stay," she declared almost silently.

A voice whispered from behind her, "You must not take what is not yours."

She spun about and came face-to-face with the very apparition they'd been hoping to summon. Only the day before, she'd come to this garden calling for Dafydd Gam, but in that moment, she wished him far, far away.

Burke had only come to meet this ghost, and once he had, he would leave.

"I haven't stolen anything," she whispered. "And I promise I won't, only please go."

One of his bushy brows arched high while the other dipped low. His ghostly mouth turned in displeased confusion.

Enid glanced over at Burke and the gathering. They were all quite distracted by their song. Now was her opportunity. "I need you to stay out of sight for a day or two."

Dafydd Gam folded his arms across his chest. His broad shoulders pulled backward in defiance.

"I am not above bribery," Enid said. "I will bring you sweets from the kitchen."

He tossed her a look clearly meant to convey what a ridiculous idea that was. He even motioned at his translucent belly.

"Or—" Enid thought quickly. How did one go about bribing a ghost? "I will solemnly vow not to pilfer any daffodils next spring."

He was beginning to look more than a little put out with her. It had been a half-baked offer, really. No one ever stole daffodils from Dafydd Gam's garden. Not ever.

"I have nothing to offer just now, but I will think on it. Only, please, go. He will leave once he meets you, and I am not ready for him to desert me yet."

Dafydd Gam held up a single finger.

"One week? You'll stay away for one week?" She knew the guess was optimistic.

He shook his head, keeping that one finger extended.

"One day?"

He nodded and disappeared.

One day it was, then. She had one single day in which to either convince Burke Kennard to remain even after his reason for coming had been accomplished, or to think of an offer tempting enough to convince Dafydd Gam to extend his "one day" into a week. Or two.

"And did Mairwen marry the squire, or was she convinced to go forward with the marriage to the aged knight?" Burke's entire attention was on Mr. Jones, the blacksmith, who most certainly knew how to weave an intriguing tale.

"Sadly, her father's will carried, and she was forced into the arranged match. The squire, bereft of hope, followed Henry to France and was killed at Agincourt." Mr. Jones sighed loudly. "Upon hearing of his death, Mairwen died of a broken heart."

"Why is it the unfortunate squire or the heartsick Mairwen aren't the ones haunting these gardens rather than Dafydd Gam?" Burke addressed the question to everyone at once. *Everyone* turned immediately to Enid.

She held her hands up in a show of innocence. "Leeks and daffodils," she reminded him.

"And how is it you know he is Dafydd Gam?" Burke asked. "Does he introduce himself as such?"

That gave her pause. Generations of her family had known who he was, but who had been the first to discover it? Dafydd Gam never said anything beyond the one sentence.

"We've simply always known," she said.

He readily accepted her answer. "We'll have to ask him, I suppose." His gaze slid around the garden. "If he ever makes an appearance."

Enid covered her blush of guilt by turning to face the gardens as well. "It is very strange. Who would ever have guessed he would stay away so long?" *I am going to be struck down by a vengeful deity.*

"I think I had best walk Miss Pryce back inside. Her family will be wondering what has delayed her so long." Burke's manners were impeccable, as always.

Before beginning their trek to the house, he turned back and waved to the townspeople. They waved back enthusiastically. He'd won them all over so quickly and so easily.

I want him to stay, Dafydd Gam. Somehow I will find a way to keep him here with me.

A second afternoon passed without a single sighting of anyone no longer living. Burke had expected his stop in Brecknockshire to be a quick one, a few hours at most, and yet he wasn't the least put out. Mr. Pryce had allowed him to peruse his small library in the hope of finding something expounding upon the history of their ghost. Mrs. Pryce, though clearly awed by Burke's exalted connections, had, nonetheless, not treated him any differently than she had when he'd first arrived. He and Trevor had passed a late evening sharing tales of academic woes and explaining, with a level of detail only a fellow scholar could appreciate, their individual areas of expertise.

Enid, however, was the very best part of his unexpected sojourn. He couldn't help smiling every time he saw her approach. Their conversations were, without exception, enjoyable, entertaining, and far superior to any he could recall having with anyone else of his acquaintance. She clearly did not have the deep passion he did for 15th-century Welsh history, but she never belittled his intense interest and even offered insights into who in the surrounding areas might have tales to share with him. And she spent all of the past two afternoons with him in the garden, watching for their ghost.

Trevor had joined them on an impromptu picnic. Enid had, during Burke and Trevor's admittedly long discussion of least-favorite subjects in school, drifted off to sleep, curled into a C on the picnic blanket. Trevor had eventually wandered to the far side of the gardens to examine a tree he found particularly intriguing, he being a botanist.

Burke leaned back against the trunk of a nearby tree— one apparently too dull to capture Trevor's attention—and took a moment to let the idyllic nature of his current situation settle over him.

Wales truly was a magical place.

His gaze drifted, as it so often did, to Enid. He'd despaired of ever meeting a lady like her, one who eschewed false pretenses and who exuded such a love of life. His income was insignificant, the Mouldsworth estate and fortunes being very tightly held in entailment. Unlike the rest of his family, he was not willing to crush himself under piles of debt in order to live exorbitantly. Most young ladies of the *ton* would consider him inarguably ineligible. But Enid lived a quiet and, by the standards of the gentry, simple life. She, having a brother in Burke's precise circumstances, understood the principles of economy. If any lady might be willing to consider him as a prospective suitor, she might.

Lud, he was getting far ahead of himself. "One would think I was on the verge of dragging her off to Gretna Green at any moment."

"You must not take what is not yours."

Burke's head jerked in the direction of the stern voice. There, translucent, menacing, and plain as day, stood a ghost. An honest-to-goodness ghost.

A ghost.

He'd not entirely dismissed the possibility that the specter was real but was still entirely unprepared for coming face to face with one.

"Good afternoon." The rote greeting felt utterly ridiculous in that moment. His thoughts were too jumbled and circling in too many directions for clear thinking.

He'd formed in his mind an image of how he believed Dafydd Gam had looked, and the specter did not resemble that imagining at all, and not simply because this Dafydd Gam was not solid.

The original Gam had received that name in reference to a problem with his eyes, though there was some debate as to whether that something was a squint, eyes that crossed, or an eye that was missing. There appeared nothing out of the ordinary in the ghost's eyes. Surely the Pryces' predecessors would have known this about the well-known historical figure. Burke had assumed that aspect of his person had been their means of identifying the ghost as the famous Welshman.

That riddle, however, slipped to the back of his thoughts, another one taking its place. *You must not take what is not yours.* Had he been accused of plotting to kidnap Enid? He supposed he had hinted at that.

"I meant my comment about Gretna Green in jest," he told the ghost. *Ghost. Good heavens.* "I don't actually intend to run off with her."

The ghost set his fists on his hips and glared at Burke with unmistakable doubt.

"I swear to it. Indeed, I cannot imagine she would go with me even if I asked. I'm not at all certain she will allow me to return here again." And once she knew he'd seen her garden ghost, Enid would consider Burke's business in Brecknockshire as complete. He'd have no choice but to leave without having earned even the smallest bit of her regard.

He could not allow that to happen.

"I don't suppose you could be persuaded to keep out of sight for another day or two?"

The apparition threw his hands upward, gaze following suit. Apparently he found Burke's request particularly annoying.

"I am only asking for a few days," Burke said. "You needn't even stay away altogether, only whilst Enid and I are together. So long as she doesn't know I've seen you, I won't have to leave."

The ghost shook his translucent head, not in refusal or denial but in growing irritation. Could ghosts be reasoned with? Burke was not at all sure, never having made the attempt himself.

Burke knew Dafydd Gam—if this spirit was, indeed, the famed Welshman—had been married. Many 15th-century marriages were arranged, so his might not have been a romantic connection. But love was universally understood. "Surely you can appreciate the urgency of winning a woman's regard."

The ghost's eyes turned downward. In a quiet, sad voice, he repeated, "You must not take what is not yours."

Somehow Burke knew the remark was not directed at him. The phantom had addressed the censure at himself. There was a self-defeat to the moment that did not at all fit the character of a man who had been almost ruthless in battle, never shirking from a fight or a challenge.

"No, one must not take something that belongs to another," Burke said. He threw caution to the wind. "Including another person's name."

That brought the ghost's eyes to him once more, but not in anger or shock or fear. A painful hope filled his features.

"You aren't Dafydd Gam, are you?"

The ghost sighed but neither nodded nor shook his head. Was he forbidden from doing so? Was this some form of punishment?

Burke rose and walked slowly toward him. "Can you tell me who you are?"

The ghost simply watched him, quiet and still, but with an intensity that set the hairs on Burke's neck on end.

"If we could sort out the mystery of who you are—" He didn't finish the question; he didn't need to. Everything about the apparition suddenly turned pleading.

The ghost's identity was tied to his imprisonment in this garden, perhaps even to his pet phrase. He was trapped, both physically and linguistically.

"Oh, no." Enid, apparently, had awoken. "You promised."

Burke turned back to face her, ready to apologize, though he wasn't at all certain what vow he'd broken. She, however, was not looking at him. She stood and walked right past him, directly to the ghost.

She plopped her hands on her hips. "Dafydd Gam. What is the meaning of this?"

"He is not Dafydd Gam," Burke said.

"Of course he is." But doubt entered her tone. "Isn't he?"

"We've had something of a conversation," Burke explained, "and I am convinced he is not the legendary cohort of Henry V. I am further certain that his extended sojourn in your garden has been pressed upon him, only to be ended when someone discovers his actual identity."

Enid stepped closer to the still-silent specter. "Is this true?"

Again, no nod, no shake of the head. Yet, somehow the answer was conveyed.

Enid pressed a hand over her heart. "Oh, you poor soul. Have you waited all this time for someone to solve your mystery?"

"I believe he has."

She turned fully back to Burke, clasping his hands and

looking earnestly up into his face. "We must help him, Burke. We must."

How could he possibly refuse? "It might take time."

"I do not mind if you don't."

"I would not mind in the least."

✳ ✳ ✳

"He has always been Dafydd Gam." Mr. Pryce was struggling to accept the change in his family specter's identity. "Who else could he possibly be?"

That was precisely the question Burke, Enid, and Trevor had been attempting to answer for six hours now.

"Have you come upon anything?" Enid asked her brother.

He looked up from the genealogical pages of the family Bible. "The only names in here match those buried in the churchyard. None of them ought to be wandering the earth for all eternity."

Enid leaned her chin into her upturned hand. "Perhaps he isn't a Pryce."

"Perhaps not," Burke said, "although it would have explained his presence on your family estate."

"The garden hasn't always belonged to the estate," Mr. Pryce said from his position near the fireplace. "It was part of Grandfather's mother's dowry."

Now they were getting somewhere. Burke caught Enid's eye and saw that she, too, understood the significance of that tidbit.

Trevor bent over the family Bible once more. "I assume this was your paternal grandfather."

"Of course."

"He was married to—" Trevor pulled out the final syllable as his gaze slid over the page. "—Mair Bleddyn. So, the Bleddyn family likely first discovered our ghost."

"I can't say the land was the Bleddyns' as long ago as the Last War for Independence." Mr. Pryce was managing to be both a help and a hindrance.

"Are there still Bleddyns nearby?" Burke never had been able to let a mystery go unsolved. "Perhaps we could ask them."

That suggestion set off a chain of events. Over the next few days, they visited the Bleddyn estate, only to be sent to speak with the Rhyses, who suggested they look over the parish records. When they found very little there that dated back far enough, the vicar proposed they talk with the butcher, who shared a great many diverting tales, none of which were particularly pertinent. They returned to the Pryce home with as few answers as they'd had before.

"What if we are never able to discover his identity?" Enid's enthusiasm hadn't waned, but she had grown increasingly less certain of their success. "The poor man will be trapped in our garden for eternity."

Burke reached across the carriage and took her hand, something she had permitted him to do more and more often of late. "We will free him somehow."

"But no one can tell us anything of these lands four hundred years ago."

Her downcast expression was rather more than he could bear. "Please, do not lose hope. We have not exhausted our resources yet."

Trevor chuckled lightly. "If you're trying to perk the girl up, you'd best do it properly. Slip across the carriage and sit beside her. I'll not tattle."

Burke literally jumped at the opportunity. He sat next to her. Emboldened by the welcoming smile he received, he raised her hand and pressed a light kiss there. "If we cannot sort the mystery out here, I have access to a great many records and writings at Cambridge, some of which are quite old and rare. We might even convince your brother to undertake a similar search at his university, inferior as it is."

Trevor grinned as he shook his head.

Enid did not share their lighthearted mood. "You are leaving?"

Though hers was not a tone of heartbreak, she did sound genuinely disappointed. That was a good sign. "I need to return to Cambridge. I have classes to teach and students who are depending on me. Not to mention a dog I sincerely hope has missed me."

"Yes, you mustn't neglect the dog." Her teasing tone was rather strained.

"He is being looked after, but I can only trespass upon my neighbor's hospitality for so long, just as I can only press upon your family's generosity a short while longer." He let that hover in the air between them, knowing that if she asked him to stay or told her affection for him would make his departure a misery, he would find any excuse to remain.

"You will send word if you discover anything?"

That was her concern? He, too, wished to free the ghost trapped in her garden, but he'd thought she might at least express some wish for him to remain, or, at the very least, some real regret at the necessity of his departure.

He nearly asked, nearly confessed his own regrets. But tender feelings were regarded as such for a reason: they were, by definition, tender. That risk was real and personal, and the undertaking was anything but simple. "If I find any information, I will be certain to pass it along," he said.

They spent the remainder of their ride in silence, sitting side by side, but not touching and not looking at each other. Perhaps there'd simply not been enough time for her to grow fond of him. Perhaps she'd simply not been interested enough to try.

What do I have to offer, really? A life of economy. An exalted family I am rather estranged from. Years of listening to me wax poetic about events and people who passed hundreds of years ago.

They were having a diverting adventure, nothing more. And he was her friend, nothing more.

He could not have felt more alone if he had been a ghost trapped inside a botanic prison.

Seven

"This is tragic." Mother dropped dramatically onto the fainting sofa in the sitting room.

Enid had expected the news of Burke's imminent departure to be taken badly by her mother, but she'd not anticipated the tears. "He promised to write if he finds anything helpful in identifying our ghost."

"He promised to write? To *write*?" Mother could not possibly have sounded more appalled. "Enid, I thought you'd won more of his regard than that."

"It seems you thought wrong." *We both did.* She kept her expression as unaffected as she could manage. "We have enjoyed a diverting interlude, not unlike my time in Bath."

None of the gentlemen there had proven interested, either. But, then again, none of them had proven interest*ing*, so their apathy hadn't wounded her.

"But Mr. Kennard seemed so perfect for you. You share the same odd sense of humor. Though his connections are

40

among the best in the kingdom, he did not turn up his nose at our comparatively low station. And he loves Wales. You would likely have returned again and again after you'd married."

Had Enid been eating anything, she would have choked. "You have made a very big leap from 'he might be intrigued' to 'he intends to marry me.' Nothing even tiptoed close to that."

"But it might have." Mother closed her eyes, as if unable to endure the sight of anything whilst in such deep mourning.

Trevor wandered into the sitting room. "Burke suggested I visit him in Cambridge this winter. He offered to introduce me to James Donn." Mr. Donn must have been someone in the world of botany for Trevor to sound so gleeful at the possibility of making his acquaintance.

Mother was suddenly alert. "You must take your sister with you. She can meet this James Whomever, and then she can visit with Mr. Kennard."

Good heavens, this was quickly growing ridiculous. "Mother, I cannot visit a single gentleman, not even in the company of my brother. You know that."

"Desperate times—"

Trevor, bless his soul, took matters firmly in hand. "If Enid wishes, I will speak highly of her frequently and enthusiastically throughout any visit I make to Cambridge. I will even issue an invitation to Mr. Kennard for a visit here, if that meets with everyone's approval. But I will not destroy my sister's reputation, or my friend's. We, none of us, are that desperate."

Though she appreciated Trev's support, Enid couldn't entirely agree with his sentiment. She *felt* that desperate. Perhaps not to the point of destroying her good name but of doing something to keep a grip on her last threads of hope.

"I mean to take a turn about the gardens," she told the others. "I will not be gone long."

"But Burke is likely to depart at any moment." Trev kept his voice low, allowing their conversation to be a private one. "You will not have the opportunity to bid him farewell."

She scarcely had the strength to prevent her shoulders from dropping in defeat. "I know," was all she could manage.

He seemed to understand. "I am sorry more didn't come of this past week, Enid. I truly am."

He was giving her the same look one might give an ailing puppy.

"I will recover from my disappointment. It stems, after all, not from losing something I already had but from the pangs of unrealized possibilities." She told herself that would translate to less pain and a shorter duration of it. The consolation was an extremely small one. "I will recover."

He accepted her brave words, though he didn't appear to entirely believe them. "Should you come across our troublesome ghost, see if you can't convince him to scratch his name in the dirt or something equally helpful."

"I will."

The garden, however, was empty when she stepped onto its winding path. Not even the breeze joined her there. Fitting.

She forced her thoughts to dwell on the late summer flowers, the number of weeks remaining until autumn, the vaguely remembered aroma of the bakery she'd walked past many times in Bath, anything other than Burke and his smile and his company. And his desertion.

The garden sat at the back of the house, but the road leading visitors away from her home ran directly past the garden's far edge. Cruel fate conspired against her once more, as she found herself within sight of that very road just as Burke, atop his bay, rode away.

He didn't look back.

She didn't call after him.

As he disappeared from view, she sighed. "I wanted him to stay."

"You must not take what is not yours."

Enid didn't turn at the sound of the familiar voice. Indeed, she'd never before been less pleased to be visited by the family phantom. If he had only stayed away as she'd asked him to, Burke might still be there, watching for the ghost he'd come to meet.

"I hadn't meant to claim possession of him," Enid told her visitor without looking at him. "I know full well he is not mine, just as I am not his."

"You must not take what is not yours."

She pulled a breath in sharply. "I know. You have told me that all of my life. I have taken nothing. I am claiming nothing. Now, please, leave me be."

"You must not—"

"Stop saying that." She spun about, facing the ghost at last. "I only wished for his company, to claim the tiniest bit of his affection, but it is not mine. I cannot have it. You need not continually remind me of that."

In the face of her quickly hardening tone, his ghostly expression softened, and his tone followed suit. "You must not *take* what is not yours."

He'd never emphasized that particular word before.

"Not *take*. But—But I might *ask*, is that what you are attempting to tell me? That forcing him to give me his affection could never work because it is not mine to *take*?" She wasn't entirely certain she was making sense, but a bubbling sensation had begun inside, and she couldn't stop her thoughts from chasing one another in this new direction. "Or—Or perhaps you are saying that he could not make claims to my heart because he did not know that it was his already."

Something resembling a smile touched the ghost's face.

She had struck upon the message he'd meant to convey. "I should tell him how I feel while I still can. But he has gone already. I will never catch him now."

The specter's almost-smile became an unmistakable

one. A gust of chilled wind rose on the instant, followed immediately by the fall of rain.

"You mean to delay him?" She couldn't say just how the ghost was controlling the weather, only that she had been handed an opportunity, and she meant to take it.

Burke stood beneath the overhang at the blacksmith shop, watching a typical Welsh downpour. The rain had begun quite suddenly, and he'd been left with little choice but to seek refuge.

Mr. Jones joined him there after a time. "This here is a wet rain."

"Is there any other kind?" That earned him a laugh, as though *he* had been the one to say something ridiculous.

"Legend has it, when Aberedw Castle was being built, the rain fell so long and so hard and so wet that the builders simply floated the stones directly where they meant to place them."

Jones seemed to be forever weaving a tale. Burke was glad of it. He needed the distraction. His heart, he knew, had been left behind in a certain garden beside a certain house where a certain young lady lived.

She hadn't even been on hand to bid him farewell. Had he meant so little to her that she could not spare even a moment for his departure? Even passing acquaintances generally offered a "Godspeed" when one or the other was beginning a journey.

"Did you ever discover the identity of our ghost?" Jones asked. "It's an odd thing no longer thinking of him as Dafydd Gam. A bit of a blow to the local pride, in fact."

"We didn't." The failing felt more personal than it should have. He did not, after all, hail from this part of the country and had no direct interest in local matters. But he'd disappointed Enid, and that pricked at him severely. "It seems he may be tied to that garden a bit longer."

"Legend has it, those spirits who don't manage to leave this world are trapped here because the weight of their regrets prevents them from floating upward."

"Perhaps he took what was not his."

Jones nodded. "That *is* all he ever says to anyone."

The rain was coming down in sheets and creating deep, wide puddles in the road. Burke likely wouldn't get far that day. "Perhaps the ghost regrets not leaving in a timely manner to avoid uncooperative weather."

"I think you struck nearer to the truth with your first guess, that he's a thief regretting his crimes."

But that didn't sound right to Burke. "I can't imagine such a thing weighing him down for hundreds of years."

"Then maybe he was a would-be thief who regrets not seizing an opportunity when it arose all those hundreds of years ago." Jones took one last look at the downpour before returning back to his forge.

Could the ghost truly be regretting not *stealing something, when he'd spent so long warning others not to?* Perhaps it hadn't been a warning, but a repetition of something he'd been told during his lifetime, perhaps the very words that had prevented him from taking whatever it was he'd let be in the end.

Burke stayed near the open doorway but turned back to face the blacksmith. "Of all the things you call yours, which would you most regret if you could not claim it?"

Jones stopped with his forging iron aloft. "No need to even give it thought, Mr. Kennard." After two more blows, he continued. "If I hadn't claim to my Molly's heart, to being her husband, her love, her friend, that'd steal all the joy from my life. I'd regret that with my every breath."

"Love." Burke nodded at the painful truth. He'd lost an opportunity to pursue that very dream, and the missed chance weighed on him. How much greater must the anguish be at the loss of known and realized and actual love?

Somewhere behind the sound of falling rain and the pounding of Jones's irons, Burke heard a voice. A small, distant voice, but a distinct one just the same. He turned back toward the doorway, straining to hear it better.

The voice was calling his name. Only a moment after that realization, he saw a figure, in the rain, running toward him. Who in heaven's name would be out in this weather?

Enid! He recognized her.

He snatched his outer jacket from the hook where it was drying and rushed out to her, holding the garment above both of their heads. "Have you taken leave of your senses? Coming all this way in this downpour? You'll catch your death."

"Dafydd—the ghost—said if I came after you, I would find you before you left. He brought the rain to slow you down."

She'd come after him? Burke didn't know whether to shake her or hug her. "If you'd wanted to say goodbye, you could have done so when I left your home."

"I couldn't bear it." Her words shook with shivers as water ran in rivulets down her face.

"Come inside the smithy's. It's dry and warm." He set his arm across her back, hurrying her toward shelter. He caught Jones's eye as they stepped inside and received a nod of understanding.

"I had to come find you," Enid said.

"We can hang your spencer nearer the forge. It'll dry there."

She worked at the buttons on the front of her jacket as he hung his on its previous hook.

Jones returned with a woolen blanket. "It smells of horse," he warned.

Smell was the least of their concerns. Burke traded Enid the blanket for her jacket. She had wrapped herself up by the time he returned to her side.

"Now, what is it that was so urgent you had to come running after me in the rain?" His heart, he swore, sat paralyzed in his chest, waiting to hear words he feared she would not speak.

"We cannot take what is not ours." Her words echoed those of the mysterious garden dweller. "You had to leave because you didn't know."

"Didn't know what?"

She took a shaking breath, though whether from nervousness or the chill in the air, Burke couldn't rightly say. "That you wouldn't be taking something that didn't belong to you. That it is yours for the claiming already."

He didn't dare trust his hopeful interpretation of her words. "That *what* was mine already?"

"You didn't—couldn't say anything because you thought that laying claim to my affections, to my heart, would be wrong because you did not believe it was yours, that you would be taking something that didn't belong to you. It was the very reason I couldn't ask you to stay, because your time and your attention and your affections aren't mine, at least I don't know that they are. He, the ghost, felt we needed to know that, that I ought to tell you."

"Enid." He sighed her name, relief like he hadn't known before sweeping over him. She loved him. She might not have said so directly, but the meaning was clear.

"My heart is yours, Burke. If you want it."

He wrapped his arms around her and pulled her to him, kissing her soundly, fervently. In a gesture so suited to her buoyant and enthusiastic personality, Enid threw her arms about his neck and held fast to him, eagerly returning his kiss.

"Oh, my darling," he whispered, keeping her in his embrace. "How close we came to throwing all of this away. If I'd left, not knowing your feelings, not telling you mine, I would have always regretted it. Always."

"But you haven't told me yours," she pointed out. "Not really."

"I am not terribly good at speeches, but when this rain lets up and I return you home, I promise to do my utmost to convince you that my heart is rightly yours."

She pulled back enough to smile up at him. "Then may I keep it? I have vowed, you realize, not to take what is not mine."

A vow not to take a heart that did not belong to oneself. His mind began racing. That would be a regret indeed, if the one making the vow truly loved the person he'd promised not to pursue. Unrequited, or perhaps simply *impossible* love was, indeed, a tremendous weight on a heart and soul. A regret of enormous proportions.

"Enid, that is it. You have stumbled upon the answer."

"The answer to what?" She watched him with expectation.

"The ghost. We—" He motioned to Jones, a few paces away—"have been speaking of the things that tie a soul to this earth after life: weighty and crushing regrets. What if your ghost is trapped here because he never could claim the heart of the woman he loved?"

Her eyes grew wide. "Yes. That would explain his insistence that I not make the same mistake."

The pieces were falling quickly into place. "And who would feel that weight more than someone who loved a woman who was promised to another, especially if she loved him in return but could not escape the other match."

Enid pulled in a sharp breath. "You mean Mairwen and her squire."

Burke nodded. "Does anyone know what his name was?"

"If anyone does, Mr. Jones will."

But when they posed the question, they received a disappointing response. "I'm afraid his name's been lost to history. He's known only as Mairwen's squire."

"Do you think it would be enough?" Burke asked.

"It has to be," Enid insisted. "We may not know his name, but we know who he is. We know whom he loved. We know why he is trapped. Surely that is enough. Surely it must be."

"If there is any mercy in this world, it will be."

Enid rested her head against his chest. "I hope you are right."

He wrapped his arms around her and held her, relishing the feel of her in his arms. He certainly hoped he was right about a great many things.

Eight

The rain hadn't entirely stopped, and the ground was a muddy quagmire when Burke and Enid arrived back at the Pryce estate and rushed headlong into the garden. She held tightly to his hand, unwilling to release him for even a moment. What a risk she'd taken, hying after him in the storm, laying bare her heart. But having the reassurance that his regard was hers to claim made every moment of uncertainty worth it.

"Where could he be?" Burke asked, glancing around at the empty garden. "Surely he must be anxious to move on."

"We have to steal something." She was certain that much was necessary this time. "And we must choose something he cannot ignore."

"Enid. Look just over there." He pointed with his free hand toward a shaded corner of the garden.

"Good heavens. A daffodil." She had never in all her life seen one this late in the season. Not ever.

"That is what we must take," he said. "I know it is."

They carefully made their way over the soggy earth to the bright yellow bloom. They each wrapped a hand around its green stem and pulled, uprooting it, mud clinging to its roots.

A sudden, cold wind picked up, and there he was, their ghost. He didn't speak this time. He simply watched them, hope in his eyes.

"We know who you are," Enid said. "We do not know your name, but we know that you loved Mairwen. We know she loved you but was promised to another, that you could not take what was not yours. We know who you are, and we know that you have suffered long enough."

She heard the sigh he emitted, watched as it shuddered through him. Sunlight burst through the clouds, illuminating him. He looked up toward the source. A smile slowly spread across his face.

Inch by tiny inch, another form appeared. A woman with flowing black hair. She stood directly in front of the long-trapped squire, reaching a hand out in invitation. He took her hand in his and raised it to his lips.

For the first time, likely in his entire sojourn as a lost and wandering soul, the nameless squire spoke a new phrase. "My love," he said. "My Mairwen."

Burke's arms wrapped around Enid as they watched the scene play out. She leaned her head against him.

"Come, my dear," Mairwen told the squire. "We have been apart too long."

But he hesitated. "I must not take what is not mine."

She raised her free hand and gently touched his face. "My love, I have always been yours."

As quickly as it had come, the ray of light disappeared and, with it, the reunited couple. The garden ghost was free at last.

"We've done it, Enid," Burke said. "We've done it."

"We should tell my parents."

SARAH M. EDEN

He kissed the top of her head. "That is likely not all we should tell them."

She did not fight her smile. "May I ask one thing of you before we tell my parents?"

He turned to face her directly. "Of course, dearest. You may ask me anything."

"My parents will insist on a very staid and proper and terribly boring courtship, which means this is my last opportunity."

He looked intrigued.

"I'd very much like you to kiss me again."

That was, it seemed, invitation enough. There, in the no-longer-haunted garden, as the rain began to fall once more, Burke held her tenderly and kissed her deeply, pausing only long enough to whisper against her lips the most beautiful words she could imagine in that moment. "Take my heart. It is yours. Forever."

About Sarah M. Eden

Sarah M. Eden is the author of multiple historical romances, including the 2-time Whitney award Winner *Longing for Home* and Whitney Award finalists *Seeking Persephone* and *Courting Miss Lancaster*. Combining her obsession with history and affinity for tender love stories, Sarah loves crafting witty characters and heartfelt romances. She has twice served as the Master of Ceremonies for the LDStorymakers Writers Conference and acted as the Writer in Residence at the Northwest Writers Retreat. Sarah is represented by Pam van Hylckama Vlieg at D4EO Literary Agency.

Visit Sarah online:
Twitter: @SarahMEden
Facebook: Author Sarah M. Eden
Website: SarahMEden.com

It's You

by Annette Lyon

Other Works by Annette Lyon

Band of Sisters
Coming Home
The Newport Ladies Book Club series
A Portrait for Toni
At the Water's Edge
Lost Without You
Done & Done
*There, Their, They're: A No-Tears Guide to Grammar from
the Word Nerd*

One

October 31, 1924—American Fork, Utah

Anna Brierley certainly didn't expect a party to be thrown in celebration of her arrival, but she also didn't expect a funeral to mark the occasion. She'd spent only one night at the home of Aunt Wilma and Uncle Milton Ingersoll before donning her dreary black dress again, though for someone she'd never met. Her uncle had assured her that the city didn't typically plan funerals for the last day of October, but the deceased's extended family couldn't attend on any other day.

"And besides," Aunt Wilma had added, "it's the twentieth century. No one puts stock in superstitions about spirits walking the earth for All Hallows' Eve." Her words had been followed by a disdainful snort.

Anna found herself at the funeral services, sitting in the grand Alpine Tabernacle, which must have held two thousand in its pews. They were all filled in honor of the passing of one David Rushton.

While she was grateful that modern fashions didn't insist on corsets as they had for her grandmother's generation, her black dress still felt uncomfortable and stifling. Its presence was enough to fill her with sadness as dark as the black sateen itself. She sat through the service, surrounded by hundreds of people she did not know, and felt entirely alone in the world.

An orphan.

At the thought, she had to dab her eyes with the corner of her kerchief. Aunt Wilma noted the action and gave Anna a slight nod of approval.

As if I'm crying over this Rushton man, she thought.

Not at all. She'd technically been an orphan since she was only a year old, when her parents caught scarlet fever and never recovered. But Anna's grandparents had taken her in and raised her, giving her a loving home. Five years ago, her grandfather passed away after a bout of tuberculosis. And two weeks ago, Grandmother's heart gave out.

Even though Anna had been an orphan for nineteen of her twenty years, she only now felt like one. She had no memory of her parents, so their deaths held no sting. But now she really was alone. The spud farm she'd grown up on had been sold, and seeing as she had no money and no employment, she'd been sent down south to live with relatives. She hoped to find work here; American Fork was many times larger than Shelley, Idaho. Perhaps she still might. She wouldn't know until she could start looking for a position.

The service ended, and a procession comprised of a few mourners—mostly family and close friends—headed north, toward the city cemetery, with the casket leading the way on a wagon bed. Anna's aunt and uncle fell into the line and walked with the mourners, Uncle Milton walking beside his wife, who held a black umbrella over their heads. Anna took her place behind them and walked toward a hill. The day was drizzly and gray, with clouds wrapping about the nearby mountains like wispy scarves. The mourners passed trees that had shed their colorful leaves, which nearly covered the ground like golden wallpaper with deep orange accents.

Free from the confines of the pew and the stuffy air of the tabernacle, Anna breathed in deeply, enjoying the smells of autumn in spite of the sprinkling rain. She loved the woodsy odor of wet trees and shrubs, loved walking over leaves, knowing that each step released a bit of the fragrance of fall. She passed several houses with twisting plumes of white smoke, another sign of the season; people were lighting their wood-burning stoves again. She hadn't realized how much she'd missed seeing wood smoke until she saw it. Many houses in the area—especially on Main Street, as the Ingersolls' was—boasted radiant heating throughout, as well as luxuries like electric lights and indoor plumbing. While she would be happy to never again use a chamber pot or an outhouse, she knew that the smell of wood burning for warmth would always be something she craved because it smelled of *home.*

They climbed the hill, higher and higher, until the ground leveled out a bit. That was where the cemetery had been built. A stone wall clearly bordered at least part of the area; the group came from the southeast corner, and the wall went both north and west from there. But the cemetery grounds themselves seemed to go on and on. Anna could make out headstones that looked no bigger than raisins at this distance, and many were spread far apart. Could such an immense space ever fill up? The wagon led the way to the plot where David Rushton would be laid to rest, and the crowd, much smaller than had been at the tabernacle, gathered about for the graveside service.

Even though this moment was for Mr. Rushton, respected citizen and beloved father, Anna felt curious eyes looking her way and taking her in. She took a half step closer to Aunt Wilma, hoping that people would know she belonged with them. The prying looks didn't feel judgmental, just curious. Perhaps a face or two in the group would one day be someone she could call a friend.

With that thought, she lifted her chin and let her gaze pan across the throng as the bishop made his remarks. After he finished, the pallbearers carried the casket from the wagon and lowered it into the open plot, which had a pile of fresh dirt beside it. The process was slow, the men using long ropes to lower the casket. Anna found her attention turning restless, shifting from the casket to her aunt to the wisps of cloud on the mountain, to the mourners, to her rumbling stomach, to—

Her eyes stopped at the sight of a woman at the back of the crowd. She seemed taller than everyone else, which was odd, but that wasn't what first caught Anna's attention. Rather, it was the fact that the woman wore *white*. Anna then realized with a start that she could see the woman from the shoulders up, yet unless she was seven feet tall, that was impossible.

She must be standing on something to see better, Anna reasoned. *Maybe on the cemetery wall.*

Except that the grave lay more than two hundred feet from the wall. Anna studied the woman, who seemed to be watching the proceedings with the rest of the group. But then, as if she heard something—or felt Anna's gaze—the woman slowly turned her head and looked directly at Anna. Their eyes met; Anna sucked in a breath and wanted to turn away, but she couldn't move. Instead of looking offended, the woman broke into a wide smile. She looked surprised and—*happy*.

She pointed at Anna, then mouthed the words, "It's you!"

Despite any misgivings, Anna questioningly indicated herself then peered about to see if the woman was speaking to someone else. There was no reason for her to know or note Anna. But no one seemed to notice the woman or react to her strange behavior. Anna looked at her again; the woman still grinned with pure happiness, a sight so paradoxical at a burial that it sent a chill down Anna's spine.

How was she so tall? And why did she know Anna—or think she did?

With great effort, Anna pulled her eyes away from the woman and stared at the ground. How much longer would the service last? How much longer could Anna stand there, silent, waiting to hurry away from the odd specter and ask Aunt Wilma who the woman was?

Her aunt must have noticed something amiss, as she leaned in and whispered, "Are you unwell? You look peaked."

"I—" Anna tried, keeping her voice low. No, she wasn't well. But she couldn't put her feelings into words. Instead, in a matching whisper, she asked, "Who is the woman over there with the long, red braid hanging over her shoulder? The one in white?" She nodded ever so slightly in the direction of the woman while keeping her eyes trained downward, on the hem of her aunt's black skirt.

Only after describing the woman did Anna realize how odd it was for a grown woman to wear a braid in public. Older woman usually wore their hair up. Younger ones often had shorter hairstyles nowadays. One long braid was what an older woman wore to bed.

Aunt Wilma searched the area, her gaze sweeping back and forth, before she leaned back in. "Which woman? There are so many, and I don't see one with a braid."

"The one in white," Anna repeated, though merely saying the words seemed to take her breath away. Unable to stop herself, she turned to look at the woman again. Yes, there she was—still staring at Anna, still smiling, looking happy. Was the woman mad, to be grinning like a fool at a funeral?

When their eyes locked again, the woman nodded

knowingly and pointed at Anna as she had before. "It's *you*."

Anna wasn't sure if she heard the words, or if they somehow went straight into her mind. No one else reacted. It was as if they couldn't see the woman.

Anna stared at the ground again. *Have I lost my mind?*

"You must be catching your death of the flu," Aunt Wilma said with a sympathetic and somewhat patronizing tilt of her head as a Rushton family member stepped forward to offer a prayer over the grave.

As he spoke, Anna had to force her head to bow. Keeping her eyes closed took more effort than a day of harvesting potatoes, and once she failed entirely, opening them a crack to peek at the woman, only to close them again because yes, the strange vision was still there. More than anything, Anna fought the urge to cry out, to tell her aunt and everyone around her that she wasn't sick or imagining things, and that they should all run away, right now, because something eerie was afoot. Or she should simply run away herself, down the hill from the cemetery and all the way back to the Ingersolls' house on Main Street, where she'd lock the doors, run upstairs to her new bedroom, and hide.

But something told her that the woman would find her no matter where she went. Anna squeezed her eyes tight again but could practically feel the woman's stare through her lids.

Who was she? Could Aunt Wilma and the rest of the gathering really not see her?

The prayer ended, and the throng murmured, "Amen."

As the people began to disperse, Aunt Wilma touched Anna's arm, and she inhaled sharply as if struck. Aunt Wilma gave her a strange look—one almost saying that yes, Anna had indeed lost her mind. She forced herself to not yank her arm out of her aunt's grip, something particularly difficult when Aunt Wilma said, "Dear, I'm afraid you're seeing things—and you poor creature, you're so pale. You're still exhausted from travel."

A nod was Anna's only response. She was exhausted, but no amount of fatigue could explain what she'd seen in the rainy cemetery. She said nothing more as she followed her aunt away from the burial plot. Before she stepped beyond the cemetery wall, Anna couldn't help but look back one last time and hope the whole thing had been a figment of her imagination.

Not only was the woman still there, but she had turned, so she again faced Anna. Without anyone in front of her, the woman clearly hovered above the ground in what looked like a nightdress with lace at the bottom and on the cuffs of her sleeves and a ribbon tied into a bow at the neck. She held a candlestick with a half-burned candle, which was lit, its flame flickering slightly, but not going out, even when a gust of wind nearly displaced Anna's hat from her head.

Through it all, the woman continued to stare at Anna with the same knowing smile.

Aunt Wilma adjusted her umbrella so it covered both of them better. Her voice broke into Anna's thoughts. "Come. No need to fret over David Rushton. He'll rest in peace. Let's get you home and to bed with a nice bowl of soup."

Not until Anna had walked past the cemetery wall did she realize that the woman had no umbrella. She stood—hovered—in the rain, yet her candle burned bright, and her personage remained entirely dry.

Two

That afternoon, Anna went to the high school in an attempt to get a teaching position. The amused smiles she got from the staff told her plenty—how they thought that the education she'd received in little old Shelley, Idaho, amounted to nothing, and her teaching certificate didn't count, either. Did she look as if she'd just fallen off a turnip truck? Her clothes weren't as stylish as theirs, but she wasn't entirely naive and ignorant of the world. If they could have seen her spitfire of a headmistress, Miss Alice, they might have had a different opinion.

As she made the forty-five-minute walk back across layers of fall leaves, through the mist of an impending rain shower, she avoided puddles and pondered what to do next. The principal, Mr. Hatch, did say he'd add her to the list of substitute teachers. If he ever called, she'd have a chance to prove herself to him and the rest of the faculty.

She passed beneath a tree, and water droplets fell from the leaves onto her hair. Anna hurried past, then pulled her scarf up like a hood, which she probably should have done from the outset. Her ears welcomed the protection.

She would try for a position again next school year, or perhaps after Christmas break, if a teacher got married and moved away or something else happened to open a spot. In the meantime, she needed a job. The biggest reason was to earn money toward an independent future, but she also needed something to keep her out of the house so she didn't feel so obligated to her aunt and uncle. They wouldn't want to give her charity forever, and she certainly didn't want to be the recipient, either.

She turned onto Main at the tabernacle and, two blocks later, found Uncle Milton sitting on the porch steps from the corner of 100 West. He looked up as she unlatched the metal gate and went through. He appeared to be waiting for her.

"Still looking for paying work?" he asked, chewing on a piece of grass.

"I am," Anna said, happy to not go into detail. She eyed the grass stuck between Uncle Milton's teeth and covered up a smile. She had a feeling that Aunt Wilma, who went out of her way to look the part of the wife of a wealthy businessman, wouldn't approve of her husband chewing grass.

The habit reminded Anna of the farm that had been her home for as long as she could remember. For a moment, it also made her feel a tad lighter in her step, and she felt more comfortable around Uncle Milton immediately. Had the steps not been damp with recently fallen autumn rain, she would have sat beside him, but she didn't want to get her second-best dress muddy.

"Figured you'd like to get out of the house a bit," Uncle Milton said. He glanced over his left shoulder at the house and chuckled as if he knew full well that Anna hadn't been inside much today—and didn't want to return, either.

If so, he'd guessed correctly. She wasn't used to such elegant surroundings. The second floor alone had two bathrooms and five—five!—large bedrooms. The dining room had a bowed window that looked onto Main Street, and the next room was a recent addition: a sunroom where Aunt Wilma reportedly spent much of her time in the summer, reading or feeding her pet canary, the window screens open for fresh air. And that didn't count the kitchen, the basement, or the grand staircases and entryway, with their elaborate woodwork.

Anna preferred smaller, humbler accommodations. She would have been quite happy to stay outside for some time, even if it meant getting a bit damp—although the rain had eased and sun shone through the clouds now.

"Talked to Jedidiah Sorensen," Uncle Milton said. "Said he could use some help over at the church building. It's paying work."

Anna tilted her head. "Paying work . . . at the church?" The congregation was run entirely with volunteers and lay leaders.

"Oh, it isn't church work, precisely," Uncle Milton clarified. He pulled the grass out of his mouth, studied it, and cast it aside, then slipped a new blade inside. With it clasped between his teeth, he went on. "It may keep you busy for a few days—maybe a week or more, depending on what you find."

Intrigued, Anna stepped closer. With one hand, she wiped a spot beside Uncle Milton as clean as she could, laid her scarf on top, and sat on it. "What is the work?"

"We used to have a woman in the congregation—a spinster." He squinted as if remembering. "She grew up here, and all her family passed on before she did. She used one of the church closets to store some of her things. Nobody minded except Mrs. Pye, who thought the church should charge a rental fee. But she didn't have two pennies to rub together; she couldn't have paid one. In her final months, she moved from house to house, with members of the congregation caring for her. Keeping her things at the church was easier than moving them around all the time." He sighed and shook his head. "She was only fifty-some-odd years old—a little younger than my Wilma—but to look at her, you'd have thought she was much older. Anyhow, she's been gone a year now, and some folks are getting antsy for her things to be cleared out—as if they have some urgent use for the space." He narrowed his eyes and added, "Come to think of it, I think she died exactly a year ago today."

Anna felt an odd thrill at the idea of going through the belongings of an unknown woman—an oddly intimate task for a stranger to perform. Yet she found herself wanting to do it.

"What was her name?" she asked, curious now—and glad that she'd been chosen to go through the woman's earthly belongings rather than a man who might not appreciate the things that were close to a woman's heart.

"Nanny Mae Workman," he said, enunciating each syllable.

"Nanny Mae," Anna repeated.

Uncle Milton nodded. "She taught school for years, but eventually came down sick with some lady trouble. Had to quit teaching, and it turned out that she had no savings— she'd donated all she could to orphans and young people trying to get an education and whatnot. So folks took turns hosting her in their homes. She spent her last two months with us, actually." Uncle Milton twisted so he could see the front of the house and pointed at one of the bedroom windows. "She slept in that room, right there. Always thought it was sad that she and Wilma didn't exactly see eye to eye."

He'd indicated the same room Anna herself slept in last night.

"Interesting." A little chill trickled along her arms now, making her feel jittery. Silly. What did it matter if an elderly woman, now dead, had once slept in the same room Anna did now?

Maybe Nanny Mae's life is my fate, Anna thought with dismay as she turned from the window. *I'll be an old maid, all alone in the world, teaching students until I'm too frail to keep up. Then I'll be carted from one house to another, having no real home, until I finally die.*

Uncle Milton didn't seem to notice her unease, because he went on. "We meant to move her to a neighbor's house because she didn't have the strength to manage the stairs anymore, but she passed before arrangements could be made."

"How sad."

"If you're willing—and I told Jedidiah you probably would be—you'll be going through the old woman's things and deciding what to throw away, what to keep, and where to keep anything worth saving. So, you willing? Because he's expecting you in the next . . ." He checked his pocket watch, holding it out from his face and moving it closer and farther away until his aging eyes focused on it. "About twenty minutes. You'll just make it if you start walking now."

"Um, all right," Anna said. "I'll let Aunt Wilma know."

She hurried inside, changed into a dress better suited for working around dust and dirt, and wrapped a shawl about her shoulders. On her way out, she flew through the kitchen, where she called to her stunned aunt, "I'll be working at the church!"

And she was out the back door. She rounded the corner and passed Uncle Milton on the porch, still chewing on grass, and waved as she passed. "Thank you."

"The least I can do for a young lady who won't lecture me on chewing grass—and who won't tell the missus about it." He grinned and raised an old, leathery hand in a wave.

Anna chuckled, lifted her skirts, and headed northward across Main Street, hurrying across the damp road and avoiding the occasional puddle. She would arrive a bit later than Mr. Sorensen expected, but hopefully that wouldn't be a problem. He wasn't the bishop, just the groundskeeper.

When she arrived, she found him working in the flowerbeds, pulling out dead annuals in preparation for winter. He straightened, wiped some of the dirt from his hands, and extended one to Anna. "Pleasure to meet ya," he said with a nod. "You're welcome to go on in that door and get to work. I'll be out here if you need anything."

"All right," Anna said. She went up the side stairs of the church and peered into the door. An office appeared to be on her right, and a long hall stretched in front of her, with rooms on the left side. Unsure where to go, she returned to Mr. Sorensen. "Could you direct me to Miss Workman's belongings? I'm afraid I'm unfamiliar with the building."

"Oh, of course. Silly me. I forget that not everyone has lived in this town as long as I have. I think the closet is locked." He chuckled and led the way, wiping his muddy boots on a mat outside before entering. He led her down the hall, and as she followed, she looked up at the chandelier and an upstairs balcony. So pretty.

She followed Mr. Sorensen to one of the rooms off the hall and from there to a closet she probably wouldn't have noticed otherwise. He found a kerosene lamp, which he lit and handed to Anna. "This here will help you see inside better. Don't worry about making a mess; that's the first step in organizing, no matter what."

"True," Anna said.

"Take your time," he said, heading back outside. "It's best we clear the space as much for her as anything—let her rest in peace and all that."

The outside door closed behind him, leaving Anna alone. Her brow furrowed as she repeated his words in her mind. *Let her rest in peace?* What might be keeping Nanny Mae Workman from resting in peace? Standing there with the lamp, Anna suddenly didn't want to look into the dark space for fear of what she might find.

Don't be silly. It's nothing more than odds and ends collected by an old woman. Nothing that can hurt you. Have a strong backbone and get to work.

She straightened her posture, put her shoulders back, and stepped forward, determined to do the job she'd come for. A nail stuck out from the wall about four feet from the floor, perfect for holding the lamp. With it hanging, Anna could look over the space quite easily. The closet wasn't large, and it didn't have nearly as much stored inside as she'd expected.

Ridiculous that you were afraid of this even for a moment.

Anna withdrew one wooden crate and then a second. Wanting to sit somewhere other than the floor, she carried one of them down a hall until she found an area that was probably the main entrance to the building. Off to the side was the chapel proper, which explained why the hall had no classrooms on the right side—that's where the chapel was. She walked over to the chapel door and peered inside. Rows of pews faced the podium on her right. Three arched stained glass windows—two on the far side, one to her left, which was the back of the room—had climbing vines and flowers. The afternoon sun shone through, creating warm colors.

This would do quite well as a place to sort through Nanny Mae's belongings. She set the crate onto the floor in front of the first pew, then returned to the closet for the second one. With the lamp resting on the side of the podium, Anna settled onto a bench to sort through the contents of the first crate. Before long, she found herself enjoying bits of history she uncovered as she looked at and touched items that had once meant something to a real person—a woman much like herself, with no family and no prospects.

Sitting there in the glow of the stained glass windows brought a peace and simple beauty that Anna reveled in as she worked. She had yet to be in this room during Sabbath services, but she'd admired the windows in passing. At this late afternoon hour, they looked richer in color than she would have guessed. Slanting rays of sunlight glanced off the hardwood floor.

She found several journals, which she decided must be kept for the sake of history. Would reading them be wrong?

I'll decide later, she thought as she stacked them on the floor and peered into the crate for what was next: stacks of paper and cards. She came across several yellowing dance cards filled with names of young men. Anna smiled. Proof that Nanny Mae hadn't always been old and frail. Anna pictured her young and full of life, going to dances, flirting with young men, having her eye set on a special one.

The dance cards seemed to speak of a vibrant young woman who had enjoyed friends and a social life. Why hadn't she married?

Anna found more cards from birthdays and other special occasions. She paused to read words penned by Nanny Mae's parents, a grandmother, an aunt. More and more, she seemed to have once been a typical young woman living a typical young woman's life. Yet she'd died alone, with no place to call home, and no family. Did any of the neighbors who had taken her in consider her a friend?

Troubling thoughts continued to build in Anna's mind, one after the other, as she sorted through the first crate. Her fingers touched some heavy paper—a black backing and something else glued to the front. She gently freed it from under an old Bible, revealing it to be an old photograph. She made out sky and clouds on a top corner, and as she slipped the photograph out further, she made out the top of a house, pine trees, and finally, people standing before the house. The picture was sideways, so Anna pulled it out all the way and turned it so she could study it with the proper orientation.

Staring back at her were three young adults, two women and a man, all in clothing a couple of decades older than the fashions of Anna's day. The woman on the left looked like Anna's own mother—she'd grown up in this city, so it might be her. But Anna didn't recognize the other two. The clothing looked old-fashioned, even compared to Shelley fashions; her hometown tended to be woefully behind on such things. She turned the photo over and found another piece of paper glued to the back, bearing with the words *Ellen, Howard, and me.*

Ellen. Anna sat back and smiled. So that *was* her mother. The man—Howard—was tall, with dark hair. He wore a pinstriped suit and a mischievous smile. Anna had a feeling that if he hadn't needed to stand so still for the photographer, he would have been laughing.

The other woman—likely a young Nanny Mae—wore a broad hat, long skirt, and a shirtwaist not unlike the old-fashioned thing Anna wore to the funeral, only pale colored, with a brooch at the neck. Her hair could have been any number of colors; with only a black-and-white image to judge by, there was no telling besides the fact that it wasn't very dark. But something about the woman's eyes caught Anna's attention; she looked closer. The young Nanny Mae seemed familiar. Not her clothing—especially not the hat.

But there was *something . . .*

Anna furrowed her brow, trying to puzzle it out.

Ignore the hat. What if her hair weren't in a pompadour? It could be brown or blonde or . . . red.

She imagined the woman with long, red hair well past her shoulders, in a braid hanging over one shoulder. With a sudden realization, Anna dropped the picture. It fell to her lap, where it lay as she stared at the image, unable to take her eyes off it. She knew that face. She'd seen it that morning.

But how could the woman from the cemetery be Nanny Mae Workman? The picture looked exactly like her, as if she hadn't aged a day. Anna tried to find some rational explanation. Perhaps the person Anna had seen was a close relative, like a daughter.

But Nanny Mae never married and had no children.

Maybe the woman at the cemetery was her sister.

She had no family at all. But if she had, any living sister would look much older than that.

Anna set aside the unsettling memory of the woman seemingly hovering above the ground; that bit had to have been her imagination.

But there was no getting around the fact that the woman at the cemetery had recognized Anna. Had smiled and called to her. Anna tried to swallow, but her mouth had gone dry as sand as the details all came together.

Was the woman at the graveyard Nanny Mae's . . .

Anna cut off her thoughts before the word *ghost*—not that that did much good. The woman died exactly a year ago today. And today was All Hallows' Eve.

As she tried to repack the crate, her shaking fingers refused to obey, making her drop several journals and notebooks and sending the stack of dance cards all over the floor, near the podium and under the bench. She dropped to her knees to pick them up, needing to get the crates back to the closet right away. Needing to leave. An urgency to escape came over her, even as part of her mind whispered that if the spirit of Nanny Mae could find her at the graveyard, she could find her anywhere. That there could be no escape.

The more Anna tried to hurry, the more she fumbled with the papers and books. The lamplight flickered, making her look up. No draft or breeze had passed through the room to cause such a thing. It flickered again. Gooseflesh broke out across her arms.

You're far from home, she thought, shaking her head disdainfully. *You're tired. And you're imagining things. Now clean up and get back to the house.*

All well and good, but the lamplight flickered a third time, and now she heard footsteps in the hall, drawing closer. They moved fast, as if the person was jogging.

"Mr. Sorensen?" she called, but it came out as a squeak and likely didn't make it past the doorway. Would Mr.

Sorensen have come so far into the building while covered in dirt and mud? She highly doubted that. Then who was it?

Or what?

Her throat tightened, making each breath difficult and shallow. She hugged a notebook to her chest and waited.

Another squeak of the floorboards. Closer this time. Drawing nearer and nearer. Someone—or *something*—was approaching. Fast.

Three

Charlie Beck strode along the street as he headed home from a long day's work in Mr. Mitchell's apple orchards. Harvest time was always the busiest of the year, so Mitchell hired extra hands. Charlie clasped his hands behind him and arched to crack his back, then tilted his head, one ear to shoulder and then the other, to stretch his tight muscles. It felt good, but he knew from experience that come morning, he'd be extra sore all over. At least he had the day off tomorrow; not all hands were so lucky as to get Saturday free.

The sun had just dipped behind the horizon behind him; the edges of long shadows began blurring as dusk gradually took over. When he was a dozen yards from the corner across from the church, a yellow glow spilled onto the street from the arched window above the side door.

Odd. Maybe Sorensen's fixing something inside. Usually the elderly man worked the grounds, but there was no reason to think he couldn't be making repairs inside—except that Mr. Beckstead from up the street was the one always called on for such matters. He knew about electric lights and fixing plaster and such.

Nothing about the situation was suspicious per se, but some quality of the air or the night made Charlie slow his step and stare at the glow. Was something amiss? Maybe he should check the grounds to be sure Sorensen wasn't lying somewhere, hurt.

Charlie stood on the street corner, ready to cross, when the light in the upper window increased until it became so bright that he had to shield his eyes and squint. Even so, he peered at the arched window, which showed the balcony of the second floor.

There, clear as day, stood a young woman carrying a candle with a flame far too small to account for the intense light. She seemed to glow as she stood on the balcony, holding the wooden railing with one hand and the candle with the other. Transfixed, Charlie took in her long red braid hanging over her left shoulder and her white gown, which appeared to be a nightdress. Who was she? And what was she doing on the second floor of the chapel, alone, in her nightclothes?

She moved suddenly, turning directly toward the window, and looked out. Charlie felt her gaze land on him as if it were a weight.

She can't see me from there, he assured himself. Even so, he took a step back and nearly twisted an ankle on a stone. *Outside, it's twilight. Where she is, it's light as day. She can't see me.*

Except he knew that she had. She still looked right at him. Smiling broadly, she pointed at Charlie; he could almost feel the touch of her finger through his shirt. Nothing about the moment made sense, yet it felt as real as picking apples had minutes ago. The woman turned her hand palm up and bent her fingers, inclining her head to the side at the same time—beckoning him to come. He raised his eyebrows. Surely he'd imagined *that*.

She laughed—somehow he could hear it. She beckoned again, then said, "It's you. Come." She turned and ran down the hall. She and the light vanished.

Charlie shook his head, wondering if he'd passed out and was dreaming, or if some of the men at the orchard had given him something stronger to drink than cider. Maybe some of them were playing a trick on him. Whatever it was, he felt compelled to investigate.

He drew his shoulders back, took a deep breath, and strode across the street with purpose. If the chapel door was locked, he'd know it had all been his imagination. He'd go home and to bed, never mentioning the matter to anyone. But if that woman was inside and needed help . . .

She *had* told him to come. And seemed to recognize him . . .

At the base of the steps, Charlie's attention was caught by a different glow. He paused and looked at the two tall stained glass windows that bordered one side of the meeting hall. Was it his imagination—again—or did he detect a faint light behind the windows? Maybe the woman had fled there.

He hurried up the steps and tried the door. The knob turned easily, so Charlie pushed the door open and went inside. He glanced up at the second-floor balcony and shivered slightly before hurrying down the long hallway. He passed classrooms and offices and kept going, heading toward the meeting hall.

He reached the main entry to the building, then turned toward the chapel door. Sure enough, lamplight spilled over the threshold. He hurried over and peered inside. A lamp sat on the lectern, which explained the faint light he'd seen through the windows. He did indeed find a young woman, but not the one he'd been looking for.

Instead of red hair, this girl's was a chestnut brown. She wore a simple navy dress rather than white. And she stared at him, clutching something to her chest. Was she, too, a phantom? He didn't recognize either woman. At least this one didn't glow or run from him.

He stepped into the chapel and asked, "What are you doing here?" Her eyes widened further. Only then did he realize that his tone might have come out sharp and unkind. He tried again. "I mean, do you need anything?"

The girl's face seemed to drain of all color. She looked at something on the floor, and then her face snapped back up to meet his. "You!"

Before Charlie could say another word, her eyes rolled into the back of her head, and she fainted to the floor. He rushed into the chapel and knelt beside her. Not knowing what else to do, he rolled her onto her side and put the back of his hand to her forehead as he'd seen physicians and midwives do. Was she sick? Delirious? She had a swelling bump on her forehead—no doubt from where she'd hit the floor. It would turn into a good-sized, multicolored goose egg. Good thing she'd been kneeling on the floor instead of standing, or she might have been hurt far worse.

He pushed away all thoughts of the specter he'd seen through the window and focused his attentions on the young woman who'd collapsed. She'd seemed genuinely frightened. *Maybe she saw the other woman.* But what had sparked the sudden fear and exclamation of "It's you"? She was clearly afraid of *him.*

It's you. The red-haired woman in white said the same thing. Was this unconscious young woman really a ghost or some otherworldly apparition?

He'd held her arm to roll her. He'd touched her forehead. No shadow from other realms could feel corporeal—solid, warm—could they? A little pink slowly returned to her cheeks and lips; surely phantasms from the beyond didn't pale with fright.

So she is real, he thought. Had they met before? He didn't think so, but then, how did she recognize him?

Her eyelids fluttered opened, then blinked once, twice. She stared into the grays and purples of the shadows of the vaulted ceiling, and her eyebrows came together as if she couldn't figure out where she lay or what had happened.

"Are you all right?" Charlie asked quietly, hoping to avoid terrifying her into another fainting spell.

She closed her eyes again without looking at him, then put a hand to her forehead and took a deep breath. "What— what happened?"

Charlie almost didn't dare speak, knowing that as soon as he did, she'd open her eyes, see his face, and be scared again. The idea shot a distinct sense of disappointment through him, though he couldn't have said why. He didn't know the woman—not even her name. Yet he knew he'd never forget her face or the feel of her cool skin under his hand as he'd checked her forehead. He eyed the mess of papers on the floor and turned to picking them up. He could help tidy what she'd been cleaning up.

"You fainted," he said with his back to her so he wouldn't frighten her again. "You're in the chapel. I saw a light and came inside to make sure nothing was amiss." By the time Charlie finished, he'd gathered a hefty stack, but the corners pointed every which way. The papers would never fit into the crate in such a state. He sat on the floor, legs splayed, and began sorting his load, adjusting individual pages so they were oriented correctly. He purposely kept his head somewhat bowed.

"I feel so queer," the young woman said weakly. "Almost as if I had a dream, but I wasn't asleep, was I?"

"Not unless you can dream in ten seconds," Charlie said in an attempt to lighten the mood. He lifted his gaze to the windows. What dim sunlight had remained when he'd been walking home was fading fast; the stained glass windows didn't glow with pinks and golds as it did during meetings held at sunset. Instead, long shadows from the pews created varying shades of gray throughout the room, shades made starker by the light coming from the burning lamp.

Someone or something could easily be hiding in such shadows. He shoved the worry away. He was a grown man now, not some schoolboy who played at ghosts and goblins.

"Let's get this cleaned up," Charlie said cheerfully. "It's getting dark, and I imagine you want to get home soon so you aren't walking alone in the dark."

The girl moved to sit, but then groaned and touched the swelling goose egg at her hairline, grimacing. She didn't lie back, though; she leaned against the bench seat and closed her eyes again.

Charlie had picked up most of the mess—all but a few photos and cards sticking out beneath the girl's skirt, but he wasn't about to collect those until she moved. He might have a face ugly enough to scare a girl silly, but he was a gentleman. He stayed close, with his arms at the ready to catch her if need be; her clear lack of strength made him uneasy.

"Where you do live?" he asked. He didn't trust that her constitution was strong enough to get her home unaccompanied. The city had only three or four thousand people, so the fact that he didn't recognize her meant that she didn't live in the immediate area. Every resident knew everyone else within several miles in all directions.

"I live on Main Street," she said, sounding a bit stronger now. Steadying herself on the pew, she gradually pushed herself from the floor and sat on the bench. "With the Ingersolls. I'm their niece."

"Ah. That explains it." Charlie gathered the final papers that had been beneath her skirts and tucked them behind the rest of the stack as he sat beside her on the bench, resting the papers on his lap. "I know exactly where they live. I'd be happy to see you home to make sure you're safe. I don't have one of those fancy automobiles like your aunt and uncle, but I'd be happy to walk with you—after you have your strength back, that is." He held out a hand. "My name's Charlie, by the way. Charlie Beck."

She would certainly look straight at him now; there was no avoiding that. If she fainted again, he'd catch her.

"Anna Brierley." She shook his hand and looked into his eyes. And didn't faint. She also didn't pull back in horror. Even better, she didn't withdraw her hand. Instead, she kept it nestled in his and studied his face. "Do I know you?"

"I don't believe we've met, no," Charlie said, quite happy to hold her hand and be in close proximity to a beautiful girl. She seemed to grow prettier by the second, and only part of that could be attributed to the fact that he was seeing her by moon and lamplight. "I apologize for startling you earlier. I was on my way home when—" But stopped there. No need to mention what he'd seen; Anna might think he was delirious. "That doesn't matter. I do apologize. I certainly didn't mean to startle you."

"It wasn't your fault," Anna said. "I must still be tired from traveling. Or maybe I caught a cold from being out in the rain." She smiled as she spoke—a pretty smile with curving, pink lips he had a hard time looking away from. Charlie had an urge to make her smile wider—at him.

What would it be like to kiss that mouth? That thought was quickly followed by another. *What are you thinking? You've only met her—and you terrified her half out of her wits.* And he here he was thinking about her pretty smile? About *kissing* her?

Control your thoughts. That thought sounded like one of his father's admonitions. Good advice.

Charlie cleared his throat and forced his gaze away from her smile. "Are these your family records?" He lifted the stack from his lap. While gathering them, he hadn't paid attention to what the papers were, but he now looked down at a photo on the top of the handful—a photo of three people, two women and a man. And it was his turn to feel faint.

The man was obviously his father. He didn't know the woman on the left, but the other one . . . She had the very same face as the woman he'd seen through the window minutes before. He'd have known her anywhere—the dark, piercing eyes, thin eyebrows, heart-shaped mouth. Her hair was in a pompadour instead of a long braid, and she wore a fancy dress that looked like the ones in pictures of his parents' youth.

The photo had yellowed, and the edges were worn. This wasn't a new photograph. It couldn't be explained away as young people dressed up in a previous generation's garb. If he'd had any doubt as to that, one detail confirmed it: a sign off to one side read *Mitchell's Orchards*, but there weren't half as many trees as there were now, and the trunks were much thinner. Besides, the man in the center was clearly his father, only younger, twenty-five years younger, he guessed.

Does this mean I really did see a . . .

He grasped the back of the bench with one hand and looked away from the picture, his mind feeling muddled and unsure.

"Are—are you well, Charlie?"

Anna's voice sounded much stronger now—stronger than he felt. She placed a hand on his forearm—a gesture of concern he appreciated, but even so, he flinched slightly. She pulled away as if she'd touched a hot stove, and he immediately wished he dared ask her to put her hand back.

"Oh, I'm fine," he said with as much bravado as he could. He forced his lips into a smile. Judging by her raised eyebrows and cocked head, he wasn't fooling anyone. "I'll *be* fine," he amended.

He glanced at the photo again, shuddered, and moved to put the papers away, but Anna stopped his hand.

"I remember now," Anna said. "It was that photograph."

"What do you mean?"

"My mind felt like pea soup when I first woke, but now

I remember what scared me. I saw that picture, and then you walked in, and . . ." She studied the photograph, and Charlie took the opportunity both to avoid looking at it and to admire Anna's profile.

She looked at him again and scooted a few inches closer, so they almost touched, although she didn't seem to notice that part. He most certainly did, and welcomed it. "Do you know who they are?"

Charlie pointed to the man. "I recognize my father in the middle, but I don't know the women."

"This one is my mother, and I think the woman on the right is Nanny Mae Workman. These are her belongings I was asked to sort through."

He looked at the woman again and nodded. "I can see the resemblance now that you mention it. I knew her much older, of course."

"You look so much like your father, you could be twins," Anna said. "When you appeared in the doorway, I almost thought—" Even though her voice cut off, he knew exactly what she'd been about to say.

"That you'd seen a ghost?"

She lowered her eyes and picked at her fingernails, laughing. "It's silly, of course. I probably got caught up in Nanny Mae's memories, and then there you were, with the face I'd just seen in a picture."

Four

Charlie took a moment to answer. What were the chances that Anna Brierley would think she'd seen a ghost right after he could have sworn that the woman in the photo had looked at him through the window? A woman who looked precisely like a young Nanny Mae Workman.

He scrubbed one hand across his mouth, trying to puzzle it out. The whole thing seemed far too coincidental to be an accident. Yet if all of this was supposed to happen, who had orchestrated it? And why?

He could be hallucinating out of exhaustion. If he kept seeing things, he'd end up like Old Joe Tracey, who wandered the city mumbling to himself as he looked for the puppy he lost as a boy. Old Joe still believed he was seven years old. Everyone said that an accident had changed him at that age, but no one remembered the details. Old Joe didn't recognize his own brother, Frank, who watched out and provided for Joe as best he could. Every time Frank brought food and offered a warm bed, Joe thought he'd met the nice old man for the first time—and had no idea that he, too, was an old man.

Charlie pictured himself wandering the streets, muttering about seeing a ghost on the chapel balcony. Maybe he'd see hallucinations of her in the church window for the rest of his life. That alone could drive a man mad. Starting tomorrow, he'd take a different route home from the orchards, and he'd avoid nighttime meetings and activities at the church.

What if I see the ghost in other places? Then I'll know I've lost my mind entirely. He cleared his throat and deliberately laid the papers face down into the wooden crate. He faced Anna, glad to no longer have the woman's face staring back at him.

"It's a bit eerie going through the belongings of a dead woman on All Hallows' Eve," Anna said. "I should have agreed to do it next week." She leaned forward and touched his arm again. "Are you *sure* you're well? Need some water? I'm sure there's some in the building somewhere." She spoke as if she weren't the one who'd fainted moments ago. The color had returned to Anna's cheeks, which now seemed to glow by lantern light.

Sitting alone with her in the quiet of the chapel, Charlie found himself happily diverted for the moment. He had a feeling he could sit in a haunted chapel for days if it meant also sitting beside Anna. He might even be able to face the visions of a young Nanny Mae Workman if it meant he got to stay. He could not say why, but he felt drawn to Anna, and not only because she was pretty. The more he looked into her face, the more he realized that she wasn't the classical ideal— not really—but she radiated a certain beauty nonetheless. He wanted to be near it as one gathered about a wood-burning stove and absorbed its warmth on cold winter nights.

"How long have you been in town?" he asked, forcing his eyes to not stray to the crate.

"I arrived yesterday." Anna smoothed her skirt and shrugged. "Just in time to attend David Rushton's funeral this morning."

Charlie chuckled. "An excellent welcome to a new citizen, I'm sure."

"Oh, definitely," Anna said with mock solemnity. Her face softened. "But the tabernacle is impressive. We don't have anything that large or ornate in Shelley."

"Shelley," Charlie repeated. "Is that up by Logan?"

"Quite a bit farther north than that. It's a small town in Idaho. Much, *much* smaller than American Fork. You probably have more chickens than we have people."

"Except that we have an unusual number of chickens," Charlie said. The city was known for its chicken and egg industry.

"Granted," Anna said with a smile. "Even so, you've got a much bigger city than I'm used to, with a bigger variety of food and crops. Shelley does quite well with potatoes, and I love a Russet as much as the next girl, but I've taken a liking to your apples in particular."

Charlie took the opportunity to tease. "You don't have apples in Idaho?"

She gave him a look, then laughed. "Yours taste better. I don't know why. When I arrived last night, my aunt served fresh apple pie . . ." Her voice trailed off, and she wore an expression of pleasure. "It was a piece of heaven on a plate."

"Ever had strawberry-rhubarb pie with ice cream? *That* is an experience you won't soon forget."

"I've never had rhubarb, and I've only had ice cream a couple of times. Turning the crank is a lot of work, but it's worth it."

Charlie's smile widened. "What if I told you that you could get ice cream without turning a crank even once?"

Anna seemed suspicious at first, as if Charlie was

teasing her again, but then her eyes widened with understanding. "You have an electric freezer."

"*I* don't," Charlie said. "But I know who does. A small restaurant on Main Street serves ice cream with pie. They call it *à la mode*."

"Really?" she asked wistfully, as if she didn't dare believe it.

"Absolutely. I'll take you. But you have to promise to try the ironport." Charlie leaned an arm on the back of the bench, further narrowing the distance between them. He felt utterly comfortable now, a far cry from a minute before. He and Anna didn't know each other at all, yet he was sure they could carry on hours' worth of conversation, and he'd enjoy every second.

"What's ironport?" She leaned against the back of the bench, coming to rest by his hand. She seemed perfectly at ease, too. No one would ever have suspected that she'd recently fainted.

If he wanted to—or, rather, if it were proper to, because he absolutely *wanted* to—he could have reached out and stroked the dark-blue cotton of her sleeve.

Anna laughed. "I won't try your ironport if I don't know what it is first."

How long had he been sitting there silently admiring her while she waited for an answer? *You're looking like a fool. Behave as if you have a brain between your ears.*

"It's a drink. Sort of like sarsaparilla, a bit like cream soda. A mix of the two, really, with its own flavor," he said, the explanation coming out in a rush.

She didn't look at him as if he were foolish. In fact, there was that smile again. It made something in his chest twist deliciously.

"There's nothing like ironport," he said. "You'll like it. Trust me."

For the space of several heartbeats, Anna didn't speak. She gazed into his eyes, the twinkle in hers suddenly replaced with a more serious expression. "I do," she finally said. "I do trust you." Her voice carried a certain depth—something saying that she meant more than a visit to a restaurant.

There was the twist again. Between that and her smile, he could be happy for the rest of his days. "I imagine I could show you a lot of things you'd never see in Shelley."

"I'd like that," she said quickly. She snapped her mouth closed and shook her head, laughing at herself. "I mean . . . I don't mean to be forward. We've just met, but—" She shrugged helplessly and laughed again.

Charlie thought he caught a deepening of pink in her cheeks and liked the idea that he might have had something to do with it. "How about we begin getting to know each other better . . . tomorrow?" He'd never been so glad to have a day off work.

"Let's." Anna looked around the room. "Goodness. I didn't realize so much time had passed. I really should get home, and I feel well enough to walk. Let's put all of this away."

Let's. He liked the sound of that—it meant both of them. Charlie stacked one crate on top of another he'd only now noticed. "You lead; I'll carry. And then I'll see you home."

"Thank you," Anna said, smiling over her shoulder as she crossed to the lamp. "They belong in a closet down the hall."

He followed, thinking ahead to the morrow and what enjoyable things he could plan for Anna. That is, after the milking and other morning chores that had to be done even when he didn't work for someone else.

The ice cream might be best to save for the end of the day, after spending hours in the sun. Before that, they could walk to the original location of the fort where the first settlers of the city had stayed. Or stroll to the river and down to Utah Lake. Its enormity surprised him no matter how often he went there.

What else? Maybe one day, if he could convince some others to come along, he could take Anna up the canyon and climb to Timpanogos Cave. Sometimes youth held dances in the spectacular caverns by the light of kerosene lamps. They danced to the music of a few small instruments small enough to carry up.

Charlie put the crates into the closet Anna indicated. He followed her outside and shut the church door behind him as Anna wrapped a shawl about her shoulders and extinguished the lamp, which she left by the door right as Mr. Sorensen appeared, apparently putting his tools away. Charlie and the gardener exchanged waves, and then he and Anna headed toward the Ingersolls' house. At the corner, he couldn't help but look back at the window above the door. It was dark. He shivered and turned to escort Anna home.

Surprisingly, after talking in the chapel, neither said much on the way. The evening was cool, the air nipping at their noses and ears. The walk seemed to last only moments. All too soon, they stood on the north side of Main Street, waiting for two carriages and an automobile to pass. Night had fallen completely, and the moon was only a slight crescent, providing little light. A few street lamps and a handful of buildings with electric lighting helped guide the way.

After crossing the street, they approached the final corner and slowed their step at the same time, as if neither of them wanted the walk to end. Anna stopped completely at the corner opposite the Ingersolls' house, which had several windows lit up already. Charlie could hardly make out Anna's features now that velvety darkness had descended, but he felt her shiver. With the sunset came the autumn chill, which surely went right through her shawl. She didn't speak or move. Charlie looked over and found that her hands were clasped tightly, and she wore an expression of dread.

"Is something wrong?" He glanced at the house. "Do they mistreat you?"

"No. They're kind enough. It's not that." She looked down at her hands.

Charlie wanted to reach out and lift her chin so he could see her eyes again, then make a joke so she'd smile. "I hope I'm not being too bold when I say that I'd like to help if I can. You can trust me with whatever it is."

Her face lifted to his, and she smiled wanly.

A small smile is better than nothing.

"I really *can* trust you, Charlie Beck, can't I?"

"Absolutely." He reached for her clasped hands and held them between his. She didn't pull away. Her skin felt like ice. "Your aunt needs to get you a good pair of mittens," he said, hoping for a smile. All he got was a nod. He needed to stop being silly and return to her—and her concern. "What is it?"

"You'll think I'm crazy."

He'd had the very same thought earlier. "I doubt that. Tell me."

She didn't answer, just looked at her hands in his for several seconds. Charlie resisted the urge to break the silence. Anna finally spoke. "That picture you saw. The one with your father . . . Your resemblance to him isn't the only thing that startled me—that frightened me. There's something more."

Charlie felt a sensation not unlike a spider crawling up one's back. "Does it have to do with Nanny Mae?"

A quick nod. Anna licked her lips then looked into his eyes and spoke quietly. "I think I saw her ghost."

Maybe I'm not going mad. The thought was a tremendous relief—for him. Anna's brow remained deeply furrowed. Whatever she was thinking, it wasn't pleasant.

"Did you see her in the chapel too?" Charlie asked.

"No. It was this morning at the cemetery." Her expression changed to one of confusion. "Wait, what do you mean, 'too'? Did *you* see Nanny Mae?" She pulled her hands from his and covered her mouth. He must have looked guilty, because she grinned with relief and grabbed both of his forearms. "You *did* see her."

A flood of emotions made thinking hard for Charlie. Beautiful, kind, smart Anna was holding on to him. And she'd seen the ghost of Nanny Mae Workman. How exactly was one supposed to behave under such circumstances? His mother always quoted the newspaper's etiquette columns, but he doubted whether even those would have sound counsel for this situation.

Anna began pacing, first going a few yards back the way they'd come, then returning, all the while talking so fast that the words seemed to come out like bullets. "I was at the burial, standing in the crowd with my aunt, and I saw a woman—the same one from the picture—looking right at me. Her hair and clothing were different, but it was definitely her. She wore white. At a graveside service. No one so much as glanced her way. And she carried a candle—outside, in the daytime, when the sky threatened rain. I asked Aunt Wilma who she was, but she thought I was coming down with the flu. I didn't want her thinking that her niece was completely daft, so I left it alone. I could tell that no one else saw the woman. The queerest part—and the most unsettling—was when she looked at me and pointed."

Anna mimicked the gesture, pointing into the darkness. "Gave me the jitters, I tell you. And then she smiled. I remember because, like the white dress—or was it a nightdress?—either way, it didn't fit at a burial. She said, 'It's you,' as if she already knew me."

Breathless, Anna stopped right in front of Charlie and locked eyes with him. "I could have sworn that she'd been *looking* for me. And tonight in the chapel, I came across the picture of her, and then you came in right after that, looking just like your father." She held out her hands helplessly, palms up. "What does it all mean?"

"I have no idea." Charlie wished he did. But the one

thing he did know was that his experience sounded eerily similar to Anna's. "You're cold. Let's keep walking."

Anna slipped her hand through the crook of his arm. First, they crossed the street to the Ingersoll house, and then they strolled around the block as if they'd done so a thousand times. Her hand felt as if it belonged there, as if his arm had always missed a piece of a puzzle, and her hand fit the spot.

"When did you see her?" Anna asked.

"About one minute before I saw you."

Her step came up short, and she turned to face him. "You saw her *tonight*?"

He nodded and encouraged her to continue walking; telling the story in the darkness, without looking into her face, seemed easier than the alternative. "I was walking home from the orchards. When I reached the church, a bright light came through the window above the door. The rest of the building was quiet with no church events or meetings, so I stopped to look. And then I saw her. The window was almost a perfect frame. She was smiling and had a white dress and candle like you described."

"And a long, red braid?" Anna asked.

"Yes." Charlie wasn't sure if the emotion he felt was relief that he wasn't alone or fear over what it all meant. "She pointed at me and spoke."

Anna pulled back slightly and paled. "What—did she say?" Her voice had grown faint.

"The same thing. 'It's you.' Then she added, 'Come,' and disappeared down the hall. I ran into the church to see if something was wrong. And found you."

They rounded the third corner of the block and slowed to a stop, looking at each other.

"Anna, how is any of this possible?" Charlie asked.

"And what does it mean?" she added, voicing another question.

Somehow, his excitement over sharing ice cream tomorrow waned as new, troubling questions loomed. In silence, he and Anna walked around the last corner of the block, to the Ingersolls' gate, which Charlie opened for her.

Anna stepped through to one of the paving stones and turned around. "Thank you for walking me home."

"My pleasure," Charlie said with a tilt of his head as if tipping his hat.

In spite of their outward pleasantries, something more, something almost tangible, connected them. He glanced at the house, where the large window beside the door was open a few inches. In the sitting room on the other side, someone could probably hear them. Anna looked over too and nodded in understanding.

"May I call on you tomorrow at noon?" Charlie asked. The day might not look like he'd first envisioned, with a tour of the city with ice cream afterward, but he needed to see her again. Soon. Together they'd at least try to untangle the mystery that fate had handed them.

"I look forward to it. Good night, Mr. Beck." She gave a proper nod, then followed the paving stones to the porch.

Charlie disliked the formality, but he understood the need, particularly if her relatives were the overly protective type. Mrs. Ingersoll, at least, had always seemed particularly conservative and straitlaced. Charlie and Anna didn't need anyone putting their noses into their business, ghostly or otherwise.

He waited as Anna climbed the porch steps. She reached the door and turned the knob. Charlie hoped she'd look back one more time. She paused before pushing the door open and did seem about to look over her shoulder at him—perhaps give him another smile to melt his insides?—but she simply went inside.

"Aunt Wilma, I'm home," Anna called, and the door closed with a thud.

Without Anna, the evening chill seemed twice as deep. He turned around and headed home, but the mile he had yet to walk stretched ahead like a long strip going on forever.

And as he walked, every shadow or flicker of lamplight seemed to be another ghost.

Five

"You were out a bit late," Aunt Wilma said over her glasses. She'd paused in her handwork, though Anna knew full well that her aunt could embroider practically blindfolded.

Anna chose to ignore the fact that she was an adult who didn't need to be scolded like a child, even if she was a houseguest. "I was up at the church doing some work." She moved toward the stairs, but as soon as she touched the newel post at the base of the staircase, her aunt spoke.

"Who was with you outside? I heard a man's voice."

Anna pressed her eyes and lips closed, gathering herself before forcing a smile and a pleasant tone as she turned around. "That was Mr. Charlie Beck. I felt unwell, so he escorted me home to ensure my well-being. He's very kind and gentlemanly."

"I highly doubt that, and I suggest you stop associating with him, seeing as he's the son of a scoundrel." Aunt Wilma crooked one eyebrow so high that it was a wonder it didn't disappear into her hairline.

"Why do you say that?" Anna asked airily, then had to clench her teeth. She would rather have stormed up to her bedroom, but Aunt Wilma had a way of keeping someone in place when she wanted to speak to them. Besides, Anna wanted to hear what she had to say, if only to defend Charlie. Even if his father had done some bad things, that didn't mean his son automatically followed his footsteps.

With a dismissive snort, Aunt Wilma returned to her embroidery and to rocking her chair. "I thought you of all people would have heard about the Beck family, seeing as Howard Beck broke your mother's heart and ruined her life."

A fire sprang to life in Anna's chest. "My mother's life was *not* ruined."

"Funny you'd say that, seeing as how she didn't live long enough for you to hear such things from her own lips."

Anna forced herself to keep quiet; she needed a room to stay in until she could support herself, and putting Aunt Wilma in her place would make life utterly miserable. Her grandparents had told stories of her parents' courtship and love for each other. But doubt entered Anna's mind. She'd grown up with her paternal grandparents. Would they have known details about their daughter-in-law's past? Why would Aunt Wilma say such things about her own late sister? Anna had to find out more, no matter how much she wanted to flee. If she left now, she'd regret it. She didn't ask for the story, but her silence must have been enough for Aunt Wilma to consider it a request.

"Howard Beck was your mother's beau, and she loved him with a depth I've never seen before or since." Aunt Wilma sighed. "I admit that at times, I envied her. I was the elder sister, and I had no young men clamoring for my attention. But somehow, whenever I saw them together, the jealousy melted away because they were so perfect together. Looking into her eyes, you could see the pure joy he brought her. Ellen was happy." She stopped rocking, and her embroidery fell unheeded to her lap. She gazed into the dying embers of the fireplace, seeming to be in another world. The house had radiant heating, so the fireplace wasn't precisely necessary, but it did add a homey feel to the autumn evening.

Anna's attention had caught on more than the fireplace, however. In her presence, Aunt Wilma had never before referred to her late sister as anything other than *your mother*. But she'd just called her by name—Ellen.

A not uncomfortable silence settled over the sitting room. Anna stepped away from the stairs and walked to the settee beside the rocking chair, where she sat and asked quietly, "What happened?"

Somehow, she didn't feel angry or defensive anymore. She genuinely wanted to know what had happened, as much for understanding her mother as for learning about Charlie and what his family had to do with hers.

"I don't think any of us will ever know precisely what went wrong," Aunt Wilma said with a far-off gaze. "I remember the day he called on Ellen and broke her heart. He accused her of awful, unspeakable things. Said she'd betrayed him with another man. He wouldn't listen to her protests, wouldn't let her explain anything. He believed the words of some supposed witness, but he wouldn't say who that was, either." She blinked, seemed to come to herself, and looked at Anna with tears in her normally crabby eyes. Anna couldn't help but feel compassion and sadness for her aunt— and for her mother.

"I've long believed that Howard Beck simply needed an excuse to move on. He'd had his fun but wanted to sow his oats, so to speak. A story from a 'witness' was plenty excuse to toss her out of his life. She cried in her room for a solid week, then moved north to live with extended family we'd never met. That's when she met your father." Aunt Wilma put a hand on Anna's knee, and added, "Your father was a good man, and he brought her back from complete heartbreak." The familiar hard edge returned to her jaw—and to her voice. "But I'll never forgive Howard Beck for hurting her in the first place."

"I had no idea," Anna said. That was both a truthful and a safe thing to say. She paid careful attention to not add opinion or commentary as her mind tried to rewrite history, adding this new information. Aunt Wilma couldn't know the entire story, and even if she did, Howard Beck's actions and character—assuming he had cruelly cast aside a woman who'd loved him—had no bearing whatsoever on the person his son had become.

After a moment, Aunt Wilma let out a weary sigh and returned to her stitching. Anna took the action as a sign that she might leave without offending.

"I'm quite tired," she said. A yawn confirmed her words. She covered her mouth and stood. "Thank you for telling me about my mother."

"I loved her dearly," Aunt Wilma said without looking up again. She focused on a rose petal in her design.

"Good night," Anna said, stepping away. "I hope you sleep well."

"Good night," Aunt Wilma replied absently. Then under her breath, almost too quiet to make out, she added, "I hope the dead, too, rest in peace tonight."

A shiver went through Anna at the mention of the dead, even though her aunt likely referred to Anna's mother. Considering the events of the last few hours, though, it was no wonder that talk of the deceased made her uneasy. She made her way up the stairs to the landing, where three tall, narrow windows looked out at the carriage house and gardens. Anna wanted to linger in case she could see Charlie, although he'd probably walked in another direction. She quickly changed her mind, in case she'd end up seeing something else—like Nanny Mae's ghost.

Anna climbed the second flight of stairs and went to the

IT'S YOU

northeast corner room, which overlooked both Main Street
and 100 West, where she and Charlie had said goodnight.
Normally at this hour, Anna would have gotten ready for
bed, but tonight, she felt restless and paced the room, which
was almost fifteen feet long both directions—much larger
than any bedroom she'd ever had, and it wasn't the largest of
the house. Back and forth she went to the wide windows
covered in lacy drapes, to the closet, and back again. She
couldn't think of sleep, not after learning about her mother
when she was about Anna's age. And with that information
came questions about why her mother and Howard Beck
were in a photograph with Nanny Mae.

That thought was quickly followed with reminders
about how many times Nanny Mae had touched her life that
very day. And Charlie's. She'd even said the same words to
each of them.

*Maybe we aren't the only ones. She could have appeared
to any number of people who simply haven't spoken of it.* That
made sense and eased Anna's nerves. It would mean that the
ghost's appearance wasn't necessarily connected to Anna and
Charlie.

At one point when she turned from the window to the
closet, she studied the closet door. Nanny Mae had once slept
in this room. A shelf in the closet had a stack of old
notebooks, Anna suddenly remembered. *What if . . .*

She walked to the closet with purpose and pulled the
door open. Before the butterflies in her stomach got the
better of her, Anna reached for the notebooks and pulled
them off the shelf. She found three—fewer than she'd
thought—and blew a slight layer of dust off the top. After
taking a seat on her bed, she turned on the electric lamp on
her nightstand and opened the top notebook. It held recipes
in Aunt Wilma's hand. The second notebook appeared to be
a journal written by Aunt Wilma's daughter Cora. It was set
aside along with the recipes. The bottom notebook had no
writing on the worn brown cover, but Anna instinctively

99

knew it was what she was looking for, and that the moment she opened it, her life would never again be the same.

With her eyes closed, she lifted the cover. Before looking down, she licked her lips, said a quick prayer, and finally opened her eyes. A journal. Anna didn't recognize the handwriting, but perusing a few pages was plenty to confirm that these were the words of Nanny Mae Workman, many of which she'd written while staying here.

Anna read, sometimes skipping past records of daily minutiae to longer passages, where Nanny Mae became contemplative. Her final days were filled with sadness and regret. Her final entry was only about halfway through the book, dated exactly a year before—the night she died, Anna realized with a start.

> *31 October, 1923*
>
> *I've been here only two months, but the hatred I feel from Mrs. Ingersoll is almost more than this old woman can bear. I fear she knows the part I played in her family's drama. If so, I cannot blame her for despising me. I've come to despise myself. Just think: the actions of an impulsive young woman who intended to create her own happiness instead created misery and unhappiness. At first that unhappiness was reserved for Howard and Ellen, but they healed of the wounds I inflicted. It is I who have paid the price for decades. I lost the man I loved, even though he never belonged to me. I lost the trust of the community. No man would court me. I lost the opportunity to have children. And now I face my final days.*
>
> *I pray they do not last long. I pray even more fervently, every night, that when I am dead, I may have the opportunity to set right what I made wrong—that I may bring together the families I so cruelly separated.*

Foolish, foolish girl. If I could go back in time, I would warn the slip of a thing that I was to stand back. To hold her tongue and not spread vicious lies in the form of idle gossip. Lies I didn't know then would have such a horrible effect.

As unhappy as I am living here, I have not asked the bishop to move me. I have already been too much of a burden to the congregation. I also know that I deserve any bitterness thrown into my path. Perhaps some of what I have endured will count toward any suffering God will require of me to atone for my sins.

May God have mercy on my soul.

Anna slowly raised her gaze from the book. What precisely did that last line mean? Had Nanny Mae killed herself? Had she thought her past actions particularly heinous? Both?

Anna closed the book and thought through what she knew of Nanny Mae. She filled gaps with what Aunt Wilma had told her. The picture it created was simple yet sad: Nanny Mae had fallen in love with Howard Beck and wanted him for herself. But he'd had eyes only for Anna's mother. To separate them and diminish Ellen in his eyes, Nanny Mae went to Howard and told him lies about Ellen. He was foolish enough to believe them.

Based on Nanny Mae's words, at least some of the truth had come out, and she'd been shunned by the revelation of what she'd done. Possibly by exaggerations of the truth as well. By then, Ellen had gone to Idaho. Anna knew that her parents' courtship was a quick one. Now Anna had a feeling that her mother had been so desperate for love and acceptance, so anxious to escape the rumors and Howard's disdain, that she'd married as quickly as she could. Even if Howard had had a change of heart, it would have been too late.

Anna couldn't help but wonder about Howard. Did he hear of her mother's marriage when it happened? Did he know of her death only two years later, when Anna was days past her first birthday?

Her vision blurred, and she found tears spilling down her cheeks at the lost opportunities, the heartbreak, the sadness. All for nothing.

A voice seemed to speak to Anna then, not so she heard it, precisely, but she *felt* the words as strongly as if someone had placed them in her mind.

I hope I did not scare you. I came only to fix what I made wrong.

Any fear or trepidation Anna may have felt at the thought of a ghost now melted away in the face of an intense, warm love encircling her. The voice spoke again.

Your mother was a wonderful woman. I hope you forgive me.

Anna wiped her cheeks and gently closed the journal. She fell asleep with it under her pillow, still in her work dress.

A nna awoke with a start the next morning, opening her eyes and looking about, feeling disoriented. *I had the strangest dream last night,* she thought, then rolled to her back and realized that she wasn't wearing her nightdress. She looked down; she was still fully dressed, down to her boots.

Then it wasn't a dream.

She rolled to her side and adjusted her pillow. Her fingers touched a notebook, and everything rushed back— sorting through Nanny Mae's belongings in the church, seeing the photograph of her with Anna's mother and the man she now knew was Howard Beck, who looked like a carbon copy of his son, Charlie.

Charlie!

Anna sat bolt upright at the memory. His dark hair, kind eyes, strong arms. His sense of humor. How they'd both seen Nanny Mae. How they'd both known that the experience was significant in some way.

And now I know why.

She got up and changed into a fresh dress. She brushed through her hair and braided it, finally flinging it over her left shoulder. Not until she looked at her reflection did she realize that she'd copied Nanny Mae's style. Anna's hair wasn't as long, but the effect was strikingly similar.

I never wear one long braid, Anna thought, running her fingers down the silky twists. Instead of taking it out, she decided to keep it for the day as a tribute to the ghost who'd stepped into her life.

As promised, Charlie arrived at noon. Anna had packed a basket with a picnic lunch for them. She'd slipped the journal inside and a blanket over the top. She came out from the kitchen door to meet him with the basket over one arm. He looked wan, almost ash-faced. And no wonder. They'd parted after discussing an unsettling circumstance.

Wearing her broadest smile, she crossed to him. "I have just the thing for us to do first," she said cheerfully. "And I promise that I'll turn that frown the other way 'round by the time lunch is over."

That alone eked a tentative smile out of Charlie. "Oh?"

"Oh yes." She turned to call through the kitchen door to her aunt, who was reading in the sunroom. "I'm going out with Charlie Beck. Don't expect me back until evening."

"All—all right," came the response, one that made Anna breathe a sigh of relief.

That morning, she'd explained what she could to her aunt—nothing about the ghost of Nanny Mae, of course, and attributing everything Anna had learned to the journal.

She closed the door and slipped one hand around Charlie's elbow, and they began walking.

He peered about Main Street and asked, "Did you have a place in mind for what I presume is a delicious meal?"

"Well," Anna said, unsure how to broach the subject. "I

suggest we walk up to the cemetery and pay a visit to Nanny Mae Workman's grave."

Charlie's step stopped cold. "Surely you're joking."

She shook her head, unable to stop smiling. She kept walking and tugged his arm so he'd follow. He did, and they crossed the street, heading in the direction of the cemetery. "I unraveled the mystery about our ghost."

"Shh," Charlie said. "Don't say that word so loud. People will talk."

Spoken like Aunt Wilma, Anna thought with a silent laugh.

"Last night, I learned some interesting things from my aunt, as well as from reading a journal written by none other than Nanny Mae Workman."

Charlie stiffened but didn't stop walking, which Anna took as a good sign.

"I learned that my mother and your father once courted." Out of the corner of her eye, she waited for Charlie's reaction. His eyes widened as she'd expected, so she hurried on. "Nanny Mae came between them. You can read about it all in her journal. I brought it along."

"What does that have to do with you and me? Why is she haunting us?"

"She simply wants to right a wrong," Anna said. "She recognized us because we both look much like our parents, and she hoped that perhaps she could intervene in such a way as to . . ."

"Play matchmaker from the great beyond?" Charlie finished.

"In a manner of speaking."

He shook his head and laughed. "I'm still not sure if you and I really are daft and imagined seeing her. I have no idea if my father courted anyone before my mother—they won't speak of those times. Which in itself is a bit suspicious, now that I think of it."

When they reached the cemetery, Charlie led her up a

grassy hill to Nanny Mae's grave, still new enough to have a headstone without chips or weathering. They stood before it in quiet acknowledgment of the woman who had lived her life hating herself for a poor decision she'd made one day as a young woman.

Eventually, they sat on the thin blanket that Anna had folded into the basket, and they ate lunch under a sky remarkably clear and warm for late autumn.

"So what now?" Charlie asked before popping a grape into his mouth. He chewed it quickly and swallowed, then added, "Are we now obligated to do Nanny Mae's bidding?"

"You mean by having a—a future together?" In spite of herself, Anna blushed. "Of course not. The mystery is solved, and that's enough." Not entirely the truth; she'd found herself dreaming of a future with Charlie. Of staying in town rather than applying for positions elsewhere. But she wasn't about to say so. "Nanny Mae must know by now that one cannot force matters of romance, and that—"

She couldn't finish her sentence because Charlie leaned in and stopped her words with a kiss. After a second of stunned surprise, Anna thrilled to the feel of his lips on hers and wished the moment would never end. Charlie pulled away, and her eyes fluttered open to look into his.

When he spoke next, his voice was soft, warm, and filled with unspoken emotion. "Would you be entirely opposed to seeing whether Nanny Mae is right this time?"

Anna couldn't find any words, so she shook her head until she finally managed to speak. "Not opposed at all. But Charlie?"

He held her face between his hands and stroked one cheek with his thumb. "Mmm?"

"Kiss me again. Only you'd better hold me this time. I'm liable to faint again."

Charlie happily obliged.

About Annette Lyon

Annette Lyon is a Whitney Award winner, a three-time recipient of Utah's Best of State medal for fiction, and a four-time publication award winner from the League of Utah Writers, including the Silver Quill Award in 2013 for *Paige*. She's the author of more than a dozen novels, almost as many novellas, several nonfiction books, and over one hundred twenty magazine articles. Annette is a cum laude graduate from BYU with a degree in English. When she's not writing, knitting, or eating chocolate, she can be found mothering and avoiding the spots on the kitchen floor.

Sign up for her newsletter: AnnetteLyon.com/contact
Find her online:
Website: http://AnnetteLyon.com
Blog: http://blog.AnnetteLyon.com
Twitter: @AnnetteLyon
Facebook: http://Facebook.com/AnnetteLyon
Pinterest: http://Pinterest.com/AnnetteLyon

Sophia's Curse

by Heather B. Moore

Other Works by Heather B. Moore

Esther the Queen
Finding Sheba
Lost King
Beneath

The Aliso Creek Series
Heart of the Ocean
The Newport Ladies Book Club Series
The Fortune Café
The Boardwalk Antiques Shop

One

France, October 31, 1838

"The babe is a girl child," the midwife informed Monsieur Rudolph Belrose in a trembling voice. "She's pink and healthy, sir, with a lusty cry."

Belrose didn't care if his daughter was pink and healthy. If she'd been a boy, he might have been able to forgive the fact that the child was born on the cursed All Hallows' Eve. But, after the death of his beloved wife, there was no forgiveness in his grieving heart.

It seemed that Sophia's curse was alive and well. When Belrose's father was on his deathbed, a woman named Sophia Rousseau from a neighboring estate claimed that she had a secret marriage to Belrose Sr. and that she deserved to inherit his property. Sophia said that all of Belrose's heirs from his "second marriage" were illegitimate. Yet, not even her own family would support her statements. She was turned away by the dying Belrose, and she cursed both families, saying that someone from one of the families, or connected to them, would die every five years on All Hallows' Eve, until the estates were rightfully reunited in marriage.

It had been a bother to hire servants since.

And now, Rudolph Belrose would have to remarry in order to produce an heir. If there was an eligible female of the Rousseau family, Belrose might actually consider marrying her if only to break the curse. But Monsieur Rousseau and his wife had been killed five years before on All Hallows' Eve, leaving only a young son. Belrose had to find another way to end the years of bad luck, no matter what it took. And that would begin by getting rid of this unholy child of his.

"Take her to the abbey," Belrose told the quivering midwife.

"Sir, you have not yet laid eyes on the babe," she said, her tone incredulous. "I am sorry for the loss of your wife, but her child is your child as well."

"Silence," he commanded. "Her birth on this day of all days surely caused my wife's death. The child is ill luck indeed. I will not have the fates brought down upon my land by raising this imp."

The midwife hung her head, her hands clenching until they were white. "What shall I tell the nuns when I deliver her to the abbey?"

"Tell them she was abandoned by a peasant on the side of the road." Belrose could not look at the sniveling woman now, or else her weakness would become his weakness. He would grieve for his wife in private only.

"And her name?" The midwife's voice was a whisper in the cold stone hallway.

Belrose's throat went dry as he fought the rage and grief battling inside of him. "She has no name. For you see, the murderer of my wife deserves no honor."

Two

Twenty Years Later
1858

Joan of Arc stood atop the crumbling stone ramparts, raised her sword, and looked over the vast field of dead enemy soldiers. "The Lord has avenged the people of Orléans! Enemies, return to England, or face the wrath of France!"

"Joan?" A woman's voice cut through her speech. "You're late milking the cows."

Joan lowered her arm and sighed, then stepped down from the low stone wall that bordered a field beneath the warm October sun. There were no enemy soldiers lying dead in the field, and, although she was also nineteen years old, she was hardly the great warrior woman. But couldn't she ever have more than an hour to herself?

Sister Eloise strode up to Joan. Sister Eloise was a tall, reedy woman, given to coughing fits at night. This Joan knew because her room was right next to Sister Eloise's. The nun was of an indiscriminate age, and Joan had once asked her how old she was. The look she gave Joan was quite deadly.

"Is it that late?" Joan asked in a light, innocent voice.

The nun's plain brown eyes narrowed. "You undoubtedly heard the bells chime four o'clock, and then five o'clock. Surely you didn't miss *both* chimes?"

Joan bit her lower lip. "I am deeply sorry," she said. "I won't let it happen again." Sister Eloise looked far from convinced. Both she and Joan knew that it *would* happen again, many times most likely.

As Joan neared the small barn that sat behind the Sisters of St. Joseph's abbey, she could hear the two cows lowing. A twinge of guilt spread through her—the animals were unhappy, and it was her fault for getting caught up in daydreaming. She hurried inside and grabbed the milking stool and wooden bucket. She worked quickly, and soon both cows were sated. Then she carried the fresh milk to the back of the abbey to the kitchen.

As Joan entered the kitchen, Sister Laurette looked up from her place at the table, where she was chopping vegetables. She was as round as Sister Eloise was thin.

"About time," Sister Laurette said, although there wasn't a bit of malice in her tone. Her deep green eyes were full of amusement. "Did you fall asleep under the trees again? Or, perhaps, wander past the stream?"

"No," Joan said, in a voice breathless from traipsing across the yard with two heavy buckets. She set them carefully next to the fireplace.

"Spying on the Rousseau boy again?" Sister Laurette asked.

Joan spun and stared at the nun. How could she have known? Joan had been so careful.

Sister Laurette laughed at Joan's stunned expression. "Don't think we don't know everything that goes on here—because we do."

"*We? Everyone* knows?"

Sister Laurette winked. "Of course. But we love you all the more for it. We all know you didn't choose this life. Some of the sisters have even . . ." she dropped her voice to a whisper, "made wagers on how long you'll remain unmarried. Especially if Simon Rousseau catches you spying upon him."

Mortification shot through Joan at the thought of Simon actually discovering that she'd spied on him more than once. More than a dozen times. At first she told herself it was because of his horse—a magnificent black beast with muscles rippling all over its body. But the months had passed, and still Joan was drawn to the neighboring estate and the young man who relentlessly rode alone each afternoon.

She knew very little of the Rousseau family, except that their ancestors were known for horse breeding and that there had been a tragedy in Simon's early years. His parents had been killed on All Hallows' Eve, leaving Simon as their young heir. His uncle had come to run the estate until Simon was of age.

Joan had heard whispers about a decades-old curse on the Rousseau's land and the estate just beyond, that of the Belrose family. Every five years, a member of the Belrose family or Rousseau family had died on All Hallows' Eve. Two of the victims were Belrose's own wife and child, who'd both died many years ago. It was said that Monsieur Belrose had gone mad and refused to leave his home. No one, other than his servants, had seen him for ages.

The entire village was waiting for him to die. For, with no heir, the lands would go to the church. But who had cursed the families and why? That's what Joan wanted to know.

"You're a young, pretty woman," Sister Laurette said, capturing Joan's attention again. "Simon Rousseau could do a lot worse."

Joan's face flamed hot. She was fair of skin and susceptible to blushing—and it happened at the most inconvenient times. That's also why she kept her almost white blonde hair in a tight plait and wrapped it into a bun at the base of her neck, complete with a handkerchief tied about her hair to help keep the sun off—she burned frightfully easily.

"Simon Rousseau is a gentleman, and I am but an orphaned peasant," she said.

Sister Laurette pursed her lips together, but Joan barely noticed. It was always like this. If she ever brought up her orphan status, the nuns would go silent. None of them could tell her about her parents, just that she'd been brought in by a woman who said that Joan had been abandoned at the side of the road.

Joan felt the familiar weight of her heart grow heavy. If her own mother hadn't even wanted her, how did it make sense that someone like Simon Rousseau would want an orphaned peasant girl who'd been raised in an abbey? Still, the desire to watch him on his afternoon ride battled within her. She found that she depended on his predictability, and the days he didn't come out riding were the days that she felt most out of sorts. Like today, knowing Simon was due for his ride, she could hardly stand being here in the abbey kitchen.

Sister Laurette was still speaking to Joan, telling her the story of how another village girl had married some wealthy man generations ago. Joan had heard it all before. But this was the year of 1858. Those romantic fantasies no longer existed.

Joan mumbled an excuse to leave the kitchen and slipped out the door, ignoring Sister Laurette's knowing look. The yard behind the abbey was quiet, and Joan continued past the barn to where there was a perfect place to sit on the stone wall and watch the northern fields through a grove of trees. Only if Simon dismounted his horse and walked quite close to the trees would he be able to see Joan.

Sometimes she imagined he did just that—that he spotted her from afar and rode over the copse of trees. He would extend his hand without a word, and she would hurry forward and climb up on his horse. Then he would take her for a ride, far across the meadow and past the manor house of his estate, and they'd ride in the purple hills beyond until the day melted into night.

But that scenario was only her imagination, and Joan kept herself firmly wedged on her rocky seat as she waited for Simon to appear. She heard the sound of galloping before his horse came into view.

Thus, Joan's heart was beating erratically in advance of actually seeing Simon's tall form sitting astride his nearly black horse. Simon had grown taller this past year, his shoulders broader, and dare she notice it, his thighs more muscular. In fact, he was well-matched with the stallion he rode. Joan wasn't quite sure of Simon's eye color, but, from a distance, they seemed dark and deeply thoughtful.

She had even heard his voice a time or two as he called out to his horse, and it had only made Joan more curious.

The hoofbeats rumbled closer, and Joan both straightened and leaned behind the foliage in front of her. She wanted a good view, but she also didn't want to be spotted.

"Whoa, boy," Simon said, his voice cutting through the grove.

Joan stiffened. He sounded very close, yet she could no longer see his horse from her vantage point.

"There, there." Simon's voice came again, this time accompanied by his horse's snort.

And then he came into view.

Joan's mouth nearly fell open. Simon was walking, leading his horse by its reins. Joan's first thought was that the horse had been injured. Her second thought was the realization that Simon's eyes were not dark brown like she had first assumed, but a blue gray, the color of an impending rainstorm.

And those blue gray eyes were looking straight at her.

Three

Simon Rousseau wanted to smile, but he sensed the nervousness in the girl behind the tree. Their eyes locked, and Simon felt something hot fill his chest. She was older than he had first guessed—not a girl at all, but a young woman. Perhaps a handful of years younger than his own twenty-four.

And she was pretty. Not in the classic and coiffed way of the young women his aunt had insisted he meet in drawing room musicales. He refused to marry those young women anyway . . . for how could he subject an innocent woman to his family's curse?

This young woman possessed a beauty unmarred by rouge or dark-lined brows or masses of ringlets. She wore a plain dress, and, for some reason, Simon was pleased to note that she wore neither the white wimple nor the black habit of an ordained nun. Her complexion was remarkably fair, nearly translucent, and her hair was so blonde that it was virtually silver in the dappled light coming through the trees.

He, of course, had heard stories about an orphaned girl that the nuns were raising. And now that he thought about it—she would have to be nearly his age. But for some reason, he'd always pictured a twelve- or thirteen-year-old, who hadn't aged with the passing years.

That he'd lived next to her his entire life, yet had only caught a glimpse of her now, was strange indeed. Of course, Simon had been away to boarding school most of his growing up years and had only recently come into his inheritance, which required him to spend more time on the estate.

"Hello?" Simon spoke in a soft voice. The woman flinched, and drew even farther behind the tree, until he could no longer see her.

"I didn't mean to startle you." He took a careful step forward, and his horse lumbered behind him. "I'm Simon Rousseau, and this abbey borders my land."

"I know who you are," the woman said, her voice surprisingly low and rich.

Simon took another step forward. "Have we met before?"

"No," came the quick reply. "There has never been an occasion to meet."

Again, Simon was struck with the richness of her voice. Her words did not indicate that she had a shy personality, although the fact that she still hid behind a tree told him she was feeling quite reluctant.

"I would not be opposed to an introduction then." Simon took the reins of his horse and lashed them to the nearest tree. Then he turned back to look in the direction of the tree, where the woman's dark blue dress peeked out.

"There is no one here to introduce us," she said.

Simon chuckled, but stopped quickly, not sure if he could tease her. "Perhaps we can dispense with formalities seeing as how we've lived on bordering properties our entire lives."

The woman emitted a small gasp. "What do you know about me?"

He smiled to himself. Did she not know they lived in a village where everyone knew many things about everyone else? "Just as you know my name, I know your name, but not much else."

She was silent, and Simon waited.

Finally, she said, "I suppose everyone has heard my story, and I cannot very well avoid what people have said." He heard a rustling sound, and then she stepped out from behind the tree. "My name is Joan," she said, gazing at him.

No, she was not shy, Simon decided. In fact, she seemed a bit impetuous. Her blue eyes were sharp in color, like cold ice, but Simon sensed that this woman was far from cold.

"Pleased to meet you, Joan," Simon said, trying to recover from his surprise at her appearance.

She tilted her head. "Monsieur Rousseau."

"I've seen you here often," he said and was rewarded with a complete transformation of her face—from the fairest cream to a rosy red in a matter of an instant. Her blush was another surprise, but he didn't have time to dwell on its meaning quite yet.

"I—I prefer the outdoors," she said with a charming stutter. "When I'm finished with my chores, I like to sit awhile and listen to the birds."

Except for the fact that the birds were quiet in the late afternoons, Simon might have been wholly convinced. Was she not supposed to be this far from the abbey?

"Surely there are birds closer to the abbey?" he teased.

Her face flamed again, and Simon found that he enjoyed her complexion changes. But now he was probably teasing too much.

"None so robust as the ones in these trees," she said, looking as if she could see the birds, as well as hear them.

"The starlings are particularly musical today."

Simon realized she was teasing him back. He looked up, as if to study the branches for himself. "Ah, you are right. I've never heard such a twittering in all my life." He was rewarded by her laughter, light and quick. Lowering his head, he caught her smile before it faded. And it was a beautiful smile.

"That is what birds do, after all," Joan said with a sigh, leaning her shoulder against a tree. "Twitter all day long. How would it be to live as these birds?"

Simon took a few steps closer and leaned against a tree of his own. They were only a couple of paces apart now, and he found that his heart was hammering. Surely he wasn't nervous. "It might be a bit cold at times and a bit wet when it rains."

Joan's mouth curved into a soft smile, her gaze not quite focusing on him. "But think of the flying and all that you could explore."

"Have you never been outside of the village?" he asked.

Her eyes were less dreamy now. "I have not. A woman in my situation has limited options." Her face pinked. "But I do not mean to sound ungrateful."

"You didn't sound ungrateful," he said. "I've been fortunate enough to attend school in Paris and travel about. Though, it's my honest opinion that we enjoy the most beauty right here in this countryside."

He realized that he was staring at her quite openly when her blush deepened. He hurried to steer the conversation away from this topic. "Tell me what it's like to grow up in an abbey."

Her brows arched as she studied him. "I suppose there is nothing unusual about it to me, for I know nothing else. I would not know what might possibly interest you, unless I knew more about *your* upbringing."

Simon grinned. Joan was clever *and* beautiful. "My story is much like any other young man's who inherits his family's estate. Plenty of family secrets, a series of tragic deaths, and even a curse to overcome."

Joan's eyes widened, then her brows snapped together. "The tragic deaths you are referring to were your parents?" she asked, her face pinking again.

"Yes," Simon answered, giving her a sad smile. "It's been many years now, and I am quite used to my lot in life. As you see, we have something in common, Joan."

"We do?" she said, her expression troubled.

"We are both orphans."

"We are," Joan whispered. She met his gaze, her eyes a deeper blue than before. "I am sorry for your loss."

Simon had been offered condolences many a time, but Joan had suffered a similar loss in her life, and, therefore, he felt that her compassion was more sincere. "And I am sorry for yours."

Joan gave a small shake of her head. "Thank you, but I cannot see how we are on equal footing as you suggest. I never knew my parents."

He straightened from the tree and took another couple of steps toward her. Instinctively, and not thinking of any possible consequences, he grasped her hand. "Your loss is still great, Mademoiselle." He bent over her hand and kissed the soft skin.

She didn't move, didn't even seem to take a breath. He looked up at her, fearing he'd offended her somehow.

Her eyes were luminous and her lips parted . . . in surprise? Simon straightened and reluctantly released her hand.

"Thank you," she said, her voice a throaty whisper. Then she turned from him, gathered her skirts and stepped over the low wall separating the two properties.

Simon was too stunned that she was leaving to call out to her. Instead, he watched her move through the trees on the other side, eventually disappearing, the dark blue of her dress blending into the approaching twilight.

Four

Joan waited to run until she was sure Simon Rousseau could not see her through the trees, that is, if he were watching her at all. But she hadn't heard hoofbeats, so she knew he wasn't astride his horse yet.

Once she cleared the grove, she ran straight for the barn. Her heart pounded with a fierceness she hadn't known was possible. Not to mention the sure flame of her cheeks and neck. She was only grateful that the nuns weren't in the yard this time of the evening. They were probably gathering for the meal, which meant she would soon be missed.

But Joan couldn't face anyone just yet. Not until she had her emotions in check. She pushed through the rickety barn door, startling the lazing cows. They eyed her for a moment with their soulful eyes, then turned back to their feed.

She shut the barn door and leaned against it, pressing her hand to her chest. She'd never spoken to a man for so long before, nor had one shown her such compassion . . . and interest. She had been literally caught spying on Simon. Had he suspected that she'd been spying on him for months?

She closed her eyes and reviewed their conversation in its entirety. Soon, Joan found herself smiling, and allowing her thoughts to break down the barriers that stood between them. If she had been born into a prosperous family, then she would have been considered his equal in status and rank. But, as it was, even though they were both orphans, their lives would remain vastly different.

Then she remembered. He'd spoken about a curse. Whenever she had questioned the nuns about the Rousseau family curse, the nuns had only said, "'Tis bad luck to speak of it."

Now that Simon had so openly mentioned the curse, Joan's curiosity was magnified. With her heart rate calm and her face cool, she left the barn and headed toward the abbey. She slipped in through the back door that led to the kitchen.

Sister Laurette looked up from the oven, where she was pulling out hot bread. Her brows lifted at Joan's entrance. "Well?" she asked. "How did your visit with Simon Rousseau go?"

Joan's mouth nearly dropped open. "I—I didn't . . ." she began, but she didn't know how to reply or how to explain.

"You can't fool me," Sister Laurette continued, using a cloth to move the bread from the hot pan to a basket. "Your eyes are bright, your skin's pink, and you look like a woman who has a secret."

Joan released a sigh and moved to pull the second pan of bread out of the oven. The heat from the embers didn't help conceal her flushed face. At the moment, it was just she and Sister Laurette in the kitchen, but that could change at any moment. The cadence of many female voices floated into the kitchen from the dining room.

"He was very kind," she said quietly.

Sister Laurette smiled and nodded as if she didn't expect anything less.

Joan slid the bread into the basket. "He told me there was a curse—"

"Hush!" Sister Laurette hissed, then picked up the basket. She cast a warning look at Joan before she hurried from the room to serve the sisters.

Joan followed Sister Laurette more slowly, carrying a second basket of bread. The warm scent reached her nose, making her realize how hungry she was. She sat down with the nuns, and after prayers were said, she began to eat. But after a few bites, she couldn't eat anymore, and she couldn't stop thinking about meeting Simon Rousseau and all that he'd told her.

Tonight she would take time for personal reflection, and Joan found a way to slip outside again without anyone observing her. She walked past the barn and set off along the lane that led to the main road. The sun had set, but there was still plenty of orange and gold splashed across the sky. With no wind, the temperature was absolutely perfect.

"Joan!" someone called out.

She turned toward the abbey and saw Sister Laurette coming. "It will be dark soon."

"Not for another thirty minutes," Joan said. "Besides, I just want to walk to the end of the lane." At the look of suspicion in the woman's gaze, Joan added, "I'm not meeting anyone if that's what you think."

Sister Laurette blew out a breath. "Of course you aren't. Meeting Simon Rousseau was just happenstance."

Joan smiled. "Of course."

Sister Laurette smiled back and linked her arm with Joan's. "We'll make it a quick walk. I don't want anyone to worry about us."

They set out at a good stride, and Joan appreciated the cooling air. It invigorated her thoughts. They had neared the end of the lane, where it joined up with the main road to the village, when the sound of an approaching rider reached them.

For some reason, Joan halted to watch the horse. It was clearly a tall man, and even more clearly not Simon. This man had white hair and wore a dark cloak that billowed behind him as he rode.

"Oh! It's . . ." Sister Laurette started.

"Who is it?" Joan said, but Sister Laurette never got a chance to say because the horse suddenly veered toward them, as if the rider had lost control.

The man jerked on the reins, and the horse raised up.

Joan scrambled backward, pulling Sister Laurette out of the way. She lost her footing, and fell just as the horse's hooves came down, narrowly missing Joan.

The man was yelling something, at the horse, or at the women, Joan didn't know. But the horse seemed spooked beyond reason, despite the efforts by the rider to calm it.

Joan scrambled to her feet and helped Sister Laurette to hers. Then, the horse reared up a third time, throwing the man to the ground. Everything happened quickly, yet it seemed slowly enough that Joan would always remember how the man thudded to the ground, landing on his back, and how the horse twisted, then landed on top of the man.

"No!" Joan cried out. She propelled herself forward, rushing toward the man.

The man yelled and tried to push the horse off of him. Joan was relieved the man was still alive, but surely he needed urgent aid.

"Help!" Joan called to Sister Laurette, who caught up with her. They tried to push and prod the horse to get off the man, but it wouldn't budge.

She turned toward the man, frantic. "The horse won't move, what should we do?"

His wild gaze focused on her and, for a moment, Joan had the strange sensation that she knew the man. But that was impossible. She'd never seen him before. She expected him to tell her how to move the horse off of him, but then his eyes widened.

"You! You are dead!" he said in a hoarse voice. "Am I dead too?"

"No," Joan said. "We're going to help you."

"Don't touch me!" the man shouted, clearly delirious. But his next words sent a sharp chill through Joan. "You are the very devil returned to curse me."

Five

The days since the accident were filled with a dull numbness until Joan couldn't tell them apart. She wasn't sure how much time had passed since she'd been yelled at by the injured man on the road. The look of his wild eyes stayed in her mind, and his words wouldn't leave her thoughts. What had happened after the man had told her not to touch him was still unclear.

She remembered Sister Laurette grasping her arm. A carriage stopping. Two men working to move the horse. The same two men carrying the injured man, who still shouted at her about how she was supposed to be dead.

Joan blinked back tears as she moved from one chore to the next. The chickens in the south yard clucked and pecked around her feet as she sprinkled feed onto the ground. What had she done to make the man on the road so angry with her? Sister Laurette said that he was in too much pain to be in his right mind and that he would have shouted at anyone so.

But Joan knew there was something more. What about the sense she had felt that she'd met the man before? When Sister Laurette said he was Monsieur Belrose, Joan couldn't imagine how she'd ever think she'd know someone like him—the village recluse. Perhaps he was as mad as the rumors claimed.

"Joan, there you are!" Sister Eloise's reedy voice rang out.

Joan was abruptly pulled out of her melancholy thoughts. She turned to see Sister Eloise hurrying toward her, bent slightly forward like a long piece of grass in the wind. Sister Laurette was a few paces behind, breathing heavy from her rush.

Joan's chest constricted. Had something terrible happened to one of the nuns?

"You're wanted in the main hall," Sister Eloise said.

"It's a servant from the Belrose estate," Sister Laurette added in a huff. "He's requested your presence most urgently."

"What does he want?" Had the old man died and she was being blamed?

"We don't know," Sister Eloise said, lowering her voice. "But you better come with us." She grasped Joan's hand and tugged her toward the abbey hall.

A black carriage with two large horses was parked in front of the hall. Joan involuntarily shivered as she passed by the carriage. As they walked into the cool interior of the hall, it took a moment for Joan's eyes to adjust to its dimness after the brightness of the sun.

The servant was a small man with darting eyes. He gave Joan a half bow as she came to a stop. "Monsieur Rudolph Belrose requests your immediate presence," he said.

Joan folded her arms. "What does Monsieur Belrose want with me?"

A small gasp came from behind her—either from Sister Eloise or Sister Laurette.

The servant lifted his chin a notch, his eyes flitting to the left, then the right. "He is ailing, Miss, and has a dire request he needs to make of you."

"Ailing?" Joan said. Of course he was. "Are his injuries extensive?"

"Quite," the servant said. "He has two broken ribs."

Was Belrose angry then? Did he blame her for his predicament? Perhaps he thought she'd spooked his horse, starting the entire incident. "What could he want of me?" she said in a small voice.

"Only to have a word, Miss." But the tone of the servant's voice was dark.

Sister Eloise and Sister Laurette stepped nearer to Joan, flanking her sides. "We will accompany you," Sister Eloise told Joan.

"No," the man said, his eyes focusing directly on Joan. His eyes were black and deeper than a pool of water. "It is to be a strictly private meeting, and you must come right away. We cannot delay any longer."

Joan couldn't look away from the depths of the man's eyes. She assumed that Monsieur Belrose had a tight grip on all of his servants, and they certainly followed all of his commands. But what did that have to do with her?

Sister Laurette grasped her arm, speaking to the man. "She will remain here then. She is under our care."

"I will go," Joan said. She felt compelled to put these strange twist of events behind her, and it would start with finding out why Monsieur Belrose thought she was a curse in his life.

"Joan," Sister Eloise whispered.

But Joan had made up her mind. She would go with this servant and hear the old man out, if only to clear her name.

"Do you need to change your clothing?" the man asked.

Joan didn't care about her appearance when faced with

meeting a deranged man. She knew there was mud and bits of straw on her shoes, and her skirt was brushed with dirt. Her hair was slightly askew from its normally neatly braided bun.

With a reassuring glance at the two nuns, Joan followed the servant out into the sunny day. Fittingly, dark clouds had moved in, scattered across the blue sky. They reached the black carriage, and Joan climbed up into it. The red velvet upholstery upon the interior bench was the most luxurious thing Joan had ever sat on.

But she wrinkled her nose. The inside of the carriage smelled as if it had been stored in a deep, dank cellar. And perhaps it had. Joan couldn't ever remember seeing this carriage pass along the road before.

The servant shut the carriage door, then joined the driver at the front. Joan spent the next twenty minutes alone in the musty carriage as it lurched along. When it finally came to a stop, Joan didn't know if she should be relieved or more afraid. What did Monsieur Belrose want with her? Would he blame her for his spooked horse?

Joan should have known that the interior of the gray stone mansion would be dim. Candles burned in sconces, but they seemed feeble, as if they were afraid to cast too much light in the grand hall that Joan entered.

"This way," the servant said in a stiff voice.

Since he didn't offer to take her cloak, she kept it on. But she soon became grateful for this because the room that she was led to was as frigid as a winter's day.

She didn't know what to expect, but it wasn't Monsieur Belrose sitting in a large chair, a glass of brandy in one hand, and a pair of spectacles in the other. His blue eyes seemed to pierce right through her as he stared at her from across the room. To his left, a fire burned heartily in the grate, but it didn't seem to give off any warmth, just like its master.

"Leave us," Monsieur Belrose said to the servant who had brought Joan.

The heavy wood door shut behind Joan, leaving her utterly alone with the strange man with cold eyes.

"This will not take long," the man said, rising to his feet ever so carefully, "so you need not make yourself comfortable."

If he'd been standing closer to Joan, he would have towered over her. As it was, the distance brought little comfort.

"It's unfortunate we met in such a way," Belrose continued.

Joan didn't know what to do with her hands or where to look. Her heart was so high in her throat that she could barely breathe.

"I am sorry," she began, hoping to soften the look in the man's eyes.

He lifted a hand. "It's better you do not speak, for this is already difficult enough."

Joan pressed her lips together, feeling a sharp pang of nausea in her stomach. Why had she insisted on coming alone?

Belrose turned toward the windows, his profile to her now. Could he no longer even bear to look at her?

"I had never thought to see you again," he began in a low voice.

So she had seen him before? When? Had he visited the abbey?

"But there is no denying who you are," he said with a short laugh. But his laugh was bitter and harsh. He turned to face her fully, and with the slant of light, and play of shadows, Joan suddenly knew.

"You are my daughter," Belrose said the same moment the realization coursed through Joan.

She felt her breath leave her body, and her legs barely held her up.

"And you look just like me," he exhaled, as if the words were distasteful to speak aloud.

This man is my *father?* Joan thought. Questions tumbled through her mind, colliding until her head throbbed in pain.

His gaze was steady on hers, unflinching. "And you, my daughter, will break the family curse."

Her mouth opened, but none of her questions came out. She simply stared at the tall man with the white hair and blue eyes. The angle of his nose, the cut of his chin . . . How had she not seen it before?

His lips curved into a half smile. "I think you need a drink, Joan."

The use of her name startled her. Of course he knew it. He was her father. He crossed the room in slow strides and poured something from a decanter into a crystal cut glass. When he pressed it into her hand, she became aware of the weight of the glass. She lifted it and took a deep swallow.

The brandy burned her throat, but she took another swallow, then handed it back to him.

"You may want to sit after all." His tone was almost gentle. He motioned toward a chair, and she crossed to it.

Once she was seated in the dark wooden chair, she began to tremble.

He sat across from Joan and told her all about a woman named Sophia Rousseau and how Sophia had cursed Belrose's father . . . which meant Joan's grandfather had been the one that had the affair with Sophia. Her curse stated that every five years, on All Hallows' Eve, a member of the Belrose or Rousseau family would die. Over the years, aunts and uncles, servants and delivery boys, and then Simon's parents, and finally Belrose's wife had all died . . . Joan's *mother.*

Her mind reeled. She had a father. She'd had a mother. She'd had grandparents.

"When your mother died giving birth to you, I hadn't considered another possibility to join the families." Belrose leaned forward, his eyes boring into hers. "But now we can break the curse."

Joan simply stared at him.

"Tonight you will marry Simon Rousseau," he said in a low, urgent tone, "for tomorrow is All Hallows' Eve."

Six

Simon reined his horse to a slow canter as he approached his stables. The sun had set, and he'd stayed out far longer than he'd intended. He could blame Joan for that—they'd only spoken for a few moments, if that—but thoughts of her had continued long after she left.

Perhaps in the light of the morning, he would come to his senses. She had looked like some sort of ethereal being, and, if he hadn't known she was real, he might have thought he'd completely imagined meeting her.

Simon entered the stable, where the groomsman waited. "Jacques, there you are."

"There *you* are," Jacques said. If their relationship was more formal, Jacques would have sounded cheeky. But the old man had worked at the estate for as long as Simon could remember.

The other horses in the stable went on alert as Simon approached. He was proud of his growing collection and had been breeding the horses for the past couple of years. He hoped to restore his ancestors' former prestige in fine horse breeding. So Jacques had never been busier, and he'd even hired on more stable boys.

"Out late today?" Jacques asked.

"I rode longer than expected." Simon's stomach felt small and tight. "And now I'm starving."

Jacques gave a rumbling laugh. "I'm sure ol' Mrs. Mauriac is already reheating your supper, counting the moments it will take for you to walk from the stables to the main house."

"That she is," Simon agreed. Madame Mauriac had also been working at the Rousseau estate since before Simon could remember.

"She's been a bit on edge this evening," Jacques said.

"Oh?" Simon asked. And, for a moment, Simon wondered how Jacques could know so much about what went on at the house. But that was the way of servants: they always seemed to know everything.

"Tomorrow is All Hallows' Eve, you know," Jacques said, his tone ominous.

Five years before, Simon's uncle had passed away on All Hallows' Eve. And by the look in Jacques's eyes, Simon could see that the servants had spent the day, if not weeks and months, speculating on who would be next.

"I'm healthier than any horse in this stable," Simon declared. "Don't you worry about me. If anyone will die, it'll be old man Belrose." He gave a dry laugh, but it didn't sound right, or feel right, to joke about the curse.

Jacques looked down at the dirt-packed floor.

They both knew that if tomorrow Simon was fine and Belrose was fine, the curse would reach someone else. Perhaps Jacques, who was getting on in years, or even Madame Mauriac, who'd complained recently of mysterious pains.

The sound of an approaching carriage drew Simon's attention. He exited the stables to see a bulky black carriage lumbering toward his house. Before Simon could reach the house, the carriage came to a stop. A tall man stepped out, his shoulders narrowed with age, but Simon would know him anywhere.

Belrose.

Simon's heart quickened as he strode toward Belrose, whose cool blue eyes studied him as he approached. Simon had heard of Belrose's accident and was surprised that the man was out and about.

"To what do I owe this pleasure?" Simon asked, although he could very well guess that the man's unexpected visit had something to do with the impending All Hallows' Eve.

"There's no time to waste," Belrose said, his voice low and scratchy with age. "Tonight, we will break the curse."

Simon couldn't help but stare at him. He'd only crossed paths with Belrose a handful of times, and it hadn't been for many years now. Was this just another of his rumored eccentric episodes?

"And how are we to do that?" Simon asked, folding his arms.

Belrose stepped closer and pointed a long finger at him. "*You* will marry my daughter."

"Your what?"

"Sophia Rousseau said the curse would only be broken when our two estates are joined by marriage," Belrose said in a flat tone. "My solicitor is drawing up the papers now, and the special license for the marriage should arrive any moment." He narrowed his piercing gaze. "Surely, you didn't think you'd marry for love."

Simon shook his head, trying to organize his thoughts. "You have a *daughter*?"

It was only then that Belrose looked away, and Simon saw something flit across his face—was it doubt? Or regret?

"She has been . . . away for many years. Since the death of my wife."

Simon exhaled. "And what does your daughter think of marrying me to break the family curse?"

Belrose's hard gaze shot to Simon. "She will do as I ask."

For some reason, the image of Joan flitted through Simon's mind. He thought of their simple conversation that afternoon and how the sun's rays had danced across her pale skin. Of how her cheeks had flushed when he teased her. Of how his aunt would be mortified that he'd entertained any thoughts whatsoever about an orphaned peasant girl.

But now, he looked into the icy blue of Belrose's eyes, and knew . . . knew that family members had died prematurely because of the curse. Physicians might be able to explain away their causes of death. But, when Simon's uncle had died by choking on a piece of meat nearly five years ago to the day, Simon had felt that his days were numbered and that he couldn't possibly subject an innocent woman to the curse from marrying into his family. Her very life would be in peril.

If he but married Belrose's daughter, the curse could be stopped once and for all. It would only take the sacrifice of two members of the families . . . then come what may. Simon let out a slow breath. "I'll do it, Monsieur Belrose. I'll marry your daughter to break the curse."

A smile crossed Belrose's face, and Simon suspected that it was a rare thing for the old man to smile. But just as quickly, the man's face straightened. "You will travel with me in my carriage. We cannot waste another moment, and I do not want to risk you changing your mind."

Simon then realized that he was looking into the face of a man who was afraid of his own mortality. How much grief this man must have faced when his wife died on All Hallows' Eve so many years before. Then, with each passing year, he must have wondered if he would be struck down next. Perhaps Belrose was not so eccentric after all.

Simon glanced down at his clothes. He supposed that any young woman who was willing to marry a stranger sight unseen would probably forgive him for not donning wedding clothes. Not that he had any wedding clothing available per se, but he'd have to arrive at the Belrose place in his riding clothes.

He climbed into the Belrose carriage and sat upon the dark velvet cushions. As the carriage traveled, Simon closed his eyes. What if the curse couldn't be broken? What if there wasn't a curse at all, but just horrible ironic coincidences of people dying every five years?

But Simon was already on his way, and the fear in Belrose's eyes had been the same fear in Simon's heart. Something had to be done; something had to be tried. And Simon was willing. He just hoped that Belrose's daughter wouldn't be disappointed in him. Perhaps someday Simon and his wife would grow to be friends, or at least two people with a common purpose. And, if it would save lives, then what did it matter that a dream or two would be crushed?

As they crossed the border into the Belrose estate, Simon sat straighter, gazing out the window. This land would all be his someday. The combination of the two estates would make it the largest property in the county and ideal property for raising horses. He could imagine it now—barns neatly lined up, immaculate stables, people coming from all over Europe to purchase his fine horses.

The carriage rumbled to a stop, and Simon sat forward on the bench, curious about the woman he was about to meet and soon marry. Was she a good rider? Would she make a good companion?

Monsieur Belrose exited the carriage first and led the way into his home. Simon followed, stepping into the cooling night. He passed through the front doors and gazed about. The home had seen better days. It fit every bit of Simon's imagination of what the home of a recluse might look like. The main hall was dim and drafty, and massive tapestries of hunting scenes and shipyards adorned the walls.

Belrose crossed the hall and opened a heavy door to the right. Simon followed and stepped into an exquisite library filled with books. A fire flickered in the grate on the opposite side of the room. Several books sat upon the credenza in the center of the room, some open, others marked with a ribbon.

"Ah, you've arrived," Belrose said to a man, who was sitting in a chair by the fire. The man rose and offered a deep bow, displaying the thinning hair atop his head. "May I introduce Monsieur Simon Rousseau." Belrose turned to Simon. "This is Monsieur Carriveaux. He has brought the special license and will act as witness to the marriage between you and my daughter."

Simon grasped the man's hand and shook it. The feel of the other man's palm brought a sharp sense of reality of what he had committed to. As if all the men felt another presence at the same time, they turned toward the door and found a woman standing there. The shadows in the room couldn't conceal the fairness of her skin or the lightness of her hair, nor did the shadows hide the tears in her eyes.

"Joan?" Simon said. He didn't realize he'd spoken her name aloud until Belrose gave him a sharp look.

"You know my daughter?" Belrose asked.

She was Belrose's daughter? But she was an orphan who lived at the abbey. He looked from Belrose to Joan. The family resemblance was now unmistakable. He opened his mouth to speak, but nothing came out.

"I can explain," Joan said, stepping into the room, her voice low. She cast a furtive look at her father. "I met Simon only this afternoon." Now she was looking at Simon. "I've only known about my parentage for a few hours."

Simon tried to understand, but his thoughts were too convoluted. Belrose interjected, telling him of how the curse had taken his wife's life and how he had been too grief-stricken to raise his daughter. Instead, he allowed the villagers to believe Joan had died as well.

"And your name is truly Joan?" Simon asked in a quiet voice.

"Joan Victoria Belrose," she answered.

Her tears had dried, but Simon could see the emotion splashed across her face. *She* had agreed to marry him . . . knowing his identity. "And you have agreed to your father's plan?"

She blinked rapidly. "I have, for it is the only way."

He barely knew the woman standing before him, but he was impressed with her willingness to sacrifice. She had just discovered her true parentage, and now she would be marrying a practical stranger.

Simon looked over at Belrose. "I don't have a ring."

Belrose gave a slight nod and crossed the room, stopping at a large cabinet. From within one of its drawers, he removed a small box. He returned with a heavy gold ring inlaid with what looked to be emeralds. "This was my wife's," Belrose said, handing the ring to Simon.

Simon gazed down at the ring, feeling its weight in his hand. Then he looked up at Joan. Her expression was calm, serene. He wondered if she was truly ready to take this step. They would be married for life, and they could only hope that it would break the curse.

Keeping his gaze on her, he sank to one knee and held out the ring. "Joan Victoria Belrose, will you do me the honor of becoming my wife?"

Joan's eyes widened, then her face softened into the smallest of smiles. "I will."

He grasped her delicate hand and slid the ring onto her finger. Then he stood, still holding her hand.

"Are you ready?" Monsieur Carriveaux asked.

Joan nodded, so Simon answered, "Yes. Marry us, please."

Seven

I n any imaginings Joan had ever had of her wedding day or wedding night, she'd never imagined this. Curled up alone on a massive bed in a dark, cold room, while her new husband slept in the adjoining room on a couch.

The fire in the Rousseau bedroom had gone out hours ago, and Joan hadn't the heart to get up and stir it back to life. Instead, she stared at the fading embers, thinking over the events of the past day. Everything in her life had changed so suddenly after she'd met and spoken to Simon for the first time.

She discovered she has a living father. She learned she is an heiress to the Belrose estate. And she'd married Simon Rousseau, a man who was handsome, kind, and self-sacrificing, yet a stranger in every way. The one thing she knew they had in common was their loyalty to breaking the curse.

Joan turned on her side and saw the gray light peeking through the slivered opening of the heavy curtains. Dawn was approaching at last. The next hours would certainly be fraught with tension . . . as the Belrose and Rousseau families wondered if their lives would be spared after all and if the curse had truly been broken.

She kept her gaze on the opening between the curtains. She had no idea which direction this room faced or what lay beyond the windows. Stables? Fields? A road leading to the village? But whatever was out there was her new home now. She was Mademoiselle Joan Rousseau. And once her father died and his property transferred to Simon, she would be the wealthiest woman in the village.

And perhaps the most lonely.

She already missed the sisters at the abbey and hoped to visit them soon. She also hoped that the curse was well and done and there would be no funerals to plan and attend. Finally, she climbed off the massive bed and crossed to the windows. Pulling one curtain open, then the other, her breath caught as she gazed out at the estate.

She could see the abbey in the distance beyond the copse of trees she used to hide in. To the right was a series of stables that looked like they were in various states of repair, and there, not far from the stables, walked Simon, leading a horse to what looked like a fenced-in arena.

Joan leaned her forehead against the cool glass and looked down at her husband. He walked with surety and confidence, not like a man who'd just entered into a marriage of convenience. So he wasn't curled up on a couch, fretting and worrying about the change in direction his life had just taken.

Yes, Joan decided, she would be his wife in name and in contract, but would he ever see her as anything more? Or did he have other women in his life, set up somewhere in Paris? Joan released a sigh, realizing again how little she truly knew about the man she'd married.

The piercing blue eyes of her father came to her mind, and she realized that she had no idea how their relationship would be from here on out. She'd done his bidding, so now what? Would she become his beloved daughter—or a daughter he'd only reclaimed for a single purpose?

Her eyes burned, and she blinked back the impending tears. Exhaustion swept through her body, but she wondered if she'd ever sleep a peaceful sleep again. Turning from the rising sun, she climbed back onto the bed and pulled the covers over her.

Closing her eyes, she found herself whispering a prayer for life, for happiness, for new friendship. Were these too much to ask for?

"Joan," a voice said, floating through her mind. It took her a moment to realize someone was speaking to her. She must have fallen asleep at last.

Opening her eyes, she was startled to see Simon standing next to the bed, peering down at her.

"Joan, are you well?" he asked in a gentle tone.

She pushed up on an elbow. The sun was high in the sky—she must have slept for hours. "I—I didn't sleep last night. I suppose my body finally gave out."

He sat next to her on the bed, offering a slight smile.

Instinctively, she drew the covers closer. A man was sitting next to her on her bed—her husband, no less, but it was still a strange thing.

He seemed to sense her unease, and he stood. She immediately regretted her modesty. They had not discussed consummating the marriage—did a man and woman even discuss such things?—but Joan couldn't help wondering what his intentions were. He had every right to exercise his husbandly privileges.

"I saw you out with the horses," she said, then regretted it for her face immediately felt hot.

He had turned toward the window though. Perhaps he was a man of propriety after all.

"Training them is my indulgence." Simon stepped closer to the windows. "With both of our properties, we can create a bit of an empire. Attract horse buyers from all over Europe." He stopped, then turned toward her, regret on his face. "I'm sorry, I didn't mean to put our union in that light."

Joan drew her knees up, keeping herself completely covered. "It's all right," she said, knowing that this type of open communication with her husband was a good thing, even if they were speaking about hard issues, like why they had married in the first place. She met his dark eyes and felt a warm shiver travel through her. He looked exceedingly handsome this morning. He hadn't yet shaved, and his shirt gaped at his throat, showing his tanned skin.

"Well, here we are, both alive," Simon said, folding his arms, his eyes questioning. "Should we check on your father?"

Joan rested her chin on her knees. "It's odd to hear the word *father* in relation to me."

Simon was quiet for a moment. "Do you feel cheated? I mean, you discover that you've had a parent all along, and now . . . you're married to someone not of your choosing."

Joan looked away from him, knowing that her emotions would show freely upon her face. "I've gone over it all in my head. Why my own father would send me away, an innocent and helpless babe, and never once claim me as his own. Then we met by chance on the road . . . What if we hadn't met? Would he have died today?" Her throat thickened as she said the next words. "Would you have?"

Simon lowered his arms and crossed to the bed. This time, when he sat on the mattress, Joan didn't draw away. "I suppose we'll have to wait until midnight to know if the curse has really been lifted."

This surprised Joan. "So, you don't believe it's completely real?"

"It's real," Simon answered in a somber tone. "I just

hope our marriage is enough to break an evil that is decades old." He reached for her hand, and she let him grasp it.

The action brought new tears to her eyes. If nothing else, they were in this together. And now she had to ask the hard question, the one that had kept her up all night, more so than dwelling on her childhood. "Do you think the curse requires that our marriage be consummated?"

Simon didn't move, didn't seem to be breathing.

Joan wanted to take the words back, but what if theirs wasn't considered a true marriage until . . . Her face went hot. But there was no hiding now.

He didn't release her hand. If anything, his grasp tightened. "The curse was spoken long ago, so there is no way to know if the threat has changed in wording over the years. But I would never take advantage of you. When you are willing and ready, Joan, then I'll be happy to live the truest form of husband and wife. Whether it's in a month, or a year."

Joan stared at their linked hands. She had watched Simon from afar for many months, much of the time wondering what sort of man he was. Now she knew.

"Are you like other women then?" Simon's voice was soft. "You want a love match? A man to woo you until you swoon?"

"I am not so far removed from reality as that," Joan said, wishing she could hide the melancholy of her voice. "I was raised as an orphan in an abbey, after all. I never had many expectations beyond those stone walls."

"Surely you had dreams."

Joan couldn't deny this. She gave a slight nod but didn't meet his eyes. And she couldn't deny that some of those dreams were about Simon himself, although she'd never tell him that.

"Then I have work to do, Wife." Simon leaned forward, until he was close enough to kiss her. He smelled of grass and wind and sky. "You are generous and beautiful and intriguing. And even though the circumstances surrounding our marriage are not made of a young woman's dreams, I feel blessed. I don't think it would be too hard to fall in love with you."

Joan didn't know whether to inhale or exhale. The heat from his body seemed to touch her own skin. And then he pressed his lips against her cheek, ever so briefly.

Before Joan could respond, he let go of her hand and stood. "I will send word to your father that we are both well."

His words startled her in a new way. She had not considered *her* own life to be at risk, but of course it was. She was a Belrose and now a Rousseau.

She could only nod, for it seemed that all her words had fled.

Eight

Was it possible to fall in love with a woman that he had only spoken to for the first time the day before? And was now married to? Simon removed the small key from his pocket and opened the intricately carved wooden chest stored in his parents' former bedroom. He had not looked upon his mother's miniature portrait for years, but today, he felt an urgency to do so.

He had something to ask his mother. Whenever he looked at the miniature, he felt her presence, as if she were somewhere close watching over him. The lid protested as he opened it, and he lifted the layer of linen that covered the miniature. Taking out the picture, he turned it toward the oil lamp he'd brought into the curtained room.

As the years had passed, Simon had remembered less and less about his parents, but he never forget his mother's deep brown eyes and the warmth and kindness there. Genevieve was her name.

"Mother," he whispered, "my new wife is sweet and delicate like a bird. She will bring new light into this house, and I think I'm falling in love with her already."

His mother didn't respond, of course, but he was sure that she would approve of Joan. How could she not? Who else would dare marry into a cursed family? And who else would gaze at him with such trust in her blue eyes?

"What is your advice?" he whispered to the picture. "How shall I woo my wife?"

He thought of the small bits that he did know about Joan—how she'd been watching him from the copse of trees for months and how he finally took the initiative to speak with her—the fairy-like woman he'd seen in the woods. She had been reticent, yet she was wholly untouched and unaffected by the world. Her innocence shone brightly from every part of her. How could someone born to such darkness carry such light? And how could he preserve it?

Simon looked at the portrait of his mother a moment longer then placed it back beneath the linen and closed the lid. He knew now that he would do everything in his power to bring happiness to Joan and to push out the darkness from the Rousseau estate.

That was when he heard a scream.

Joan was his first thought, and Simon tore out of the bedroom, and ran down the corridor, his feet pounding on the wooden floor, rattling the portraits on the wall, and the oil lamps on the tables, as he passed by.

Passing down a flight of stairs and around a corner, he burst into Joan's room. He stopped cold when he saw Joan. She lay on the floor, her body twisted, her head turned facing the ceiling. Blood trickled down her forehead, pooling on the carpet beneath. Disbelief and anger rocked through Simon. Was she still alive?

"Joan!" Simon called out, crossing to her and kneeling.

He touched her throat with a shaking hand. Her skin was warm and pulsing with life. "Thank the Almighty," he said, leaning close to stroke her face. "You're alive."

She blinked her eyes open, then she groaned. Tears filled her eyes.

"You're all right." Simon touched her hand. "What happened? I heard your scream, but . . ." He looked from the gash on her forehead to the floor. Had she fallen and hit her head on a table?

"There was a man . . ." Joan said faintly.

Simon stared at her. "Someone did this to you?"

"Yes," she said, then she closed her eyes.

"Joan, stay with me," Simon said, pulling her carefully into his arms and lifting her near weightlessness. He carried her to the bed and laid her upon it. Then he rushed to the door and called to Madame Mauriac.

When the housekeeper came bustling into the corridor, Simon explained what had happened and told her to send for the physician. Once she'd left, Simon turned back to the bedroom. Joan's eyes were still closed, and he didn't know if that was a good thing. He went to the wash basin and soaked a cloth, then started to clean up Joan's forehead. Thankfully, the bleeding had stopped, but its swelling might prove to turn into a deep bruise.

Joan's eyes fluttered open.

"How are you feeling?" he asked.

"He tried to kill me," Joan whispered.

A cold shiver pricked the back of Simon's neck. Who had been in the house and why did he attack Joan? Then the shiver traveled to his heart, twisting it in a suffocating realization—since today was All Hallows' Eve, people believed that someone in their families was supposed to die today. Except Joan and Simon had now legally joined the estates, so the curse should now be broken.

"Simon," Joan said, her voice raspy.

Her eyes had cleared, and she was staring straight at him.

"What if there wasn't a curse after all?" she asked. "What if it was a story created by someone at your home or mine to conceal a murder?"

Simon wanted to tell her no, that it was impossible, and that the curse was real. But . . . these thoughts had impeded his mind too. If what Joan was suggesting proved to be true, that would mean a murderer had lived among them for decades. An evil man who carefully chose a new victim every five years. Someone who had killed both of his parents. That didn't explain how Joan's mother died in childbirth, but perhaps there was something sinister behind that as well.

Joan grasped Simon's arm. Her eyes had grown wide and reflected the fear that he felt growing in his heart. He laid his hand on her shoulder, feeling an overwhelming urge to lock every door and block every window in his home and protect Joan. "Do you remember anything about the man who attacked you? What he looked like? What he was wearing?"

She shook her head, then winced at the motion. "I didn't see him," she said in a voice just above a whisper. "He came in while I was looking out the window. I didn't even hear him until it was too late to turn around and see who it was."

Simon let out a breath. "Did he speak to you?"

"No," Joan said, her voice drifting away. "Although I sensed he wasn't much taller than me. He wasn't a large man, but he was strong and determined." She shuddered.

Simon pulled her into his arms, holding her gently against his chest. She leaned into him, and her softness blended into the edges of his body.

"What if he knows he's failed," she whispered, "and he goes to find my father?"

Simon drew away from her. She could very well be

right. "I'll send someone over to check on your father and warn him."

"We should insist that he come here, and we can stay together as a group."

"Joan, the entire staff at both households are at risk."

"Don't you see, Simon? The attacker must already be a member of one of our households."

Simon thought through his employees, Madame Mauriac, Jacques, the newly hired stable boys, the two kitchen maids, the butler, and his valet. The only employees who could have carried on a decades-old plan would be Madame Mauriac and Jacques—both of whom Simon immediately dismissed. They were like family to him.

"What about your father's staff? Did you meet any of them yesterday and have any impressions?" He could see that Joan was trying to think, but the pain must still be throbbing through her head.

"I met the housekeeper, Monsieur Carriveaux," she said. "And the older servant who fetched me at the abbey in the first place."

"What was his name?"

Joan drew her brows together. "I don't recall. But he was at least as old as my father."

"We'll find out," Simon said, turning toward the doorway as a man entered. It was the physician, and the man hurried in and set his black bag on the table near the bed.

"She's awake and talking?" the physician asked. Without waiting for an answer, he crossed to Joan. "That's a very good sign. I'm Doctor Colville. How are you feeling?"

"Tired," Joan said, grimacing as the doctor probed the skin around the gash. "But I didn't sleep much last night either."

"Drowsiness is to be expected," Doctor Colville said. "You need several days of rest, and I've brought a salve to apply three times a day." He looked over at Simon. "What happened here? Do I need to report this to the police?"

"Yes. She didn't see the attacker, but we don't think this was his first attack."

The doctor raised his brows. "What do you mean?"

"There may be a killer behind the curse. But I need to write up some things," Simon added. "So the police can have a full report of my suspicions."

The doctor turned back to Joan. "I need to do a few sutures. It will only take a moment."

Simon crossed to the other side of her and held Joan's hand as the doctor began his work. She closed her eyes, clenching her jaw tight, but she did not make a sound. When the doctor finished, he applied the salve to Joan's forehead, then cleaned his hands. "If you remember anything more," he said, "no matter how small, write it down."

"I will," Joan said, her eyes an even deeper blue against her pale face. "Thank you."

The doctor turned to Simon. "She was very fortunate. The bleeding was minimal, and it closed up nicely. But the attacker meant business."

Nine

Darkness had fallen by the time Joan opened her eyes again. Simon had been in and out of her bedroom, and when he hadn't been there, Madame Mauriac had stayed with her, the door locked. Every man was a suspect since the one thing that Joan could be sure of was that the person who'd attacked her was a man.

Now, Madame Mauriac stood by the window and turned toward Joan. "You're awake again, Love. How are you feeling?"

Joan reached for the glass of water by her bed and took a deep swallow. Her head ached, but her mind was clear. "Better, I think," she said, drawing the covers off and moving her legs to the side of the bed.

"You shouldn't get up yet," Madame Mauriac said, coming toward her. "The physician said—"

Joan held up her hand. "I just want to walk about the room a little bit. I'll sit down again if it's too much."

Madame Mauriac pursed her lips, but stepped back to let Joan stand.

Her head immediately began swimming, and she paused, taking several steady breaths. She didn't know if it was the head injury that made her dizzy or just the event itself and the thought of what might have happened to her.

"Where's Simon?" she asked, walking slowly to the wash basin. The water had been changed, and she dipped her fingers into it, and splashed her face with the cool water.

"He's with your father and the constable now," Madame Mauriac said, hovering close to Joan as if she expected her to collapse at any moment.

Her father had arrived a couple of hours ago—safe. But even then, Joan felt like she had been thrust into a convoluted world, one in which she was a married woman, had a living father, and was now in fear of her life.

"I must see him," Joan said, looking toward the windows. The curtains were pulled shut, and the only thing beyond was darkness.

"Your father?" Madame Mauriac asked.

"Simon," Joan said. "Take me to him." She couldn't explain it. But she knew she wouldn't feel better unless she was in his presence.

"Let me go and fetch him."

"No," Joan said, reaching for the woman's arm. "I don't want to be in this room any longer." Bits of the memory were returning. The feeling of knowing someone was in the room with her . . . The half-moment when she started to turn and was struck and all went black.

And now, the walls seemed to be shrinking around her.

Joan kept ahold of Madame Mauriac's arm as they walked out of the room and down the corridor. As they descended a flight of stairs to the main floor, Joan heard voices coming from one of the front rooms—the library? Or a parlor?

When Joan opened the door, three pairs of eyes turned

to look at her. Despite all of her tumultuous feelings about her father, she was glad to see him.

Simon spoke first, stepping forward to meet her. "Joan, what are you doing out of bed?"

Joan reached for his hand. The very touch of his warm skin calmed her troubled heart. "I don't want to be in that room any longer."

"Is everything all right?" he asked.

"I don't know," she said, her voice faltering. Tears burned in her eyes, and she realized she should have just stayed in bed, even if she did have to deal with the horrible memories. She didn't want to break down in front of him.

"Come and sit," he said, guiding her toward a set of chairs next to a cheery fire.

For some reason, the sight of a perfectly normal fire brought her a bit of ease—that, and Simon was near again. How had she come to depend on him so quickly?

He pulled a second chair close to her and sat. "Better?"

She tried to smile, but the tears started again. Simon held out a handkerchief, and she took it gratefully. "I'm sorry," she began. "I don't know what's come over me."

Simon called over Madame Mauriac and asked her to bring Joan something to eat.

At the mention of food, Joan realized she was famished. She'd eaten a bit of soup after the physician left, but nothing since. As they waited, her father and the constable continued to speak in low tones. It sounded like her father was telling the constable about the deaths that had occurred every five years on All Hallows' Eve.

A shudder passed through her at the thought of all the wasted lives over the years. "Has there been any progress?"

Simon leaned closer. "The constable has sent out all of his runners to question any man who works or has worked on either of our estates. I'm afraid we don't know much more than that."

Joan nodded and leaned her head back. If all these years

the curse had been a cover-up for a sinister killer, then her childhood spent in the abbey had been in vain. She loved the sisters she'd been raised by, but she'd also missed out on what her true life should have been. She was still motherless, that she knew. But what about her relationship with her father?

She watched him from her chair as he waved his hand at something the constable said. His hair was white, although his shoulders and back were straight, as if age hadn't traveled to the rest of his body. He also had a certain vulnerability about him; she could see it in the lines about his face and the somberness of his eyes.

She now didn't view her father's choices to banish her to the abbey as cruel and heartless, but she saw them as actions made by a man who was afraid, a man who grieved for his wife and wanted to protect his daughter from a terrible curse.

A loud knock sounded at the front door. Simon stood and crossed to the half-open doors of the library. The butler must have opened the front door because Joan soon heard the voices of men coming from the entrance. She half rose to her feet as the voices grew louder.

Suddenly, the library doors burst open, and a man came in, half dragging a boy with him. "This lad's got something to say."

Joan recognized the cap the man wore—he was one of the runners sent by the constable.

"Frederick," Simon said, crossing to the boy and drawing him up by his jacket. "Do you know something?" Simon's voice was much kinder than the runner's, but it was firm nonetheless.

"He saw something," the runner said. "But I had to drag it out of him. Don't know if you want this sort of lad working in your stables."

Simon's gaze narrowed, but Joan couldn't tell if he was more displeased with the runner's roughness or the boy's apparent insolence.

"Monsieur Jacques didn't come back from fixing the barn fence," the boy said.

"How long ago was that?" Simon asked, his voice growing more urgent with each word.

The boy looked down at his scuffed boots. "More than an hour ago."

"It must have been soon after I questioned the old man," the runner added.

Simon's brow furrowed, then he glanced over at Joan's father. They exchanged a look that could only mean one thing: they both wondered if this man named Jacques was in danger. Joan's heart started pounding in response. Had this man, who worked for the Rousseau estate, become the latest victim?

"Did he say he was returning to the stables?" Simon asked. "Perhaps he went to his cottage."

The boy shook his head. "He told me not to leave the stable until he returned."

The constable stepped forward. "Has this man Jacques done anything unusual in the past few days?"

"Jacques has been working for our family since my father's time," Simon interrupted. "He always keeps his word, which makes me think that something has happened to him."

Joan's father joined the gathering of men, saying, "Or . . . he could be the culprit."

"You couldn't be more wrong, Belrose." Simon met the men's gazes.

"Actually, your new father-in-law is quite right," a new voice spoke in a deep tone that Joan hadn't heard before.

They all turned and found a man standing in the doorway of the library, his hand raised, holding a pistol.

Joan gripped the back of the chair she stood next to.

The man's peppered hair was tied back, but about his face hung loose pieces, slick and gray. His heavy eyebrows were bushy and wild, taking on their own life as the man swiveled his gaze about the room, the pistol moving with his gaze.

Simon stepped forward, and Joan gasped as the man with the pistol aimed it straight at Simon's chest.

"Jacques! What are you doing?" Simon's tone was equally angry and edged with disbelief.

Joan realized this man must be the stable master, the one who'd gone missing, who'd been working for Simon's family for decades.

"Stay back, Simon, unless you want to fulfill the curse."

"There is no curse, is there, Jacques?" Joan's father said.

Jacques swung the pistol toward Belrose, and Joan's heart stuttered. The expression on Jacques's face was that of a man whose anger ran deep. He seemed here to enact his revenge—for what, she didn't know—but this evening could only end in disaster. Joan looked about the room, desperate to find something that she or one of the men could use in defense. The fireplace andirons were on the other side of the hearth, too far to reach without drawing attention to herself.

Belrose continued. "I know now who your mother was."

Joan stared at her father. It seemed that everyone in the room was holding their breath.

"Sophia," Belrose said. "She *was* wronged by my father, wasn't she?"

Jacques nodded, his limp hair brushing against his face.

"And you are my . . . half-brother?" Belrose finished.

The air left Joan's chest. It was all starting to make sense . . .

Color flooded Jacques' face, and his eyes hardened. "You've been raised with every privilege, while I . . . have been mired in horses' muck."

"I understand," Belrose said in an even voice, taking a step forward. "You created the story of the curse so that you could get rid of the Belrose and Rousseau heirs, until there was no one left but you."

Jacques sputtered, his mouth working. "How did you know?"

Simon answered, his own face pale. "You forgot one thing, Jacques. If every single person in the Belrose and the Rousseau family died, both estates would revert to the town and be governed by the abbey."

"Not if I could prove that I am a Belrose and a Rousseau by birth," Jacques snarled, his complexion deepening.

"You're illegitimate," Belrose announced, his voice far from calm now. Instead, he'd drawn himself up to his full height, and his tone was steely. "No judge would hand over an inheritance to an illegitimate child, unless the father had declared him an heir before his death. But my father is long dead, and so is your mother."

Jacques's pistol hand trembled, and his eyes started to water. Joan hoped that the man was about to give up the pistol. He would already be facing life in prison, but perhaps he could find some redemption for his soul.

She released the chair back and surprised herself by stepping forward. "Put down the pistol, Sir," she began. "Your parents are gone, and they would want their son to live an honorable life."

Jacques's face crumpled, and tears coursed down his cheeks. His chest shuddered as if he were trying to hold back a sob.

Joan took courage from the way the man seemed to be experiencing remorse and a change of heart. She'd heard about it nearly every day during her growing up years at the abbey. She took another step, until she was near Simon. "We understand your pain. It's time to let it go now, and seek forgiveness for your actions."

Jacques' attention was fully on Joan now, and he blinked through his tears. Even though he had brutally attacked her, her heart swelled with compassion for him. Who knew what his mother might have told him? But, he had been an innocent victim of his birth status. "Please," Joan said.

"Please turn over the pistol, and let's stop the real curse of revenge."

The color in his eyes deepened, and his face tightened. Then he lunged straight for Joan.

Time seemed to move slower, yet so fast that Joan didn't fully comprehend what was happening. His arm extended, and his finger pressed the trigger of the pistol. Her father crumpled to the ground, and Simon and the runner tackled Jacques to the ground.

Belrose must have leapt in front of Joan and been shot. She sank to the floor, grabbing for him, screaming, "Father!" Blood soaked his shirt on his shoulder and chest, and his eyes were unfocused and staring.

"No!" Joan screamed again. "Father, look at me."

Then she realized a second person was kneeling over her father—Simon. He pulled off his jacket, then ripped part of his shirt and bunched it up, pressing it against the bullet wound. The entrance wound was higher than Joan had at first thought.

She exhaled, adding prayers to her desperation. Perhaps there was a chance her father would live. Somewhere in the background, the constable and runner subdued Jacques and led him out of the library. But for the moment, all Joan could see was her father—the pain on his face, the pallid color of his skin.

"Save him, Simon," she whispered over and over.

Simon called out for Madame Mauriac, who appeared almost instantly, as if she'd been hovering nearby in the corridor. "Call for the physician."

The woman scurried away. Joan's eyes met Simon's, and she saw the same worries there.

"We won't let him die, Joan. Not so soon after you have found him."

She nodded, hoping desperately that Simon was right. Then her father's eyes opened and focused on Joan. In his eyes, she saw his apology for all their years of separation. She knew that he couldn't change the past, and, even if there would be no time together in the future, he'd finally been a true father to her—if only for a moment—when he'd protected her.

She grasped his limp hand and squeezed it gently, telling him in this one action that she understood, that she forgave him, and that if he survived, they'd face their new life together.

Joan didn't know how much time had passed when the physician finally arrived, but she felt exhausted when he came into the room and took over.

She and Simon sat on the sofa together, hands clasped, as the doctor worked to remove the bullet.

And then her father was able to rest. He was breathing steadily, his eyes closed, his expression calm. The physician insisted that he stay on the floor, unmoved, for a couple of hours. Joan didn't want to leave him, so she stayed next to Simon on the sofa, curled up against his side, his arm around her.

Ten

As the night wore on, Joan dozed off and on, leaning against Simon as they sat together on the couch. His mind spun, making any and all sleep elusive. When the runner arrived, Joan stirred awake. Only then did Simon release his new wife, so he could help the runner move Belrose up to a bedroom.

Joan followed them up the flight of stairs, and Simon knew it was because she didn't want to remain in the library by herself. The physician also sent a nurse to watch over Belrose throughout the night.

"I can help too," Joan said, stifling a yawn, when Simon came out of her father's bedroom.

"You should rest," he said, guiding her along the hallway to the bedroom she'd been in the night before.

She hesitated at the room's entrance. The fire had been lit and two oil lamps burned, so it should have seemed welcoming and cheery, but Joan wouldn't step inside.

"I'll take you to another room." Simon led her to one of the guest rooms across the hall. As he led her inside, she clung to his hand.

"Don't leave me," she said. "I know that Jacques is in custody, but I don't want to be alone."

Simon wrapped his arms about her, pulling her close. "I wasn't planning on leaving you."

He felt Joan nestle against him. She didn't treat him like a stranger now. He kissed the top of her head, then guided her to the bed. Pulling back the blanket, she climbed in. Then he joined her, propped up on pillows, and she curled against him and closed her eyes.

It was only then that Simon found himself relaxing. Jacques had been arrested, Belrose was resting and being watched over by a nurse, and Joan . . . his new wife . . . slept in his arms. Just before Simon drifted off to sleep, he silently thanked his mother. He didn't doubt that she was still somehow watching over him.

Some hours later, Simon woke with a start to sunlight streaming in through the window.

He lifted his head, only to see Joan still nestled at his side, smiling up at him. Simon couldn't remember ever having seen anything more beautiful.

"You're awake," she said.

He couldn't help but smile. "Heard anything about your father?"

"I just spoke with the nurse. The physician should be arriving within the hour, but my father slept peacefully and even awakened for a few moments and swallowed some broth." Her eyes fluttered. "Climbing back into bed was probably what woke you."

"Hmmm." Simon slid his arm around her. "I like that you climbed back in." As he knew it would, her face flushed bright red.

"This is strange," Joan whispered.

"A good strange?" Simon teased.

165

"Yes, I think so." Her smile was shy now, but she didn't draw away.

So Simon kissed her. Her mouth felt soft and delicate, and her body was warm as she pressed against him, kissing him back. He pulled her closer and kissed her harder, feeling the slowly igniting flames throughout his body as their limbs tangled together and her fingers moved to the back of his neck.

He wasn't sure where he ended and she began, but there seemed to be no past or no future. Just the present moment.

"Simon," Joan broke off, breathless. "I didn't mean to be so forward."

He laughed, squeezing her against him. "*I* did, my love."

Her breath caught as she seemed to comprehend what he'd implied. But he hoped she didn't mind. He'd never spoken truer words in his life. He kissed her again, taking his time, until time itself seemed suspended. It wasn't until he heard voices outside the bedroom door that he touched earth again.

"The physician," Joan said softly. "We should speak to him."

Simon groaned. Reluctantly, he disentangled himself from Joan, then helped her from the bed.

She flushed as she stood and tried to smooth out her skirts and fix her hair.

"You look beautiful," he said.

She looked up at him, and his heart stumbled. Her gaze was open, trusting . . . and loving.

"Come, Wife," he said, extending his hand. "Let's see how your father fares."

She smiled and placed her hand in his, squeezing his fingers lightly.

Simon couldn't wait to return to return to this room again and take his wife into his arms. But most of all, he couldn't wait to start the rest of his life with this enchanting woman by his side.

"Are you listening?" Joan asked.

Simon arched a brow and blinked his eyes.

She laughed. "You weren't. How about we order the morning meal sent up to the bedroom?"

Grasping her other hand, he lifted it to his mouth and kissed it. "I can't think of anything better."

That blush again. Simon was completely charmed.

It took Joan practically tugging his hand to get him out of the bedroom, and they walked the short distance to where Belrose was convalescing. They entered the room while the physician was packing up his instruments into a satchel. Belrose was awake, and his eyes brightened when his gaze landed on Joan.

She rushed forward. "You look so much better."

"Thank you," Belrose said, his voice scratchy.

"How are you feeling?" she asked.

"I'll be well soon enough." Belrose's brow furrowed. "What about you and Simon?"

"We are well, thank you," Joan said.

"Thank you, Sir." Simon stepped to the side of the bed. "Thank you for bringing Joan and me together, and thank you for saving her life."

Next to Simon, Joan wiped her eyes. "Yes, thank you, Father." She leaned over him and kissed his cheek.

The man's face reddened, and Simon hid a smile. Like father, like daughter. But Belrose looked pleased, and Simon thought he saw moisture in the old man's eyes.

"We'll leave you to rest now," Joan said, straightening. She turned to Simon, and he was more than happy that he'd soon have her all to himself.

As they left Belrose and stepped back into their bedroom, Simon felt as if he were stepping into a new life, one that held great promise of happiness, one that would chase away all the darkness and replace every shadow with light. Sophia's curse had only been a threat, and Jacques had breathed life into it, keeping it a deadly reality for years.

But now, Jacques was locked up, and the Rousseau and Belrose families were forever safe.

"Joan," Simon whispered, pulling her close and burying his face into her hair. "The curse is truly broken now."

Her arms tightened about his neck, and she whispered back. "Yes, my love. I believe it is."

About Heather B. Moore

Heather B. Moore is a *USA Today* bestselling author. She writes historical thrillers under the pen name H.B. Moore; her latest is *Finding Sheba*. Under Heather B. Moore, she writes romance and women's fiction. She's one of the coauthors of The Newport Ladies Book Club series. Other works include *Heart of the Ocean, The Fortune Café, The Boardwalk Antiques Shop,* the Aliso Creek series, and the Amazon bestselling Timeless Romance Anthology series.

For book updates, sign up for Heather's email list: http://hbmoore.com/contact/
Website: www.hbmoore.com
Facebook: Fans of H.B. Moore
Blog: MyWritersLair.blogspot.com
Twitter: @HeatherBMoore

The Sirens' Song

by Lisa Mangum

Other Works by Lisa Mangum

After Hello

The Hourglass Door Trilogy:
The Hourglass Door
The Golden Spiral
The Forgotten Locket

One

"Attention, passengers, this is Allison King, entertainment coordinator for the Odysseus Star Cruise Line. We have a number of special treats in store for you tonight—no tricks! The masquerade ball will begin at 7:00 in the main ballroom on Deck A. Our legendary chefs have prepared a 'spooktacular' buffet on Deck B. And Count Dracula himself will be hosting an arts-and-crafts party on Deck C.

"And for those of you who have registered for the Storytelling by Starlight event, please gather at the departure area in fifteen minutes.

"On behalf of Captain Williamson, First Mate Michaels, and the rest of the Odysseus Star crew, I would like to personally wish everyone aboard—"

The crackle of the ship's PA system cut in, obscuring the last words of the overly perky Allison King.

"A happy Halloween," Oliver muttered, shaking his head and leaning his elbows on the railing overlooking the ocean, grateful for the small moment of solitude he'd managed to find.

The cruise was four days into the trip, and the passengers had been celebrating all day. Loud music, all-night dances, endless food. The cruise line certainly knew how to throw a party. Even the weather was in the holiday spirit: a full October moon, a brilliant sky dotted with stars, and a cool breeze that carried with it the hint of a coming storm. The night-black waves rippled far below him as the luxury liner cut inexorably toward Greece like a silent, oncoming leviathan.

Oliver was four months into his six-month contract as the lead physician with the cruise liner, and while he was proud of his immaculate uniform, complete with gold caduceus and red-and-gold bars on his epaulets, he wished he was somewhere else this Halloween. Anywhere else.

A pack of kids dressed as pirates ran along the deck. As they careened around the corner and disappeared from sight, he swallowed past a scratch in his throat.

"Ready for your storytelling gig, Doctor?" Derrick asked as he walked past. His housekeeping uniform glowed orange under the string of pumpkin lights wound around the deck.

"As ready as I'll ever be," Oliver replied with a smile. "Congratulations, by the way. I heard about you and Allison."

Derrick grinned. "Yeah, I kinda didn't think she'd say yes. I mean, is it weird to get engaged on Halloween?"

Oliver's smile froze. Memories of Cate flooded through him. Hot. Then cold. A tingle in his lips, as though a ghost had breathed a kiss into his mouth. The coldness numbed his tongue, spread down his neck, through his nerves, and lodged in the corner of his heart he had locked away. "No," he managed before the knot in his throat threatened to choke him. "It's not weird at all."

Derrick slapped him on the shoulder. "See you around, man. Have fun tonight." He backed up as he spoke, nearly bumping into a couple dressed as Batman and Robin. His grin never left his face, and he nodded in farewell. "Happy Halloween."

"You too," Oliver replied automatically, but his memory was filled with Cate, and his thoughts scattered like leaves on the wind.

He turned back to the railing and gripped the polished wood. He could hear his wedding ring knock against the bar, and, with effort, he forced his hands to stop trembling. Blowing out a hard breath between his teeth, he stripped off his ring and held it between his fingertips. A simple gold circle, but he knew every inch of it by heart.

Long ago, he had thought it symbolized eternity—one unbroken round—but now, looking through it to the endlessly shifting waters beyond, he realized it was a zero. A hole through which his life had spiraled until he was left with this.

Nothing.

Cate had put this ring on his finger on October 31, 2004. He had been twenty-one. Young and nervous in his doctor's scrubs. She had been twenty-two. A princess in a wedding dress. The most beautiful woman in the world.

For ten years, this ring had stayed on his finger.

Now he was thirty-one. No longer young and nervous.

And his beautiful Cate was dead.

Laughter rose and fell around him as passengers began filling the walkways, heading toward the various offerings and activities of the evening. Chattering conversations overlapped each other like waves until the words were nothing but noise.

Someone bumped into Oliver from behind. "Sorry, mate," the man slurred.

He grunted at the contact—

And his wedding ring fell from his fingers.

His breath exploded from his lungs. He lunged forward, nearly falling over the railing himself, and watched, helpless, as the gold ring twirled and twisted away from him.

He tried to keep his eyes on the small circle, but with the darkness pressing in on him, and with the ship moving forward, he didn't even see where the ring landed. No splash. No ripple.

It was just gone.

Oliver tried to breathe, but the air suddenly felt heavier, thicker. He couldn't force it into his body; he didn't want to.

A sharp pain shot through his left palm, spiraling around his wrist and making his forearm throb.

Looking down, he saw blood welling from under his fingernails. He forced the muscles of his arm to relax, forced his fingers to uncurl from the fist he had made.

His heart thudded in his chest, but it felt like it belonged to someone else. It had to be someone else's blood and body and pain. He'd spent the last four months in a welcome numbness, so now, to have this exquisitely precise pain tracing its way through his veins and nerves, bridging the hollows of his heart to the hidden walls in his mind, and connecting him in a network of unrelenting agony was beyond what his body was prepared for.

He had lost so much already. Would the loss ever stop?

"Are you all right?" A woman with a blue masquerade mask paused, her gaze darting from his face to his arm and the streak of blood on his palm. "Would you like me to call someone? The ship's doctor, perhaps?" She looked at his uniform, clearly uncertain if it was the real thing or a costume.

Oliver laughed, a cold, brittle sound. The wind whipped it away, which made him glad. No one should have to hear such a sound. No one should have to *make* such a sound.

"No, thank you, miss," he managed. "It's just a scratch. I'll be fine. Thank you for your concern. Please, enjoy your evening."

She hesitated a moment longer, an appraising and appreciative look in her eyes that he could see even though she was masked.

He knew what she saw when she looked at him: a tall man with closely cropped hair the color of desert sand, eyes the color of wood. A man used to the discipline of wearing a uniform, of giving orders and having them obeyed. A man comfortable in his confidence.

A man with no ring on his finger anymore.

He hid his hand behind his back.

Oliver wasn't used to other women looking at him like that.

"If you'll excuse me," Oliver said, edging away from her and turning toward the main deck.

"Perhaps I'll see you later," she called out after him.

He hoped not. He brushed the back of his hand across his forehead, scrubbing away a layer of sweat. The crowds, the noise, the energy—everything was suddenly too much.

Despite the cool darkness, his skin felt hot, rough as sandpaper. He wanted to get away; he *needed* to get away.

But being on a cruise ship in the middle of the Mediterranean Sea in the middle of the night didn't exactly lend itself to escape. They were days away from reaching port. And it wasn't like the smaller ship-to-shore vessels were being launched tonight . . .

Oliver stopped mid-step.

He checked his wristwatch and picked up his pace. He didn't want to be late for the Storytelling by Starlight gig.

Two

The Storytelling by Starlight activity was designed to appeal to families. The largest of the ship-to-shore vessels held nearly 250 people, but by the time Oliver arrived at the designated area for departure, there was only one ship left: a small boat with ten seats, four of which were already filled with a cuddling teenaged couple and a set of grandparents.

"I'm sorry," the crew member—Nathan—said to the last family waiting on deck. "All the larger boats are in use, but this one will work just fine. We didn't expect so many people."

"Are you sure it's safe?" the young mother asked Nathan. She held hands with both her husband and her small, five-year-old daughter, who was dressed as a Care Bear, complete with fuzzy ears and a giant red heart on her stomach.

"One hundred percent," he said. "I promise. And look. Here is our ship's doctor. He will be joining us tonight."

Oliver nodded. "Permission to come aboard?" He smiled at the family and gestured for them to go first.

The father took the lead down the gangplank that led to the boat. His wife tightened her grip on her daughter's hand and followed him down.

Oliver smiled at the sight, though not without regret. He and Cate had talked about kids—she had wanted a houseful of them—but the timing never seemed to be right. He was focused on school; and then the time he thought they had vanished overnight.

It had been fast and, he hoped, painless, but it didn't change the fact that Cate's own body had killed her. She had complained of leg pain one weekend, but she was training for an upcoming 5K, and her legs often hurt. He'd chalked it up to that. She had just pulled a muscle, he said. Nothing a hot bath and a good night's sleep wouldn't cure, he said.

And she listened to him. He was her husband, after all.

If only he had suspected that a sneaky, silent clot was developing in her leg. If only he had guessed how swiftly it was growing in her vein. If only he had figured out a way to stop it from breaking free one night and shooting straight to her heart.

He was a doctor, after all. He should have been able to save her.

"Doc?" Nathan prompted. "You coming?"

Oliver shoved his memories back into the darkness and nodded once, curtly. "Yes, I'm coming."

He strode down the gangplank in three quick steps, landing hard in the boat and sending it rocking.

The little girl squealed in delighted terror. "Mama! We're sailing!"

Mom smiled and held her close. "Not yet, baby. But we are much closer to the water now. Stay close to me or Dad. Okay? We want you to be safe."

Nathan and Oliver helped everyone buckle their life jackets, and then Nathan steered the boat away from the liner and out over the dark, moonlit waves. The breeze had died down, though the temperature was still cool. The teenagers sitting on the port side of the boat cuddled even closer together, the boy wrapping his arms around his girlfriend. The grandparents sitting next to them were more prepared: they already had a lap blanket spread over their legs.

There was an empty seat between the two couples, but Oliver didn't want to crowd anyone. He made his way to the empty seats next to the family on the starboard side. He wasn't particularly in the mood for socializing, but he couldn't stand for the whole trip.

The little girl smiled shyly at him across the empty seat. "Are you gonna tell us a story?"

Oliver nodded, but without much confidence. He looked around at the passengers. Did he even know any good stories? His glance fell on the littlest passenger. She knelt sideways on her wobbly seat, her orange life jacket nearly swallowing her up. Her pink cheeks glowed, and she reached up to pull back her fuzzy bear hood.

"Halloween stories is the best," she said to Oliver, as though imparting a great secret. "Tell my favorite story about the witches."

Oliver, clearly unfamiliar with that story, looked to the girl's parents for help.

"Becca, I'm sure the doctor has his own favorite story to tell," the mother said, smoothing back her daughter's dark brown hair.

What would Cate do? he thought. Cate had been the storyteller in the family. She would know how to make this night memorable for everyone. She would know how to weave a story out of the stars and the moonlight. He closed his eyes and conjured up his favorite mental picture of her:

Cate, wearing her faded Swedish Bitters concert T-shirt,

broken-in jeans, and scuffed-up sneakers. Cate, pulling back her long, blonde hair into a ponytail. Cate, looking at him with a smile as bright as the sun and asking him, "Ready?"

Then she'd bolted down the sidewalk before he'd had a chance to answer, making him chase her. Which he had— until he'd caught her by Mrs. Bailie's mailbox, at which point he'd kissed her until they both forgot why they had been racing in the first place.

The kiss had been worth remembering forever, but it had been that singular moment *before* that had stuck with Oliver longer. The moment of anticipation. Of possibility. Of unparalleled joy.

A scream cut through his memories, jolting him back to the moment. Oliver's instincts took over. He swept the boat with a single glance: the teenagers gaped, the grandparents gasped, Nathan lunged for the starboard side yelling, "Stay in the boat!"

The small family of three was down to two.

Becca was gone.

Three

Oliver dove into the water.

He didn't think; he just took one step onto the recently vacated seat, extended his arms, and plunged into the ocean. He barely had time to take a breath. The waves cut the mother's scream in two.

When he was younger, he'd thought it would be quiet underwater, but he'd been in the ocean often enough to know it was filled with sound. The zip of bubbles escaping from his nose and mouth. The tidal hush of his blood flowing in his veins. The tick-tock of his heartbeat.

Oliver pulled his arms through the water, diving deeper in order to avoid being blinded by the bubbles. He looked around, but between the darkness filling the water and the salt stinging his eyes, his visibility was low. He wished he could call out Becca's name, but he could already feel the pressure in his lungs.

He saw a flash of orange to his right. Spinning as best he could, he kicked his way forward.

Becca's life jacket had come unbuckled, black straps drifting like seaweed.

Oliver pushed the jacket aside. Becca had to be close. She had been wearing a full bear costume, which had probably gotten waterlogged as soon as she hit the water, and without the jacket helping to offset the weight, she would sink instead of swim—

There.

Oliver looked below him and saw Becca falling as though in slow motion. Her small hand uncurled, reaching for him. Her eyes were closed, and a few small bubbles trickled from her nose.

Stroking downward, Oliver reached the little girl and grabbed her wrist in one motion. The Care Bear costume was heavy, and pulling Becca to the surface strained every muscle Oliver had.

The pressure in his lungs battered at him, demanding release, but he resisted. He couldn't give in until Becca was safe.

He swam toward the light, imagining that with just one more stroke upward, he'd be able to reach the full moon that hung low over the water. One more stroke. One more. One . . .

His head broke the surface an instant before he hauled Becca up beside him.

Nathan had kept the ship close, and Oliver was grateful that his crewmate's instincts had proven true. Six faces peered at him over the edge of the boat. Nathan shouted at the passengers to step back, move back, keep the weight evenly distributed; they didn't want to capsize the boat.

"Becca! My baby!" the mother called out. "Becca, where are you?"

"Here!" Oliver called back, his voice raw. The salt water tasted like tears.

Becca spluttered in his arms, her eyes snapping open and her mouth drawing in a deep, gasping breath.

Oliver wasted no time swimming back to the boat. He'd spent his adrenaline on the dive and the rescue. He didn't dare risk going into shock while still in the water.

"Oliver!" Nathan shouted, then threw out a life preserver. It splashed near enough that Oliver could grab it with his free hand. He looped it around Becca's small body to help support her.

"Go!" he shouted to Nathan, who began hauling the life preserver back toward the boat.

Becca clung to the white ring with both hands as she cut through the water. Her eyes never left Oliver's. Her face was as pale as the moon.

Nathan, Becca's father, and the teenage boy all reached down and pulled the little girl back into the boat. In an instant, Becca's mother had wrapped her arms around her daughter, her sobs shifting from terror to relief.

"You'll be okay," he whispered, partly to reassure Becca and her mother, and partly to reassure himself. "You're going to be okay."

He tilted his head back into the water and looked up at the moon. It had felt so far away when he'd been underwater. Now it felt close enough to touch.

He pulled a breath deep into his aching lungs, wondering if Cate had felt similar pressure the night the clot moved into her lungs, cutting off her air, and then into her heart, cutting off her life.

The salt water on his lips no longer came only from the sea.

He rubbed a wet hand over his face and turned toward the boat.

"Oliver!" Nathan shouted. He stood with one foot on the side of the boat, the life preserver back in his hands, ready to cast it into the water. "You ready?"

Oliver opened his mouth to say yes, he needed help—he was ready to be saved—but instead, a yelp escaped his lips.

A hand encircled his ankle, as cold and hard as marble, and pulled him down.

Down into the depths of the sea.

Water closed over his eyes, his mouth, his nose.

The moon receded in his vision until he saw nothing but blackness.

Kicking didn't help. The hand had latched onto him with the ferociousness of a shark, and he was helpless to break free.

Whatever it was that had grabbed him was pulling him so fast that the water blurred around him. There was nothing to grab onto to stop his momentum. Nothing to cling to.

His lungs emptied of air. A tingling sensation started in his hands and feet. His chest and throat tightened, and he felt like he needed to cough, but he also knew that was the worst thing he could do.

Oliver gritted his teeth and forced himself to look down, trying to catch a glimpse of what had captured him.

He hadn't really expected to be able to see anything, but to his surprise, he could see every detail of the creature below him.

Because she *glowed.*

The skin of her entire body was pure white, and while she looked mostly human, Oliver could see the shimmering, silver scales that coated her legs in overlapping rings from her thighs to her toes. Was she a mermaid?

No, because folded against her back were what appeared to be wings.

An angel?

Impossible. Angels flew in the sky, not swam in the ocean.

The lack of oxygen was clearly affecting Oliver's brain. He was hallucinating. That must be it. That would also explain the music he could hear trailing in the wake of the strange angel-mermaid creature. Was it possible that she was humming underwater? Singing?

Struggling to escape, Oliver kicked again and again, but the white woman merely tightened her grip on his ankle and increased her speed.

I'm going to die, Oliver thought, surprised at how calm he felt at the realization. *I'm ready, Cate. I hope I get to see you again. That would be nice . . .*

The angel-mermaid creature suddenly stopped swimming and pulled Oliver close, turning him to face her. She peered at him with bottomless black eyes, her mouth a narrow slit. Her song nearly disappeared, but Oliver could still hear the thrum and lift of the notes.

Death cannot have you, a voice said in his mind. *I found you. I caught you. You are mine.*

She wrapped her scale-clad legs around his, pressed her body close to his, and then tilted her face upward.

Like a rocket, they shot toward the sky, far above.

Four

Oliver woke with the sound of the ocean in his ears. Sand coated the side of his face, gritty and cold against his wet skin. A soft breeze blew past, rustling the leaves in the trees and bushes around him.

He rolled onto his back, quickly taking stock of his situation and being amazed by three things: one, he wasn't dead; two, there were no stars in the sky, only the round, full moon; and three, he could hear voices.

So, on land, but probably not on a *mainland,* as the liner had been fairly isolated. An island, perhaps? There were certainly plenty to choose from in the Mediterranean, some inhabited, some not. But the voices supported the former. Wherever he was, he was not alone.

He tried not to look at the sky. The missing stars created a sense of *wrongness* in him. His brain insisted the stars were there; his eyes disagreed. The edges of his vision wavered like they did when he got a migraine. He closed his eyes and focused on the voices. He didn't want to barge into a situation without preparing for it first.

"You should not have brought him here," a feminine voice said, her tone strong and unusually husky.

"I was not going to leave him. I found him," a younger-sounding voice replied, a hint of petulance beneath her words.

I found you. The words echoed in his memory. Could it be the same creature from the water?

He heard music layered beneath and between the words, but the notes were discordant, edged with anger.

Oliver rolled to his knees, then into a crouch. He scraped his soaked hair back from his forehead. A flicker of light danced between the bushes on his right. Stepping carefully, his footsteps timed to his slow and even breathing, he approached.

Pushing aside some of the smaller leaves, he created a peephole. Again, his mind and his eyes battled over the reality presented to him.

His mind said it wasn't possible. Not in the slightest.

His eyes saw three women standing around a bonfire. One of them he recognized instantly. It was the woman who had abducted him—there was no other word for it—and her white skin, still wet from her swim, emitted a pale glow. Her silver-scaled legs were lean and muscular. Her back was to him so he could clearly see where the wings attached to her shoulders. The feathers rustled and ruffled, but whether from the ceaseless breeze or as a result of her frustration, he couldn't tell.

Facing the white woman were two others. The three were similar enough to each other that Oliver's first thought was *Sisters.* Like his captor, the other women had silver scales covering part of their white skin, but the scales on the one on his left ended just below her breasts, while the third woman had scales all the way up to her neck.

What did it mean? Was it a deformity? A mark of authority? A sign of age? Oliver felt himself reverting to his three-part training: observe, analyze, act. He knew he had to stay detached, impartial, unemotional, otherwise the strangeness of the evening would drive him insane.

"You should not have gone *looking* for him," the tallest of the three said, the one with the scales up to her neck.

Then she said one more word, but Oliver's ears heard it only as a note of pure music. His brain struggled to translate the sound into something recognizable, something familiar. *Glau.* A word. A name?

When the musical note transformed into language, the sound of it shivered into his body, sliding down his nerve endings until his skin tingled on the inside. He grimaced at the pain, even as he leaned forward, hoping to hear them speak again.

"I told you she would do it, sister," the woman on the left said. "You know Glau cannot resist a challenge."

"Mol is right, Thel," Glau said, her shoulders straightening with pride. "I have done what you dared not do. What you *could not* do."

Again, as the two high notes of pure music were spoken, Oliver's brain transformed them into language, into names. *Mol. Thel.* He filed them away, trying to focus on the conversation even as the tingling sensation in his nerves increased with every word the women spoke.

The two older sisters exchanged a glance. Thel, the tallest, with scales up to her neck, rolled her head on her shoulders and snapped open her wings. "I repeat: You should not have gone looking for him. You should not have brought him here."

"But . . ." Mol prompted, her own wings unfurling and curling like a question mark.

"But—" Thel glared at both her sisters. "I am glad you did. It has been far too long since we have enjoyed a . . . guest."

189

Glau's wings twitched in silent victory, and even without seeing her face, Oliver knew she was smiling.

"Bring him," Thel ordered. "The night grows late."

"Oh, but he is already here," Glau cooed. "Or could you not tell?" She half-turned, looking over her shoulder directly at Oliver's hiding spot. Her black eyes were darker than the empty night sky. Her mouth, which had indeed been smiling, widened into something bordering on a snarl, and her small pink tongue darted out to lick her lip before retreating behind sharp-looking teeth.

She crooked a finger in his direction and beckoned him forward.

Oliver rose. His nerves responded to every sound the sisters made, increasing from a warm tingle to a hot vibration to a roaring inferno, as if a molten-hot coal had been placed in his belly, threatening to char him from the inside out.

A small portion of his soul screamed at him that this was *dangerous,* that he should turn and run back into the sea and swim as far and as fast as he could until this island was someplace beyond the horizon.

But the heat had consumed him, controlled him. He had to stay. He had to hear more of their words, their music, their song.

Without hesitating, Oliver pushed through the bushes and strode toward the bonfire and directly to the strange women who circled the flames.

Five

"He is beautiful," Mol said.

The sound of her voice, so near to Oliver's ears, rocked him, and he fell to his knees in the soft sand.

"He is perfect," Glau insisted. She touched Oliver's shoulder, and he leaned into her cold hand. He couldn't help it.

"He will do," Thel said. She folded her arms across her chest and snapped her wings closed. "I will be first, as—"

"What?" Glau shouted. "No!" She dug her fingers into Oliver, and the flame in his belly hissed in response to her anger.

"—As is my right as the eldest," Thel finished.

"But the first memories are the most potent." Mol traced the scales across her belly. "What if there is nothing left for us?"

"Look at him," Thel said. "There is enough for all of us. He is so full of memories, his emotions are seeping out of him. He is ripe and ready to burst."

The words washed over Oliver. He suspected he heard only one in ten and understood even fewer. The fire banked in his body made his skin hot to the touch, and his doctor's uniform, which had been soaking wet from his time spent underwater, was nearly dry.

"Wha—" He tried to speak, but the effort made his muscles seize up. He tried again. "What are—"

He wasn't even sure what he was trying to say. *What are you talking about? What are you going to do to me? What are you?*

"Hush, my sweet," Glau murmured to him. She ran her fingers through his hair, leaving behind tracks of heat. "Speaking is unnecessary on our island. We have everything we need right here—" She moved her hand from the top of his head down to his temple, tapping it with a hard-edged fingernail. "And here." She trailed her hand down his cheek, down his neck, down his chest, to rest against his heart. "If you let us in willingly," she said in a half-song, "it will go much better for you."

The fire she ignited was such an intense blend of pleasure and pain that Oliver couldn't stop himself from nodding. *Yes*, he thought, lightning-fast, before the *No* that rushed to his lips could be spoken.

Glau smiled at her sisters in triumph. "As simple as that."

Thel wrinkled her nose. "Is he a warrior? He smells of pain."

"Good warriors know when to fight—and when to surrender." Glau shrugged. "If you don't want him . . ."

"I did not say that." Thel moved faster than Oliver's eyes could follow. One moment she was towering over him, silver scales shifting on her skin like waves on the water. The next moment she was by his side, her arms around him, her hands cradling his head, gently helping him to lie back on the sand.

It is time to rest.

Oliver heard Thel's words in his mind even though he didn't see her lips move.

It is time to relax.

What are you going to do? He didn't know how he thought it *toward* Thel, but she smiled as if she had heard him.

We will sing you to sleep. And while you sleep, you will dream. And then we will take all the pain and hurt and sorrow from you. You will be freed. You will wake a new man.

Oh. That didn't sound so bad. His vision blurred, and he felt dizzy, as if the earth stood still and he was the one spinning atop it.

Thel stretched out next to Oliver, fitting her body next to his. Her scales were a cooling balm against his fever-hot skin. Mol knelt at Oliver's head; she brushed his hair back from his eyes. Glau knelt at his feet; her hand fit perfectly around his ankle.

Rest, Thel repeated. *Relax. Remember.*

This time, though, she opened her mouth, but what came out weren't the words Oliver heard in his head. A song poured out of her, heavy and dark and sweet and light all at the same time. Mol joined in, the two voices weaving and dancing together in perfect rhythm. Glau waited a moment before rounding out the trio. Her voice was the highest and loveliest sound Oliver had ever heard.

Rest. Relax. Remember. The three sisters sang in unison, then in harmony, then individually.

Rest. Glau.

Relax. Mol.

Remember. Thel placed her hand over Oliver's heart. The fire in his body flared into life at her touch. She leaned closer and kissed his forehead.

Remember the first, the best, the brightest. Remember it for me. Sing it for me.

The sisters' song rose in both volume and intensity. It was endless. It was powerful.

Oliver dove into the sound as if it was water. He was weightless, worry-less.

My first memory? Oliver's mind spiraled away from him, rising up into the blackness that stretched from horizon to horizon on this unreal island.

Oliver relaxed—and remembered—as the siren sisters sang the stars back into the sky.

✳ ✳ ✳

My mother finishes painting a whiskery beard on my chin with her makeup pencil. She leans back on her heels, hands on her thighs, and beams at me. "Oh, Ollie, you are so cute!"

I don't want to be *cute.* I am a pirate, and pirates are scary. Pirates are brave. Pirates fight sea monsters and have adventures and rescue princesses. I am only five years old, and even I know that.

Mom takes a picture of me, the flash bright in my one good eye. The other is covered by a black patch. I clutch my pumpkin bucket in sweaty hands. My insides feel wiggly and bubbly. Halloween is my favorite. I've waited all day for the sun to go down. I can't wait any more.

"Can we trick-n-treat now?" I ask, earning a laugh from Mom.

"Of course we can. Just let me get my shoes."

The wiggles inside me try to get out. My plastic sword swings against my hip as I hop from foot to foot. I try not to think about all the candy that is hidden behind all the doors up and down the street. I am a pirate, and I will claim it all for my own.

Ding-dong.

Someone is at the door. Someone else is already out trick-n-treating.

"I'll get it!" I shout and run, the wiggles making me go fast.

I am small, but I can open the front door.

"Trick-or-treat!" calls out the princess standing in front of me.

She is my age; her mom and dad are standing a few steps away from the door. Her hair is yellow, and her eyes are blue. The princess holds out her black bucket with spider's legs on all sides. "Trick-or-treat," she demands.

I can't move. I can't breathe.

I've never seen her before. Maybe she's new. She is . . . so pretty. Prettier than anything. Prettier even than my mom.

"Hi," I say. "I'm a pirate."

She moves her hip out, making her pink dress swish in the last of the sunlight. "I'm a princess."

I can't say anything. My heart is running faster than it did when Mr. Thompson's dog barked at me.

The princess sighs and holds out her spider to me. She shakes it. There isn't much candy in it yet. "You're supposta give me candy. That's the rule."

Suddenly my mom is behind me, opening the door even wider. I am moved out of the way.

"Hello, Mr. and Mrs. Eden." Mom waves to the other grown-ups. "And hello to you, princess." Mom grabs the candy bowl and crouches down so the princess can choose her favorite.

She picks Butterfingers. That's my favorite too. I smile without knowing why.

"What's your name, princess?" Mom asks.

"My mom and dad call me Catherine." She jerks a thumb over her shoulder. "But *I* call me Cate," she finishes boldly, just like a princess should.

"Welcome to the neighborhood," Mom says. "Maybe

you and Oliver could have a play date sometime." Mom points at me and smiles.

Catherine—Cate—looks me up and down. I drop my pumpkin bucket. "Yeah, okay." Then she twirls away and bounces down the steps.

Mom closes the door and sees me standing there. "You okay, Ollie?"

"I'm gonna marry her," I say.

Mom laughs, but I mean it. She drops a Butterfingers into my bucket as she hands it back to me. "Happy Halloween. You ready to go get some candy?"

Six

Pain lanced through Oliver, arching his back and making his heels drum against the sand. All the air in his body exploded out of him in one harsh exhale.

Thel rolled away from him, her wings spread out beneath her like a blanket. She rubbed her hand against her mouth and giggled, high and childlike. The sound felt wrong coming from such a formidable person. Her silver scales now coated her throat and the underside of her jaw. Even without the starlight, they glimmered and glowed.

"How was it?" Mol asked.

"What did you see?" Glau said at the same time.

Thel raised her arms over her head and stretched her body like a cat. She smiled—lazy, fat, and happy—and purred. "That was . . . delicious."

"My turn," Mol said, wings fluttering. She scrambled to replace Thel by Oliver's side.

Thel laughed. "No rush, my sister. If all his memories are like that one, we will feast on him for *days*. It has been too long since I have tasted such wonder."

Oliver shook his head. He felt *different*. Fire still blazed under his skin, but a part of his mind was clear, cool, and curiously empty. He mentally probed that emptiness, and a fleeting sensation of *pirates and princesses* drifted through his mind before dissipating like blown smoke from a candle.

The truth crashed in on him like cymbals. Thel had stolen his memory. Worse, she had *consumed* it.

He pushed Mol away and tried to lever himself up on his elbows, but Glau pinned his feet down into the sand.

"Let me go," he said. The words came easier to him than before. He wondered if that should frighten him.

Glau glared at him with her black eyes. "Not yet," she said.

"My turn," Mol said again, pulling Oliver down next to her. Thel still giggled, drunk on Oliver's memory.

"Thel," Glau snapped. "We need you. Anchor him."

The eldest siren sighed through pouted lips but did as she was told, replacing Glau at Oliver's feet so Glau could take Mol's empty place at Oliver's head.

Oliver, pinned down, could only stare up at Glau's dark eyes. She bent her face over his.

"Please," he whispered. "No more."

Glau's eyes were flint and steel. "It's Mol's turn."

"Why?" Oliver tried again. "Why did you take me? Why won't you let me go?"

Glau looked at Thel, whose eyes were closed in bliss, and at Mol, who was arranging her wings and scale-covered legs, and then back to Oliver. Anger turned her white skin the palest pink. "Because I heard your song. I've never heard such sorrow and grief before. I wanted it." She placed her fingers on Oliver's brow and growled, low in her throat. "We don't want your happy memories. Give Mol something sad. Something painful."

Oliver certainly had enough of those kinds of memories, and part of him would be happy to let Mol take them away, but life was about balancing the bitter with the sweet. Though it seemed like lately all his memories were bittersweet, especially when it came to Cate.

"No!" Glau snapped. "Don't think of her—"

But it was too late. The sirens resumed their song, and Oliver remembered.

I am running through the rain and the dark and the wind. I am holding Cate's hand as she runs next to me. I am laughing. We both are.

Lightning flashes in the sky, and thunder rumbles close. Cate shrieks and runs faster. Now she is pulling me along.

We are heading for the high school. The Halloween dance is already underway, and Cate and I are late. We are juniors, and it is our first date, and I wanted it to be memorable—just maybe not *this* memorable.

"C'mon, Oliver, quick before—"

Lightning. Thunder. Cate throws her laugh back into the storm, unafraid.

We slip and slide our way through the puddles and into the school. I look at Cate. She looks at me. We both burst out laughing again.

Cate's costume is ruined. I'm sure mine is as well. We're dressed up as Danny and Sandy from *Grease.* Cate has my leather jacket, which helped shield her from the rain, though now my T-shirt is soaked through. Her skirt drips water on the school carpet.

"Guess I should have driven after all," I say.

Cate smiles, and my heart flips. "I didn't mind the walk." A lock of blonde hair tumbles free from her clip and lands on her perfect, upturned nose. "Besides, a little water never hurt anyone."

"Tell that to the Wicked Witch of the West," I said.

She laughs so hard she gives an unladylike snort, which only makes her laugh harder. "C'mon," she finally manages to say. "I know what to do."

We skirt the edge of the gym, where the dance is in full swing, and head for the back locker rooms. Cate pulls me though the door. The automatic lights turn on.

"This is the girls' locker room!" I keep my voice low and glance over my shoulder at the door I should be bolting through.

"Relax. I doubt anyone is here besides us." Cate squelches to her locker along the back wall. A few spins of the combination, and the lock pops open. "I've got my lacrosse uniform I can change into, and, oh, here—" She tosses a pair of socks and a white towel at me. "For you." She bundles her clothes in her arms and gives me a stern look. "I'll be right back."

"I'll be right here," I say, pointing to the ground.

She heads for the bathroom, and I slide down the bank of lockers. Draping the towel around my neck, I pull off my wet shoes and soaking-wet socks. I worry that Cate's socks won't fit me, but either she has larger feet than I suspected or they are magic socks because they fit just fine.

Except one sock is solid purple and the other is striped.

I pull off my T-shirt and use the towel to dry off as best I can. I'm rubbing the cloth over my face when I hear Cate's indrawn breath. Then it sounds like she says, "Oh, wow."

I look at her, and I have to swallow hard. She's exchanged her costume for her lacrosse uniform. She's taken her 1950s curls out and slicked back her wet hair into a ponytail. Her makeup is mostly gone. She looks *good*. Clean and comfortable and confident. She, too, is wearing one solid purple sock and one striped sock.

I wiggle my toes. "Looks like our socks got split up."

She sits on the floor across from me, her back against a bank of lockers too. She stretches out her legs so her feet match up with mine, striped socks against solids.

"I've never understood the appeal of wearing matching socks."

"Um, because everybody does it?" I offer. Her feet are smaller than mine, but not by much.

"Not little kids," she fires back, folding her arms across her chest. "Kids wear whatever they want. They don't care if their socks don't match."

"Maybe you should start an anti-matching-socks-club."

"Why? You wanna join?"

"Sure," I say, curling my toes over the tops of hers. Her feet are warm. "I'm open to all socks, whatever size or color they may be. I'm definitely pro-sock."

She tilts her head and gives me a look that makes me suddenly aware that I never put my T-shirt back on.

"You know what I like about you, Oliver?"

"My stance on socks?" I joke, though my heart has kicked into high gear at her words. *She likes me.* I've liked her for as long as I can remember, laughed with her, longed for her, but I've never been brave enough to tell her.

She lowers her gaze and rocks her feet side to side. My feet follow her lead. She speaks to her toes, and her voice is low and serious. "I know I'm kind of . . . I know I'm not like other girls. I've never been able to wait around for someone else to want to be friends with me. I've always made my own way and done my own thing. But you've always been there for me. Ever since we met that Halloween when we were just kids."

I sense she has more she wants to say, so I don't interrupt her.

"You're my best friend, Oliver. You know that, right?"

"Yeah," I manage. My mouth is dry. I feel like the next thing she says will either break my heart—or bless it.

"We're like these socks. You're the solid to my stripe. Other people might not think we match, but we do."

My heart fills with light. *She thinks we match?*

"I'm totally a striped sock, I admit that. I'm easily distracted, I like too many different things, I'm all over the place. But you're the solid sock. Steady and reliable." She shakes her head. "That sounds lame. That's not what I mean." She purses her lips, and all I can think about is how much I want to kiss her. "I mean, you're honest and open. A what-you-see-is-what-you-get kind of person. I can trust you."

"Always," I say. My chest feels hot even without a shirt on and with a cold, wet towel draped over me.

She continues as if she hasn't heard me. "I like the kind of person I am when I'm with you." She finally looks up and meets my gaze. Her eyes are as bright as a full moon. Her smile is somehow brave and shy at the same time. "The kind of person who can say 'I love you' and not be afraid."

A roaring wind sweeps through me. I am drowning in relief and happiness. "I love you, too." I hold my breath, waiting to hear what she will say next.

All she says is "Good," but then she moves and kneels across me, straddling my legs. She leans into me, and I can smell her hair and feel her rain-softened skin and the mesh fabric of her lacrosse jersey as it brushes against my chest.

I've never kissed a girl before, but this is Cate. I know her better than I know myself, so my hands know exactly where to sit on her waist, and my mouth knows the exact moment to move forward and meet her lips.

She tastes like summertime breezes. Her lips are as hot as a fireplace in winter.

She places her hands on my shoulders, right where it curves into my neck, and electricity crackles over me, making the hairs on my arms lift. I tighten my grip on her waist, and she lets me tilt her forward, closer.

Cate—the girl who never follows when she can lead—
has surrendered. She is pliable, willing.

The kiss grows exponentially—deeper, broader, all-
consuming. The towel falls to the floor. I sit up straighter,
needing to be as close to her as I can. Her hands move from
my shoulders to my jaw.

Cate makes a sound low in her throat. It makes me
think of her laugh trapped inside a firecracker. When it
explodes, I feel the heat of it in my own body.

I can't breathe—I don't care.

I can't stop—I don't want to.

The automatic lights in the locker room click off.

Cate pulls back, and though every instinct in me
screams to keep her close, I let her go.

"I'm not sorry," she says, as if I had raised an objection.

"Me either." I barely recognize my voice. My mouth
tingles with the taste of Cate.

She rocks back on my legs, and I wince at the pressure
of her body on mine. The heat that has raged through me is
now localized.

We sit in the silent dark for a while, listening to each
other breathe. I am acutely aware of exactly where her body
is in relation to mine.

"I guess we should go to the dance," I say, though it
comes out more like question than a request.

"I'd rather stay here. With you."

The fire in my body flares, and I reach for her; I can't
help it.

"Don't move. I don't want the lights to turn back on,"
she says, but then she slowly slides off me, taking that
exquisite heat with her, and I hear her sit beside me. She
takes my hand, weaves her fingers with mine. "I know this
will sound strange coming from me, but . . . I don't want to
rush it."

I imagine I can feel her pulse in her wrist where it
presses next to mine.

"I don't want to ruin it," she adds.

"Do you know how long I've wanted to kiss you?" I say. It's easier to be bold in the dark.

"Your whole life." She doesn't say it like it's a throwaway answer. Instead, there is amazed realization in her voice. It's easier to hear in the dark, too.

She inhales, and then says quietly, "Me too."

All my words fly away from me. I am left with only joy.

The music from the Halloween dance drifts down the hallway and into the locker room. I'm surprised I haven't heard it before now.

But something is wrong. The song is too slow, a minor key of some kind. The notes warble like they are being played underwater. The sound grates on my nerves, and I clench my teeth. It shouldn't hurt to listen to music, should it?

The vocals break into two parts, three. Three voices calling out for me . . .

I turn my head to tell Cate to cover her ears, to protect herself from the sirens, but I'm too late.

The darkness cracks open, and the memory shatters into shards. Cate is gone. Glau is looking at me. She says my name.

Seven

"Oliver," Glau said again, her voice cold and sharp. The edges of her wings fluttered with every shift of her shoulders. Her pale skin was another shade darker. Her eyes cut to the side, and Oliver looked where her gaze led.

Mol sprawled on the ground a few feet away, not in relief or with satiated ecstasy, but like a discarded rag doll. Oliver couldn't tell if she was still breathing.

Thel had crumpled into a ball at Oliver's feet, nothing more than a lump of scales and wings. She might have been crying, or it might have been the wind moaning through the trees.

"What happened?" Oliver asked Glau.

She bared her sharp teeth in a snarl. "You did this. My sisters—" She pointed at Mol and Thel. "They were not prepared for that. You fed them too much!"

Freed from her touch, Oliver rolled to his feet and backed away. He only made it a few steps before the ground shifted beneath him and he fell back to the sand. The empty spot in his mind had grown larger, colder.

"I told you to give Mol something sad. All these memories filled with happiness and joy—" She spat on the sand beside the bonfire. "We cannot live on that. We need your sorrow, your grief. That is what sustains us. We need the *meat* of you."

Crouching on her hands and knees, she looked feral. Oliver scrambled back a few more yards.

She threw something at him with a roar. It glittered in the firelight and landed next to his feet. "I heard your song across oceans, across time. But your song was a lie!"

Oliver's wedding ring. His hand trembled as he picked it up and slipped it back on his finger. "How did you get this?" The coldness in his voice matched the coldness in his soul, the emptiness in his memories.

"I told you. I heard it enter the water. I heard the song it sang."

"A song of me—and Cate." He rubbed the ring with his thumb.

She shook her head. "A song of life lived—and lost." She licked her lips and crawled closer to me. "You are a dead man walking. You were supposed to be different."

Dead man walking. That was how Oliver had felt since Cate's death. Just marking time until it was his turn. Was this it? Would his death come at the hands of a siren bent on harvesting his memories?

"You think my life was nothing but happiness?" he said. He kept his gaze on his ring as a coughing laugh cut through him. He looked at Glau and smiled to see that it was her turn to flinch. "Your sisters couldn't survive my joy. You think *you* can survive my sorrow?"

Glau shifted her weight back, her body poised to either fight or flee but uncertain which would be necessary.

Oliver wasn't going to let her touch him, let her consume another memory, but that didn't mean he couldn't tell her one of his memories. Cate's death was too new, too raw. He hadn't survived it himself yet. Sharing it would likely kill them both. But he had plenty of others to choose from.

"She said no."

Glau narrowed her eyes, but otherwise remained motionless.

"We were in college, and I was still blindly, stupidly in love with her. But somewhere along the way between high school and college, she . . ." He shook his head, spinning the ring around and around on his finger. "She changed. I changed. I should have seen it, I guess. But I was buried with my medical classes, and I thought she'd always be there. She always had been."

Glau settled into the sand and wrapped her wings around her legs. Her eyes closed all the way, but Oliver could still feel her attention focused on him.

"It was Halloween." He looked up at the moon and laughed, short and bitter. "It was always Halloween with us."

Glau's mouth parted as if inhaling Oliver's words.

"We were on the bus. Cate liked to hop on a route and see where it went. We'd had a lot of great adventures that way. But that day something was different. Normally she talked to everyone on the bus, but she was really quiet. I kept trying to get her to talk to me, but she slumped against the window and wouldn't look at me."

Glau began rocking side to side, like seaweed caught in a drifting current. A low-level hum rose from her throat.

"I asked her why she was sad, and she just brushed me off.

"I asked her if I had done something wrong, and she just shrugged.

"I asked her what I could do to make her happy, and she just closed her eyes.

"I asked her—" His voice caught. Even though he knew

what happened next, and how the story ultimately ended, Oliver still remembered exactly how he had felt at that moment.

"I asked her if she wanted to break up with me."

Glau's eyes slitted open, glowing with a rainbow-streaked black light, like raindrops on oil.

"I meant it as a joke—something to force her to talk to me. I didn't start to panic until she didn't say anything at all. Then she said . . . no." He allowed the memory of relief to flood through him now as it had then, passing through him and into Glau.

Her hum faltered. She had expected agony, torment—not relief. Oliver had knocked her off balance. That was good. But his story wasn't done, and his relief had been short-lived.

"'Well,' I said, 'if you don't want to break up with me, then marry me instead.'

"She finally looked at me, but not with the happiness I expected. It wasn't terror, or disappointment, or anger, but some combination of all three. Her eyes were mean, I remember that.

"I must have spoken louder than I'd thought because the girl sitting behind us gasped. 'Did you just propose to her?' she said.

"I looked from Cate to the girl and back. 'Yeah, I guess I did. I am.' I reached for Cate's hand. She let me take it, but her skin was cold, and I could tell she didn't want me to touch her.

"The girl grabbed the handrail and pulled herself into the aisle. 'Hey, these guys just got engaged!'

"Everyone on the bus began clapping and cheering and whistling. The driver even honked the horn in celebration. Everyone was happy—except Cate. Everyone thought she had said yes—but she hadn't.

"'C'mon, Cate,' I said, pleading, begging. 'What do you say? Marry me?'

"What had started kind of as a joke suddenly became the best idea I'd ever had. I'd loved her my whole life. I wanted to spend the rest of my life with her. We were both in college. I was going to be a doctor. I'd be able to provide for her, take care of her, protect her."

Glau crawled toward Oliver as if his words were hooks and he was reeling her in.

"Instead of answering, Cate started to cry. Silent, endless tears that rolled down her face. She didn't even bother wiping them away.

"I should have dropped it. I should have taken her into my arms and held her while she cried. I should have said, 'I love you, no matter what' and left it at that. I almost did. But I didn't."

Glau was at Oliver's feet, her hum repeating the same melody over and over. New silver scales appeared on her upper thighs, reaching for her hips and her stomach.

"What I said instead was, 'Marry me, or else I'll get off the bus. Your choice.'

"And that's when Cate pulled the cord to stop the bus. The bell cut through the celebrations, and everyone got really quiet.

"'Marriage isn't an ultimatum, Oliver,' she said. 'No. My answer is no.' Her voice echoed in the bus, and the silence got awkward. Bad.

"The bus pulled over, like it was supposed to, and the doors folded open. I didn't know what to do, what to say.

"Cate said it a third time—'No'—and it was like she cast a magic spell over me. I got up from my seat, walked down the aisle, and stepped down and out of the bus. I didn't say anything. I just stood on the curb and watched as the doors closed, and the bus pulled away and took Cate with it."

Glau crouched in the sand, her eyes fixed on Oliver's ring. "Good," she murmured. "Yes. I understand your song now. You never saw her again, did you? You loved Cate, but when she didn't love you back, you married someone else.

Yet the ring carries all your memories of Cate—good and bad, joyful and sorrowful. She is gone, and you want her back. *That* is a memory I can sink my teeth into."

Oliver looked at Glau in amazement. "That's not what happened at all. Cate and I didn't marry—*then*. But we did *later*. And yes, Cate is gone, but not because I pushed her away, not because we stopped loving each other. She *died*." He shook his head. "You don't understand anything at all. Not sorrow or joy or love. You're like a child."

Glau reared back, fire flashing in her eyes. "We are the Sirens, daughters of the River God Achelous and Melpomene, the Muse of Song—we are *not* children! We have lived more thousands of years than you know. We have brought countless sailors here, either by force or by persuasion, and consumed more memories than you can imagine. I don't need to *understand* you to devour you."

"Then it's no wonder you're starving," he said.

Glau's mouth clicked shut, and a ripple moved in the muscle of her jaw. She wouldn't meet Oliver's eye.

"You take and take, but everything has left you feeling hollow. You focus on the pain because you think pain is more powerful than love, but it isn't." He nodded to her sisters, who were still unconscious on the sand. "Love is both good and bad. So is *life*. If you are only taking the bitter or the sweet, you'll never get to the heart of a man—to the *meat*, as you put it."

Glau measured him with her gaze. Her wings were eerily still against her back. The moonlight cast a silver glow on her body. "We have taken your sweet. You have told me of the bitter. You say I do not understand, then make me understand. If you give me the best of your *life*—the *truth* of the bitter and the sweet—I will let you go."

Eight

It felt like a trap.

Offer up one more memory, and Glau will let me go?

But not just any memory. One that would convince her that life was about hope. That's what it boiled down to, after all. When sorrow is more than you can bear, hope promises you that, one day, it will get better. And when your days are filled with happiness, hope is what you share with everyone around you.

Oliver had two gaping holes in his memory, vacancies like missing teeth, but even though he couldn't remember what used to be there, he still had one memory—his *best* memory—that could be the key to his freedom.

If he was willing to give it to Glau.

Oliver curled the fingers on his left hand into a fist, making his wedding ring the focal point of his thoughts and his gaze.

Could I do it? Should I?

What would Cate tell me to do?

Oliver wished he could ask her; the memory was hers, too, after all. It didn't seem right to sacrifice it like this without consulting her.

But he couldn't. Glau was right about one thing. Cate was gone, and even though Oliver wanted her back, it was impossible.

Unless . . .

Glau had proclaimed herself a daughter of a god. There was power here on the island, in the songs of the sirens.

"You said you've brought people here from all over," he began slowly. He couldn't believe the words forming in his mind, let alone that he was about to give voice to them, but the moment felt like a chance. One he had to take. "How far is your reach?"

Glau settled her shoulders and raised her chin. "No place is beyond my reach."

"Even"—he swallowed—"Hades? The underworld?" He couldn't remember which was the Greek name and which was the Roman. "Can you bring someone back from the dead?"

Glau tilted her head, considering.

"If I give you my *best* memory—" He pulled off his ring and offered it up on his palm. "—could you do it?"

Glau was silent, but Oliver could tell she was intrigued.

"She may only stay until sunrise, but, yes, I can bring her here. Then you will give me your heart. And then, if there is anything left of you, I will let you go." She stated the terms with meticulous precision.

His heart stuttered with fear and desire. He nodded, not trusting himself to speak.

Glau snatched the ring from Oliver's hand and stood up, her wings snapping open to their full width. "Done."

She took two paces to the edge of the firelight, three to

the edge of the vegetation, and then four to the edge of the ocean. Her last step submerged her feet in the water.

He followed her, wondering with each step if he had crossed the line into madness. But whatever else he had learned from loving Cate, it was that hope never dies.

The moon was still full, still hanging low in the sky, as if the time he'd spent on the island had been no time at all. The stars were still gone, the arching dome of the sky solid black glass. He kept his eyes fixed on Glau.

Water ebbed and flowed over her feet. With each washing, the scales on her toes, her legs, her thighs, glowed brighter. Her wings gathered the sea breeze, swirling it around her like an invisible cloak.

"We stand on powerful ground," she murmured, her voice melodic and strong. "This is the middle passage— where water meets land meets air meets *fire*." On the last word, she thrust Oliver's wedding ring into the sky. The moonlight ignited the gold band, and he heard a low rumbling begin beneath his feet. The water retreated with a soft hiss. The breeze built into a storm with them at the center. "This is where the song begins—and ends."

The moment Glau closed her eyes and opened her mouth Oliver knew it was too late to turn back or have doubts.

The sounds that emerged from her were inhuman. A rolling, rising tide of noise. A rhythmic pulse that forced his heartbeat into alignment with it. A song that was both harmony and melody in the same voice.

Oliver had thought her voice was powerful when it had been joined with her sisters', but as her body arched back and her wings stretched wide, as her hair flowed down her back like shadows and her scales shimmered on her skin like light, he realized the truth. Glau might have been the youngest of the three sisters, but she was the true anchor, the source of strength for the other two. She was the one who ruled them all.

He fell to his knees under the pressure of Glau's Siren song—calling, coaxing. Summoning. Demanding.

He pressed his hands against his ears trying to keep the sound out, but Glau's song filled up the empty places in his head until they rang like a struck bell. He couldn't get away from the noise. He was made of noise. He was made of song.

The moonlight gathered around the ring in Glau's hand, intensifying and building even as the song did. The gold grew so bright, Oliver couldn't look at it anymore.

A shaft of golden light streamed down from the ring, hitting the water and dividing it, pushing it aside. A hole opened up in the ocean, as black as the empty sky above, as full as the moon illuminating the beach.

A figure rose up out of the water. Tall. Blonde.

Oliver's body screamed in recognition even as his mind struggled to accept what was happening.

She was bathed in winter moonlight and Mediterranean waves.

She wore a pair of worn-out sneakers, blue jeans, and a faded Swedish Bitters concert T-shirt.

It was Cate.

Nine

Oliver whispered her name.

She looked up and, when she saw him, offered him the smile he'd fallen in love with. "Oliver?" she asked, and his heart nearly stopped.

If he hadn't already been on his knees, he would have fallen at that moment.

Glau's song cut off, and she rolled the ring into her fist. Pride straightened her spine. She didn't look as if the summoning had cost her anything. Rather, she looked stronger, hungrier, than before.

"Remember," she said to Oliver. "Sunrise."

He nodded and scrambled to his feet. All his attention was fixed on Cate, two thoughts pounding in his head in rhythm with his steps: *It can't be. It is.*

Cate stepped forward and met Oliver on the beach; her arms came around him just as his arms encircled her. Her body met his, melting into him, matching curves and hollows and hips. She was his second half, his better half. She filled the emptiness inside him. She made him whole.

Oliver ran his hands through her soft hair, tilted her head, and kissed her all in the same motion. He was already out of breath, and the touch of her mouth on his stole the rest of it from his lungs.

She was warm. That was what he kept coming back to. Her skin was warm under his hands and his lips. Her body moved and responded to his. Her heartbeat rolled and crashed like the waves below their feet.

He kissed her long and hard, greedy to taste her again. She kissed him back, giving what he wanted, taking what she needed.

He ran his hands down her neck, her back, to her hips. He lifted her up and held her even closer.

Stars speckled behind his closed eyelids. He pulled back a little, only to bury his face in the curve of her neck. He breathed in the familiar, sweet clean scent of her. "Cate," he whispered again. "I missed you so much."

He felt her hands spread across his shoulders and her tears fall on his cheek. "I'm here," she said, repeating it over and over as though she couldn't believe what had happened either.

"I can't believe I was gone when . . ." Tears blinded him. Words crowded in his throat. "You were all alone that night. I'm so sorry. I should have been there. I should have—"

Cate pushed him back and looked him in the eye. "It's not your fault. You didn't know. I didn't know. It's okay."

"It's *not* okay. I should have known. I'm a doctor. I was your *husband!*"

"You still *are* my husband," she said with a smile. She slid her hand down his arm and held his left hand. She lifted her eyebrows in a question.

He looked over his shoulder at Glau. "She has it. It's part of how she brought you back."

216

Cate nodded at Glau in greeting, her eyes cool.

"When we have completed our bargain, he may have it back," Glau said.

Cate looked at Oliver. "Bargain?"

He licked his lips and told her what had happened to him during this long, strange night trapped between reality and myth. "I promised to give her my best memory if she brought you back to me," he finished.

"But only until sunrise," Cate said.

Oliver nodded.

"And which memory does she want?"

"October 31, 2004."

Cate flinched. "You would give her that?"

"It's the best memory I have," he said. "It is her price for my freedom."

"It's our wedding day."

"Which is why I couldn't give it away without you knowing why."

Cate looked at Glau, then at Oliver. She pursed her lips in thought. Silence stretched out to the horizon.

"If I give her this one," he said low, so only Cate could hear, "she will let me go, and I'll be able to keep all the other memories I have of you. If not, she'll take it from me anyway—along with all the rest. I'll die here, and you will be forgotten."

She searched Oliver's eyes and placed her hand on his cheek. "I will never be forgotten," she said. "And you will *not* die here."

Decision made, she took his hand, and together they faced Glau. "You ready?" she asked, her tone between a tease and a challenge. Then she grabbed Glau's right hand, and Oliver took her left, which was still curled in a fist around the ring.

Cate slanted a look at him, and grinned. "She's not ready," she said, "but . . .

I am standing in the kitchen of Joshua's apartment,

217

refilling my cup for the third time. I keep hoping someone will spike the bowl, but so far, no luck. The dull ache in the back of my heart remains. It has been there since last Halloween when Cate stayed on the bus and left me on the curb. I can't believe it's been a year.

A year without Cate. No word from her. No phone calls, no postcards, no carrier pigeons. Nothing. It's like she's vanished.

It's not like I didn't try to find her, but her parents stonewalled me, telling me Cate wasn't at home, even though her car was in the driveway. Her friends hemmed and hawed and avoided me. I hung around our favorite spots, but she never came back to them.

I tormented myself with unanswerable questions. What had I done? What had I said? Why was she so sad that night on the bus? Would I ever see her again?

I couldn't face the possibility that the answer to the last one might be *no,* so I threw myself into my medical training, studying more, working more, outpacing my colleagues until exhaustion wiped my mind clear every night.

"Doctor!" Joshua comes around the island in the kitchen and slaps me on the shoulder. "Glad to see you."

I am dressed in my doctor scrubs, a stethoscope around my neck, and a name tag that reads "Frankenstein" on my chest. I've only been at the party an hour, and I'm already tired of explaining to people why I don't have green skin, scars on my skin, and bolts in my neck.

Cate would have gotten the joke.

"Thanks." I lift my cup in a salute to Joshua. "Great party."

"Hey, there's someone here to see you."

I frown. Coming to the party was a last-minute decision on my part. If someone from the hospital needed me, they would have called or texted.

"She's in the living room." Joshua jerks his head over his shoulder. He grabs a handful of chips from a bowl and wiggles his eyebrows at me. "And she's hot."

A girl? Looking for me? Impossible.

I am curious, but cautious, so I edge my way to the kitchen doorway and peek into the living room. Crowds of people fill the room, dancing, drinking, talking, laughing.

In the center, though, is a girl in a white dress, a bridal veil drawn over her face. She holds a bouquet of flowers in one hand.

I down my drink in a swallow, wishing it had more of a kick, and step out into the din of the party.

The bride turns to me as if she knows the moment I entered the room. She comes directly toward me, pushing a zombie and a French maid out of her way.

I know that walk. "Cate?" I say, confused.

She reaches me, grabs my hand, and pulls me down the hall, pushing open each door until she finds an empty room. We are in a small bathroom, barely enough room for one person, let alone two.

"Cate, is that you?"

She tosses back her veil, ditches the bouquet, and presses me against the door, kissing me hard.

I don't understand what is happening.

I put my hands on her shoulders and push her away. "No," I say. "Don't."

"I'm so sorry, Oliver," she says. "You have no idea how sorry I am."

I have dreamed of this moment for months, but now that it is here, all my carefully planned speeches are lost. All I can manage is, "Why?"

She seems to understand the depth of my question. "I'm sorry for what happened on the bus. I was mad and scared and confused, and it turned into something I didn't mean for it to. I've never loved anyone but you, and I thought that was a bad thing, so I kept wondering if maybe we *should* break up, you know, so we could both date other people, see if there was someone else out there for us—for me—but then you wanted to *marry* me, and I panicked, I guess. I ran. And I kept running. Everywhere. Nowhere. But it didn't matter, it was always the same. I was alone. And I couldn't stop thinking, 'What if he never knows how much I love him?'"

Her words flood out without pause. I am as breathless as she is.

"Of course I know," I say. "And I'm never going to stop loving you, no matter what. I'm just glad you came back."

Tears fill her eyes, stream down her cheeks. "Can I ask you something?"

I brush my thumb across her face. "Anything."

She offers me her signature smile and hikes up the hem of her white skirt. Peeking above the laces of her sneakers are a pair of purple socks: one striped, one solid. "Marry me?"

A laugh builds up in my chest, impossible to contain. I say, "Yes," and then thoroughly kiss her until her body hums beneath my touch.

I break away, grab her flowers and her hand, and together we bolt toward the front door.

We are laughing as I point my car toward Vegas.

Ten

Oliver felt Glau's hand slip from his grasp, though his hold on Cate remained secure. He could still feel the wind in his hair from the open window as he and Cate drove to an all-night wedding chapel in Vegas. No, it wasn't an open window—it was a sea breeze. And they weren't in Vegas—they were lost in the Mediterranean Sea.

He felt a touch on his cheek. He opened his eyes and saw Cate, near tears.

"You didn't even hesitate," she said. "I never knew. I mean, I *knew*, but seeing that memory from your viewpoint . . . You never doubted me, or hesitated, or held a grudge, or anything. Your heart was just happy to see me."

"Of course." Oliver's voice scratched at his throat. "My heart is always happy to see you."

A low moan rose up from the sand. Glau sat with her knees pulled up to her chest and her arms wrapped around them. She rocked from side to side, her eyes closed.

"Do you think she'll be okay?" Oliver asked.

"Do you want her to be?"

Oliver hesitated, then said, "Yeah, I think I do. She wanted to understand forgiveness, and joy, and hope. Maybe she does now." He looked at Cate and raised an eyebrow. "That wasn't the whole memory of that night, you know."

She smiled. "I know. But *I* remember that night, and that's what counts."

"Me too," Oliver said, then paused. "How is that possible? The other memories are gone—I can feel where they used to be—but I still have this one. Even after Glau . . ."

Cate tapped his forehead with her index finger. "You gave Glau *your* memory, while I was giving you *mine.*"

Oliver tested the truth of that statement and found that, yes, he could remember everything about that night. Except now he remembered standing outside Joshua's door while the party raged inside. He remembered the worry and the hope and the flowers in his hand.

"Cate—" he started.

She placed her finger on his lips. "Yes, I should have." She smiled, but for the first time it was shaky, and a little bit sad. "And don't be surprised if you eventually remember a certain Halloween dance that ended with a kiss, or an even earlier Halloween where a princess met a pirate for the first time."

A thin line of light sliced at the horizon of the starless black sky. Oliver's whole body flushed cold with dread. Sunrise.

"I don't want you to go," he whispered.

Her sad smile softened. "I won't be gone forever, you know. And I'll still remember you."

"I think about you every day."

Tears welled up in her eyes. "Don't," she said so softly Oliver thought he misunderstood. He frowned in confusion, and she continued. "Not every day. Don't keep these

222

memories forever on the forefront of your mind. Don't feast on them every day." She nodded to Glau and her silver scales and her white wings. "We aren't made to live on memories. Promise me that one day soon you'll take all the memories of you and me—of us—and you'll store them somewhere deep in your mind and your heart for safekeeping. Promise me that then you'll live your life and make *new* memories."

"I . . ." Oliver tried to say the words, but the light continued to creep up the sky, sweeping away the darkness.

"And then, when we're together again, you can tell me all the stories of all the new memories you made. Okay?"

"Cate." He cupped her face with his hands and kissed her.

She was the first to pull away. "Good-bye, Oliver," she murmured. Her tears had dried, and her blue eyes sparkled when the bright rays of the rising sun caught them.

"Ready?" she asked.

The sun rose swiftly and completely. One moment there was darkness. Then, light.

Oliver squinted and blinked and shaded his eyes against the brightness, trying never to lose sight of blonde hair and blue eyes, but when his vision cleared, Cate was gone.

He expected to feel shattered again. Torn and broken and lost. But his heart still beat, and his body still drew breath. He was still standing.

He looked around for Glau, but she wasn't there. Neither were her footprints, or his, or Cate's. The island looked different too. The trees were smaller, the bushes thinner.

Wherever Glau had taken him, she had upheld her end of the bargain and returned him home. Oliver had been set free. His gold ring lay on the sand. He picked it up, hesitated, and then put it in his pocket instead of on his finger.

A shout reached him from across the water. Turning, he saw Nathan waving from a rescue boat bearing the Odysseus Star logo, heading directly for him.

He squared his shoulders and felt hope flood through his body. "I'm ready," he said to the sky, to Cate, to himself.

Then he lifted his hand and waved back.

About Lisa Mangum

Lisa Mangum has worked with books ever since elementary school, when she volunteered at the school library during recess. Her first paying job was shelving books at the Sandy Library. She worked for five years at Waldenbooks while she attended the University of Utah, graduating with honors with a degree in English. She has worked in the publishing industry since 1997. In 2014 she was named the Editorial Manager for Shadow Mountain.

Besides books, Lisa loves movies, spending time with her family, trips to Disneyland, and vanilla ice cream topped with fresh raspberries. She lives in Taylorsville, Utah, with her husband, Tracy.

She is the author of four award-winning books: the *Hourglass Door* trilogy and *After Hello*.

Follow Lisa on Twitter: @LisaMangum

The Man of Her Dreams

by Jordan McCollum

Other Works by Jordan McCollum

I, Spy
Spy for Spy
Tomorrow We Spy
Spy Noon
Mr. Nice Spy
Tomorrow We Spy

One

When Alex became a cop, she anticipated nightmares. She just didn't anticipate hers coming true.

But for the last six years, they had. All thirty-seven times. Thirty-seven attempts to stop the inevitable. Thirty-seven crime scenes awaiting her the next morning. Thirty-seven murders.

Until today. Energy buzzed through her veins and her brain. She had to get there. She had to get there. If there was any chance she could stop it this time. She. Would. Get. There.

Alex checked the dash clock. 6:44. Why'd she have to live so far from downtown? Normally it wasn't a problem, but after this morning's dream—

This morning's dream had been different. First, it ended too abruptly. The victim wasn't dead yet. Second, she actually knew the location. Hard not to recognize the iconic brick building downtown, between its century-long history as a tobacco warehouse and the ubiquitous ad campaign for its remodeled urban lofts.

Normally, she had to analyze a dream, roll it over in her mind, scrutinize, calculate, think. Today, she could jump into action—and she was.

Alex barely managed to stop in time for the last red light before the freeway entrance. The eerie half-light of dawn bled into the dark night sky. Was it this light in the dream? She might be able to make it.

The dream *was* different—and that had to mean something. It had to. It had to mean she could do something about it. Stop the murder.

The stoplight turned green, and Alex stomped on the accelerator, though she had to slow for the cloverleaf onramp in fifty feet.

Alex leaned into the pull of the curve, then accelerated to merge onto the freeway. Should she take the Duke Street or the Chapel Hill Street exit?

Duke would be faster. No left turns that way. She punched it to cover the next mile, mentally replaying the fragments of the dream: the sky was lightening. Sun wasn't up. The victim, tall, slim, features obscured by a bulky gray hoodie, walked down the sidewalk, passing into the shadows where the brick warehouse bridged over the street. After a minute, Alex followed, living the dream through the killer's eyes.

Once the shadows were the deepest, the killer attacked, grabbing the victim from behind. He struggled, and Alex watched. She could almost feel the victim's body straining against her grasp, even as Alex's every muscle screamed for her to let go, draw her weapon, stop this. But she was powerless, as if she were the one in the chokehold.

And then the dream stopped. They never stopped before the victim was dead.

The trees and grassy hills by the road fell away to reveal the downtown's pervasive old brick. Alex zoomed across the last overpass, past the ballpark, craning her neck as if she could see what was happening in a tunnel half a mile away.

She had to get there in time.

The hill next to the road climbed back up to grade, the towering pines whipping past, in time to provide the exit ramp she needed.

Another mile. One more mile choked with lights and traffic and jockeying, filled with buildings that had gone from big tobacco to rundown bars to upscale ethnic eateries in her lifetime. Why did they need so many lights and cross streets? She didn't dare flip on lights or sirens—even from this far away, that warning could change the dream, make something go wrong. Annoyance—no, frustration, *anger*—flared at yet another red light.

In the past, the dreams had never given enough clues to solve the murders. This time was different. This time Alex would stop a murderer *before* he killed.

She hoped.

The light cycled back to green, and Alex was the first off the starting line. She scanned the streets to her right. The brick warehouse bridged above one of these cross streets. Morgan or Main?

Main didn't feel right. She sped up to get to the next light. Morgan. Had to be it. She whipped around the corner. The warehouse didn't pass over the street; a rusting covered walkway spanned the space instead.

No, no, no. It was getting too light. It was getting too late.

Too fast, Alex zipped under the walkway—and then she saw it, thirty feet later: the building-bridge. This was it.

Blue and red flashed from the far side of the tunnel underneath. Two squad cars and an ambulance. Oh no. No, no.

Her stomach foundered. She was too late. He was already dead.

Alex fought against the defeat clawing at her rib cage, forcing herself forward. The dream was different, and that had to mean something. Just not what she'd hoped, what she'd wanted. She couldn't prevent this murder.

This was where she usually came in anyway, after the fact. Prevention wasn't nearly as much of her job since she'd made homicide.

She pulled into an empty parking spot on the street, checked her badge on her belt and straightened her dark brown take-me-seriously blazer for the early morning chill. Before she got out of the car, she cleared the dream off her mental list. It gave her a little to go on, but she couldn't sit on the witness stand and say, "I had a dream." She needed evidence now. Footprints on the sidewalk. Security cameras. Witnesses.

Alex ruffled her choppy blond bob and marched across the street. She'd expect some foot traffic, but only two uniformed officers and a witness stood on the sidewalk. The October air's chill snaked through her jacket. Deserted downtown. Creepy.

Coming from the homicide detective who dreamed of killing people? That was rich.

She reached the sidewalk. No way would she barge in and commandeer someone else's crime scene, but surely they'd appreciate someone offering to help. The area wasn't cordoned off yet—unless they were done. But they couldn't have finished collecting evidence that fast. The sky was still too dark for it to have been long, and the ambulance three cars down was no coincidence.

If nothing else, the dreams had taught Alex there was no such thing as a coincidence. Analyze, observe, then act.

The dreams were cruel that way.

The pale, freckly cop reported on his radio, while the black officer interviewed the probable witness, a tall man with his back to Alex. His navy fleece set off his deep bronze skin tone, halfway between the officers', but that wasn't the only reason the witness reminded Alex of someone she used to know. Something about his stance dredged up a memory of a man she'd tried to forget.

Officer Freckle Face finished on his radio, and Alex strode up to him, pulling back her jacket to reveal the badge on her hip. "Detective Alexandra Steen. Who's in charge?"

"Uh." The officer glanced around. "Me?"

"Are you asking me or telling me—" Alex checked his name tag. "—Officer Pfeiffer?"

He squared his shoulders, stepping up to his authority. "Telling you."

Good. Someone she could work with. "Want some help?"

"We've got it under control."

"Lex?" came a voice to her left.

Alex froze. No one called her that, not since college, and even then, that was only one person. She whipped around to face the man being interviewed by the other cop.

Nick. Black ice coated her brain, making any thought treacherous.

Years of memories slid through her mind anyway. His easy laugh. Holding his hands. The sharp ache after they broke up, an ache that hardened into the razor-edged shard still lodged in her chest.

Of course he lived in Durham. Of course he'd come home, like she had. Of course she couldn't run into him any other way.

And of course, he had to be every bit as handsome still—only grown-up this time. Mature. Confident, like he'd finally found direction in his life.

Business. She was here on police business. "You're—you're a witness?"

"No."

Then her own surprise cleared enough for her to register the look in his eyes, hollow and stunned, and the streak of blood on his fleece. He was more than a witness. Alex glanced back at where she knew the crime scene was. Still no cordon, no other officers, no coroner. She knew the conclusion, but she didn't dare make the leap.

The officer who'd been taking Nick's statement cleared his throat. Alex checked this one's tag. Harrison. "Next of kin," he supplied.

Next of kin? Shock threatened again, but Alex muscled past it. Who was this victim to him? He didn't have any brothers, and his dad had been out of the picture for decades.

Still, it must be someone close to him. "Oh, Nick, I'm so sorry."

His gaze slid away from hers, and he nodded his thanks.

"You two know each other," Harrison didn't ask, tucking his notebook in his hip pocket.

"Used to," Alex murmured.

Harrison eyed each of them in turn. When neither of them elaborated further, he placed a hand on Nick's back to guide him down the street. "We should go."

The officer was trying to be sympathetic, but Nick was traumatized; couldn't Harrison see that? He'd lost someone close. They should question him here instead of dragging him off to the station. Assuming he lived here, of course.

Alex looked up at Nick again and their gazes met. She knew how it felt to have your world tilt beneath your feet, losing control, losing direction, losing safety. The way she'd felt when the dreams started. Or when he'd broken up with her in college.

She'd spent seven years trying to forget him—the bad and the good. But when he stood there, still stunned, and opened his arms, she had to hug him.

It was almost criminal how easily they fell into the embrace, how well they still fit together. She might've been obligated to hug him, but she didn't have to hold onto him quite so tightly, trying to return that same support he'd always given her. And she didn't have to remember all the times he'd held her before, the comfort and quiet strength he always seemed to have for her, how much she'd missed the security of his arms around her.

But remember she did.

Finally, Nick loosened his grasp. Harrison walked Nick down the sidewalk, and Alex followed, stopping at Pfeiffer's car. "What's your take?" she asked the other officer.

"Not much to go on yet. Victim says she didn't see him, no witnesses so far. Maybe random street crime."

Alex allowed a nod. Maybe, but she'd never dreamed of street crime before. Still, she needed to consider all the alternatives. The dreams demanded no less than exacting investigation, every time.

"Heard you know the next of kin." Officer Pfeiffer jerked his head down the street after Nick and Harrison.

"Yeah."

"Know his sister?"

Candyce? Sure, she'd grown up with them, then followed them to college.

Wait. She wasn't—she wasn't the victim, was she? Alex raced through the dream's images. Tall, slim, gray hoodie. She'd assumed it was a man, but she only saw the victim's back. Candyce was tall and still had the broad shoulders that had helped earn her a swimming scholarship.

But Candyce couldn't be dead.

Alex glanced at Pfeiffer. "Is someone from homicide assigned yet?"

Confusion etched a furrow between his brows. "No, but—"

"Coroner, anybody? You need to get a barrier up to protect your crime scene."

Pfeiffer squinted, more confused. "Coroner? For an assault?"

What? No. All of her dreams ended in death. Every.

Last. One. No one knew that better than Alex. "What do you mean, an assault? Start from the beginning."

Pfeiffer pointed behind her, to the scene. "Victim was walking down the street, and someone grabbed her from behind. She passed out, and the guy ran away. Never got a look at him. When she came to, she called her brother, and he called us."

"Gotcha," Alex said, her tone totally normal, as if this wasn't all so very wrong. Not that it was a bad thing Candyce had survived. But Alex had never dreamed about an assault. Nothing less than premeditated murder.

Maybe the attack was bad enough that Candyce might still be in jeopardy. "How's she doing?"

"Tough to say. Up half the night driving from Charlotte. Couldn't get much out of her. Probably concussed."

Down the street, Harrison packed Nick into the waiting ambulance—where Candyce must be. Only a concussion? They wouldn't need EMTs. "You called in a bus?"

"The brother did. Treating her head wound. You know how those are."

Sure—they bled like a B-movie bullet hole. "So she had a head wound, too."

Pfeiffer half-shrugged and fell into a classic cop dead-pan, downplaying the injury. "More of a scrape where she hit the pavement. Enough to look bad."

Alex turned to check the crime scene. If that dark stain on the sidewalk was blood, and Nick had it streaked on his fleece, small wonder he was worried. He could be right. Even minor head injuries could turn life threatening.

Nick could be right? It'd been a long time since she'd let herself think that.

Officer Harrison reached them. "Doesn't seem like there were any witnesses, but we'll start canvassing."

Alex barely acknowledged him, the numbness finally settling in. How could Nick be right and her dream be wrong?

A blinding flash snapped the final piece of the dream into place in Alex's mind. Alex—the killer—grabbed the guy from behind, and the scuffle began. But as the victim went limp, her gray hood fell back, revealing her hair, twisted into tiny curls. The killer jumped away from her, and Candyce crumpled to the ground, her head crashing against the sidewalk hard enough to bounce. The killer ran away without looking back, his footsteps and the dream fading into nothing.

Candyce wasn't the target. And she wasn't dead, not in the dream and not in real life.

No. Impossible. Six years of consistent dreams of death. They'd never changed. Never.

But they had. And Alex had to figure out what that meant. What it meant to see Nick.

She caught a glimpse of the retreating ambulance. When they'd broken up in college, she'd never planned on running into Nick again. But this morning, he was the least of her problems. Or maybe only the beginning.

Two

Six hours later, her regular work had pulled her away, but her mind kept sliding back to the dream. She was used to running on not enough sleep—too used to it—but this distraction was different than simple sleep deprivation.

Her computer wasn't helping. Alex tapped one finger on her desk, waiting for the program to catch up yet again. She needed to get through this paperwork and track down Pfeiffer and Harrison. They probably didn't have a status update on an assault case with zero leads, but one upside of her personal connection: it gave her an excuse to stay involved.

And she had to stay involved. If the dreams were changing, she needed a grip on this new angle, fast. She had to. Or she might come close to losing it. Again.

After another sixty seconds of waiting for the world's slowest computer processor, Alex jumped to the next item on her list. Dispatch put her through to Harrison without question. Alex introduced herself and reminded him, "I was at your assault this morning. Find any witnesses?"

"Canvassing didn't turn up anybody. Barely after dawn, so I guess that's to be expected."

Yeah, the residential side street had been eerily empty. "Any update on the victim?"

"I think Pfeiffer went by the hospital about an hour ago. They admitted her. Maybe her brother was right about the head injury."

How many times did people have to say Nick was right today? "Is she still there?"

"I think so."

Alex realized she was stabbing that one finger on her desk again and clutched a pencil to keep her hand quiet. "Which hospital?"

"Duke."

"Okay, thanks. Keep me apprised of any developments."

"Will do."

Alex hung up and glanced at her computer screen. The stupid report management program had finally caught up, and she quickly finished entering her info. She called Pfeiffer and got Candyce's room number. Her boss, Sergeant Oscarson, was occupied, so barring any mid-afternoon murders today, she was safe to do some questioning of her own at the hospital.

She managed not to grip the steering wheel too hard despite early rush hour traffic over the few blocks to the hospital parking garage. What did she hope to find? Between the element of surprise and the head wound, Candyce might never remember enough of the incident to ID the suspect—would-be killer—but Alex couldn't leave that call to someone else. Not when it involved Candyce.

And Nick.

And her dreams.

Alex tried to push aside the creeping doubts and pulled

into the muggy parking garage. Hard to believe she'd been shivering on the street a few hours ago. While she waited for the underground shuttle to the hospital, worries snuck back to her brain. Could her connection to Nick and Candyce, long ago as it was, have anything to do with the dream? Ever since the dreams started, she'd never figured out why. In all those years, she'd never dreamed about someone she recognized, never a place she'd been before, not even a killer she'd known somehow—all of which she'd come across in her non-dream cases. The one thing that seemed to tie the dreams together was that everything was unfamiliar—and the dream quickly became the only way to solve the case.

But all that had changed. Alex knew the scene. She might have even prevented it if she'd been a few minutes faster. She knew the victim, and Candyce wasn't dead.

Could Candyce and Nick be the reason the dreams had changed?

The shuttle finally arrived and Alex boarded, choosing to stand facing the doors and gripping a metal pole, like that could keep her anchored to reality instead of drowning in her thoughts.

It didn't. What did this mean for the dreams? Could this one be wrong?

She needed certainty. Till now, the dreams had given her that, in a way. Sure, she didn't know why or how they'd started, why they had to happen to her, but at least they had a purpose. They gave *her* a purpose. She'd made homicide with them. If she couldn't rely on the dreams, maybe she didn't deserve to be a homicide detective.

Could she solve this case without—or in spite of—the dream?

The shuttle pulled into the hospital stop, shifting her momentum. Alex tightened her grasp on the metal pole. She was off her game. She needed to focus, home in on the goal, get this done.

Solve this case. Figure this out.

She headed up to Candyce's room and paused in the open doorway. Candyce's athletic swimmer's frame drooped, and even her tawny brown skin betrayed a little pallor. She was obviously beyond exhausted. Nick sat by her bed, his hands clasped in his lap. Something about his slumped posture broke Alex's heart all over again, but in a different way. Because everything else was different.

Maybe she was intruding. Maybe this was a family time. Seven years ago, she would've been right by Nick's side, and some small, stupid, sad part of her wished she were there now. But the dreams weren't the only things that'd changed.

She wasn't intruding. She was doing her job. Her *calling*. Alex lifted her knuckles to knock, but the movement caught Nick's attention before she contacted the door's blond wood. Confusion flashed across his features, but he leaned back in his chair as if they ran into one another every day. "So you're a cop now?"

"Have been for a while." She should ask what he was up to—she wanted to—but she was here on business. She tilted her head for a better view of Candyce. "Are you up for questions?"

Candyce drew and released a deep breath like her entire body was deflating. "I guess."

Alex would take it. Her gaze fell to the silver letters embroidered on Candyce's hoodie. Bartlett University. Candyce's alma mater, Alex's—and Nick's. He'd pretty much lived in an identical hoodie back then. Back when he loved her.

For a second, her throat began to close around a lump, but she shoved aside the emotion. This wasn't about back then. This was about today, when Candyce was attacked. Alex came to stand at the foot of Candyce's hospital bed and put on her best bedside manner. "Have you remembered anything about what happened this morning?"

Candyce closed her eyes, thinking. After a moment, she

shook her head, then winced, one hand lifting to her bandaged forehead.

Times like these, the dreams were almost a disadvantage. Alex didn't dare plant memories for Candyce, not without corroboration from witnesses. That'd bite them in the end. Especially when she couldn't be totally sure the dreams were trustworthy.

"Can you think of anyone who might've wanted to hurt you? Maybe a boyfriend? An ex?"

Nick sighed audibly. The irony of asking Candyce about her dating history—in front of Nick, no less—was obviously not lost on either of them, but Candyce merely said no.

"Someone you owe money?"

Nick shifted noisily in his chair, like he was trying to advertise his discomfort. Candyce pinned Alex with a piercing glare. "Yeah, my bookie," she scoffed. "Of course not."

Well, if she was up to copping an attitude, she must be feeling better. "Someone from work, maybe?"

"She didn't see him," Nick cut in. Interrupting her? Normally—years ago—he'd sit there and stew in silence. "It can't be someone she knows. She doesn't even live here anymore."

Alex turned to Candyce to verify that. She did. "I moved to Charlotte after I graduated." She grimaced. "I'm sorry, but I've answered all the questions the best I can. I didn't see him, and I don't know why anybody would attack me. I guess that other officer was right—just a random act of violence."

Durham had that reputation, earned during the national crime wave of the eighties and nineties, but this didn't seem like random street crime or gang violence. The killer was surprised to see who he'd attacked. He was targeting someone—someone *else*.

"Candyce, I know random acts of violence, and something about this doesn't seem right."

Her eyebrows pulled down into a deep, furrowed V, and Nick practically shot to his feet. "Okay, I think my sister needs her rest."

"It's key that we pursue any leads in this case early on, before the clues go cold—"

"What clues?" He jutted his chin out at her, daring her to contradict him. "Nobody has anything to go on, so all we want is to recover and move on."

"Recover and move on? From your own sister being attacked? You don't want answers?"

"I know when I shouldn't push someone." And then, as suddenly as he'd challenged her, Nick shut down, sliding back into his chair.

Of course he did; he always did. He'd challenge her, and she'd challenge back and then he'd withdraw, like doing exactly what he was doing made *her* a terrifying monster.

Alex snapped her mouth shut, shoving down the heat rising in her chest. Five minutes in the same room and they were back in the same argument that ended their relationship. Next, he'd say she was too pushy, moved too fast, did too much, never gave him room to breathe—when *he* was the suffocating one. The suffocating one who somehow didn't want to move forward in their relationship.

The longer she stood here, staring at him and stewing, the angrier she'd get. If he wanted to stonewall the investigation, fine. Alex pivoted on her heel and marched out.

She was halfway down the antiseptic hall when the long-striding footsteps caught up to her. "Lex," Nick began, his tone . . . conciliatory?

"What?"

"Listen, we want to help. We're not trying to make things harder for you guys. She just doesn't remember."

Right. Alex chose not to respond.

"So pushing her won't help," he finished.

Alex looked into his warm, tawny brown eyes—the

same eyes she'd loved through high school and college. "Will time help her remember?"

Nick averted his gaze. It was only then Alex remembered how he'd told her even her stare came off as a challenge.

During their last argument. Right before they'd started shouting. Right before he'd told her, after four years of dating, he didn't want to get married. Right before she'd grabbed her toothbrush and her picture frames. Right before she'd left his apartment for the last time.

Now they were both back in their hometown, thrown together—not by fate. By her dreams. Unless her dreams *were* fate?

"Look," Nick began on a sigh. "I just want Candyce to be able to move on. I'd do the same for you."

Alex whipped around to face him again, but before she could say anything, Nick continued. "Anything I can do to help?"

Maybe he could—best not to read anything into his other offer. His neighbors had been canvassed and he'd been interviewed, but there could always be gaps. "You live in the neighborhood?"

"West Village."

The remodeled apartment building right where the attack was? She'd assumed he lived nearby, but it was still a surprise. In her mind, she could only picture him in his college bachelor pad, eating cheap takeout and playing video games. Instead, he had a place in the heart of twenty-first-century yuppie-ville. He really had gotten his act together.

She pressed on with the questioning. "Have you noticed anyone hanging around the neighborhood lately, anyone suspicious or out of place?"

Nick tucked his hands in his pockets as he thought. "It's downtown, you know? Sometimes there are shady folks around, but you don't think much of it. Homeless men, maybe. Did someone like that attack Candyce?"

She knew the answer, but she certainly couldn't tell him the truth. She couldn't tell anyone that. "Can't rule anything out yet. How long have you lived there?"

"A few years, since I started my company."

He'd started his own company? Definitely sounded like someone had given him the kick in the pants he'd needed when they were dating. She wanted to focus on the investigation, but curiosity got the best of her. "What do you do?"

"Medical database software."

"Going well?"

One corner of Nick's mouth turned up in that modest-yet-cocky grin of his. "Pretty well. Twenty employees. Just moved into a new office space."

Huh. Maybe she wasn't the only one who'd changed since college.

"I promised Candyce something from the vending machines." The cockiness of his grin wore off, and suddenly he looked so familiar that Alex's heart caught in her chest. How many times had he given her that almost-shy smile? Junior year of high school, the first time he'd sat with her at lunch. That summer, the first time he'd asked her out. Senior year, the first time he'd kissed her.

She'd never been able to say no to that smile. Something about it—about him—relaxed her honed defenses, even now. "I'll walk with you," she offered.

This wasn't high school or college or their carefree summers. This was a police investigation, and Alex had to remember that. "What do *you* think happened this morning?" she asked as they fell into step almost too easily.

"Mugging gone wrong?"

She couldn't rule that out, but why would she start dreaming up visions of muggings instead of murders? And the killer ran away when he realized it was Candyce— because she wasn't the right target.

"Random question," Alex began, "but do any of your neighbors look like Candyce, even vaguely?"

Nick narrowed his eyes, though Alex couldn't tell if he was disagreeing or merely thinking. "Nobody springs to mind."

Didn't mean there weren't any. She'd have to check with Harrison and Pfeiffer. It was the only explanation that made sense, after all. The killer was absolutely going to murder someone this morning, but it obviously wasn't Candyce. So someone else in the neighborhood must be easily mistaken for her. At least in the dream, with her oversized, bulky sweatshirt, it was impossible to tell who she was from behind.

They reached the vending machine lobby, and Nick fed the machine quarters—too many quarters. He punched in two selections, and a Snickers and a Kit Kat dropped to the bottom.

He retrieved the candy and opened the Kit Kat. Alex tried not to eye the chocolate. Stupid, the things she remembered after this long—they had the same favorite candy bar.

She wasn't the only one who remembered. Nick snapped off two chocolate bars and held them out to her. What was she supposed to do, play stubborn to spite him? "Thanks," she said, keeping her tone to its most businesslike.

"Sure."

Alex crunched into the first bite of the crispy, chocolate-coated wafers. She tried not to look at or even think about Nick standing next to her, but the memory surfaced anyway. Seventeen. Their first kiss. He'd wanted the moment to last, so just before their lips met, he pulled back, softly nuzzling her nose with his, two, three, four times. She was ready to shout for him to kiss her already when his lips touched hers. She could still taste the sweet chocolate of the Kit Kat he'd been eating, and then he gave her the last piece.

Nick touched her shoulder, pulling her from the past. She'd been gazing off into space—at him. Great.

But it wasn't awkward, though Nick might have been remembering that same moment. Even in this little hospital alcove, under the angry cicada buzz of the cruel fluorescents, everything seemed . . . natural. Easy. Comfortable in a way she'd never found with other men she'd dated. Maybe they'd shared too many of these candy bars, but something about standing here with Nick was familiar and peaceful and right.

No. Not right. Not anymore. He wasn't annoyed or having an off day all those years ago when he'd cut off their relationship. He would've apologized if he didn't mean to say she was pushy and ornery and headstrong—that he didn't want to marry her. But he wasn't sorry. He'd meant it. And there was nothing peaceful or right about dating all those years only to be blindsided. Betrayed.

Alex backed away, breaking the spell of his presence. "Hope Candyce feels better soon."

Uncertainty flashed across his face, almost a wince. "Thanks."

"Tell her I said so. I'll keep you posted on the case."

Nick nodded, and Alex backpedaled out of the room.

She didn't need her dreams changing. She definitely didn't need to go falling for Nick all over again.

She'd help him and Candyce, but that was it. She'd help them, and her dreams would go back to the way they were, and more importantly, she and Nick would go back to the way they were—blissfully oblivious to one another.

The sooner things went back to normal, the better.

Three

Alex knew the dreams, knew their patterns, knew what to expect. Every couple months, a new one, starting the day of the murder. Seeing life seep out of a stranger through a murderer's eyes. Searching for tiny clues to piece together the case. Solving the homicide. Until now.

And the next night only left things more complicated.

The dreams had repeated before, sometimes. Always the same, beginning to end. Always not quite enough to solve the case. Always another push for Alex to find the killer.

Not that night.

The dream started with the sky a little darker, but at the same unmistakable location downtown. Alex held her breath. The dream was starting earlier. If it was the same dream at all. This time, the dream began filtered through evergreen shrubs. The killer was hiding, though he'd be in plain sight if it weren't for the night's shadows.

A car's headlights swept across the other side of the hedge. Through the killer's perspective, Alex scanned the parking lot. A silver Mazda pulled into a spot.

Candyce got out of the driver's seat, the hood shielding her face. So this was a repetition. She ambled to the sidewalk. The killer moved out. The same as yesterday, he followed her, grabbed her, saw her, dropped her, fled. That part, at least, remained unchanged. A repeat.

Alex snapped awake. The red numbers on her clock glared 5:36. The dream was different—again. The killer had lain in wait. But still not for Candyce.

No answers came during her morning run or shower or coffee. Turning it over in her mind didn't help, and there was no one to talk to—she couldn't tell anyone about the dreams in the first place. Now she couldn't tease apart this tangled mess. In a distorted way, the dreams had become the one thing she could depend on, simultaneously driving her mad with guilt and keeping her sane. The content might be different, but they always had the same format, message, reason.

Now the reality she'd constructed for herself, where these dreams made sense, where they gave her purpose, where she exorcised her guilt at "committing" those murders by solving them—that was all slipping away like the Outer Banks' shifting sands. She needed a grip, needed her bearings, needed *something* to grab onto before the eroding logic of the dreams made her doubt her sanity.

Years ago, she could've run to Nick. She would have. Even if she couldn't explain the dreams to him, he'd always brought her that peace. Who else could soothe you when his sister was hospitalized and you were in the least romantic spot in the world?

But Nick had proven he wasn't the person she needed. Not if he could reject her—who she was, at heart—the way he had. He didn't want to marry her. No use in regretting that anymore. She'd moved on, finished her degree and pressed ahead without him. That had gotten her places. Like the homicide unit. Where they needed her.

Alex pulled into the station and headed straight for her desk. Not much new on the murder board. She helped a couple guys who'd dredged up a cold case she'd worked originally. Once she'd gone over the files with them, Alex consulted with another officer on the case he'd have to testify in next week. Fairly straightforward: carjacking gone wrong. They'd caught the guy driving the victim's car. Why he thought he was better off facing a jury, she had no idea.

She was about to dive into a cold case when something snagged her curiosity. Did the killer mistake Candyce for someone else because of her car?

Alex pulled up the state DMV database and typed in Candyce's first and last name. One listing popped up: a forest green Mustang.

Wait, what? Alex closed her eyes and called the new beginning of the dream back into focus. Candyce was definitely driving a silver Mazda. Was that *not* real?

Or there could be another explanation. Borrowing the car, from a relative, maybe. Their dad hadn't been in the picture since Candyce was a baby—something that'd always haunted Nick—but maybe she borrowed her mom's car. Alex deleted Candyce's first name from the criteria and narrowed the search to silver Mazdas. Once again, one listing popped up.

Nick.

A wall of static rolled in to fill her brain, obliterating every other thought.

Candyce was wearing a hoodie like Nick's favorite, down to the same university name. Coming to Nick's apartment. Driving Nick's car.

The killer had definitely targeted someone and had definitely caught the wrong person.

The realization settled on her skin like gathering frost. The right target . . . was Nick.

Alex practically vaulted from her chair—nearly running right into the wall of flesh that was Sergeant Oscarson. "Steen," her boss addressed her, "headed out?"

"I was, yeah."

"We need to coordinate this morning on the Cook homicide. You're testifying at trial tomorrow, right?"

Alex nodded.

"Good. Get up with the detectives from the previous charges."

How could she say no? As one of the minority of women on the homicide unit, she often had to testify in domestic violence cases carried to their extreme conclusion. She didn't know which was sadder: the implicit sexism or that it worked on juries.

Alex sank into her chair and pulled up the case file which listed the other investigators' phone numbers. Maybe she could track down Nick's number that easily to warn him. She alternated between searching through Harrison's assault report and taking notes on the phone with the investigators who'd handled the Cooks' worst disputes over the years. Mrs. Cook seemed to give as much as she got, but only one of them had escalated to homicide.

By the time Alex could replay the Cooks' arrest records from memory, it was lunchtime—and she still hadn't found Nick's number. She couldn't just show up at his house; he had to be at work, and she didn't know which apartment was his.

Easily solved. She switched back to the DMV database to find his apartment number. Awesome. He still wouldn't be there at 11 a.m.

He couldn't be that hard to find. If his software company was doing well enough to move into a new office, he had to be on the Internet. Alex pulled up a search engine and typed in *Nick Carpenter medical software*. Even with a relatively common name, she'd find him eventually, thanks to that one last piece of information. It was a wonder she hadn't Googled him more often.

The first result: a corporate biography page for a company called Carexa. Alex clicked and once she scrolled past the top banner, Nick's black and white picture appeared on the screen, smiling at something off-camera. Casual. Relaxed. Comfortable. His bio hit on corporate buzz words but still sounded like it was written by a human—by him, but with a quiet confidence that was new to her. His bio finished with a quote about how their software was designed to allow patients and doctors to really connect, then listed him as CEO & owner.

Huh. Alex skipped to the Contact Us page. If it was up to date, he'd probably be at their office on Market Street. She closed up the last of her files and punched Carexa's number into her cell phone. A recording answered, asking for an extension.

Great. She didn't have one. Alex half-jogged down to her car. Faster to drive there—in air conditioning in the midday heat—and march into his office than to listen to the company directory. She maneuvered over to the address, an old building with an updated Art Deco style façade proclaiming it the Bull City Business Center. She ignored the stupid hope fighting against the dread in her middle and took the stairs two at a time to get to Suite 203.

The office was appropriately modern for the gentrified part of downtown—only a few blocks from Nick's upscale historical remodel. Funky light fixtures hung from the high ceiling amid exposed pipes, and the walls hosted huge dry erase boards. Instead of cubicles, the employees milled around open tables and work spaces.

Alex strode through the doors, and a small black woman with her hair in short twists looked up from the nearest table. "Can I help you?"

"Yes, I need Mr. Carpenter."

"Nick?" The woman frowned. "He's not here. Maybe I can help you."

"'Fraid not. Police business." Alex turned away, but the other woman caught her at the door.

"About his sister? Poor girl."

Alex managed not to laugh. Candyce was hurt, and that wasn't funny, but the problem was that it *wasn't* about his sister, not even a little bit. "Her case, yes."

"He ran home to check on her at lunch. He should be back in half an hour."

Home? Meaning the address she'd found on the DMV records, less than half a mile away. Perfect. Alex thanked the woman and headed out.

Within minutes, she stood in front of the ornate white doorframe of Nick's apartment. The woodwork had to be original to the building. She'd knocked twice, but he still hadn't answered. Tension tightened along Alex's back like her spine was being tuned like a guitar string. Something was wrong. And a killer was after him.

The dream had the killer attacking in the morning, early. Lying in wait. Here. But the dream wasn't about a murder, like every other dream she'd had—so it could've gotten other details wrong, too. The time of day, the location. Or the killer could've changed plans.

Nick could already be dead.

Alex's heart rate began a slow rev, like she was pressing the accelerator every second. Where was he?

Nick finally appeared in the antique door's glass panes, interrupting the chaotic whirlwind of her thoughts. He opened the door. "Lex?" His tone said finding her outside his building two days in a row was too much to believe.

He was all right. Better than all right. More well rested than yesterday, but tall and athletic as ever—

She stopped that train of thought before it derailed her completely. "Hi, Nick." Her voice stumbled out, more awkward than the silence now stretching between them.

"Hi." She'd never been all that smooth at flirting, but not many people could make her trip over a simple greeting.

She had to stick to business. Safer for them both. "Candyce was released?"

"Yeah, she's upstairs resting. Something new on the case?"

Yes. No. Possibly. A dozen answers streamed through Alex's brain, but she managed to pin down a couple of the right ones. "Not exactly." She glanced over his shoulder, but all she could see from here were the stairs. "We need to talk."

As soon as the words were out, she remembered the last time they'd "talked," all those years ago. That cliché phrase was exactly how Nick had started the conversation. How he'd started to break her heart.

He didn't seem to notice, though, as he stepped back to let her in. He led her up the stairs into the main living area of his apartment. Exposed beams and brick hearkened back to the building's tobacco warehouse past. Alex took a deep breath, like she expected to recapture that sickly oversweet baked apple smell that had permeated the whole neighborhood on hot days when she was a child. The old home for the curing brightleaf tobacco seemed perfectly suited to the honey pine floors, and high ceilings set off the modern fixtures from gleaming ductwork to sparkling countertops.

Some of the furniture was familiar—a bookcase, the photos of the nearby Lucky Strike smokestack and a vintage barn hanging on the cool gray wall, Nick's loveably schlumpy chair—enough to make it feel like home, updated. Or maybe it was standing here with him again, away from the crime scene and the hospital. With Nick next to her, the anxiety she'd felt a minute before eased, and the quiet peace of the space seemed to suffuse her soul.

He'd always centered her like no one else could, without even trying. But she'd forgotten the downside that came with the peace—sometimes, peaceful meant slow. Immobile,

THE MAN OF HER DREAMS

practically. She took another deep breath and pressed forward with her questions. "We won't bother Candyce, will we?"

Nick waved a hand past the kitchen. "She's in the guest bedroom. She'll be okay."

Time to talk, then. "I'm concerned this wasn't random street crime."

He pulled his lower lip through his teeth but simply nodded.

"We have reason to believe Candyce was targeted specifically."

"What, she happened to stumble on a serial killer? Someone with a vendetta against her?" Nick nailed her with a *seriously?* look.

"Actually," Alex dragged out the word, "the assailant might not have realized who she was."

Nick shook his head and sauntered to the kitchen. "Of course he didn't know her. She doesn't even live in Durham."

"I mean he might've mistaken her for someone else."

"I guess, but that doesn't exactly rule out street crime." He opened the fridge and pulled out two white cartons. "Do you still like Thai?"

Alex barely allowed a "Yeah."

"Remember the first time we tried Thai food? The blackout after the hurricane—which one was it?"

"Hanna," Alex answered before she could remind herself not to remember their forced-candlelight dinner of his roommate's leftovers, barely warm enough to be edible. The night she realized she wanted to marry him.

"Great night." Nick's voice was too close and too warm and too soft, almost a sigh, like he was lost in the memory, too. Reminiscing.

He turned to her, his mouth open ready to say something. Nostalgia still hung in his gaze.

How could he remember their relationship with that

255

kind of fondness? Unless . . . it wasn't quite as one-sided as their breakup made it seem?

It didn't matter. She couldn't let him distract her. Time to focus. The case. "Listen: she was wearing a Bartlett hoodie, driving your car and parking in your lot early in the morning. Sound like anyone else you know?"

Nick paused in dishing up the pad thai noodles. "You think it's me." He stated it in a monotone, his back to her.

So much for reminiscing.

"Well, like you said, no one in Durham has a reason to come after Candyce." She couldn't mention the would-be killer had fled once seeing he'd grabbed the wrong person. "But maybe someone has a reason to come after you."

Now Nick turned around, his lips puckered into an expression that said he couldn't believe she was even trying this.

"I'm a cop, Nick. It's my job to think this way."

"I know it's your job, but I'm telling you, I don't have any enemies." The steel in his voice was strong enough to hold a knife edge. "No one is after us."

"You haven't even thought about it," Alex tried.

Nick scoffed and went back to filling his plate. "What kind of person do you think I am these days, Lex? Software guy by day, gangbanger by night? Does that sound anything like me?"

"I never said it did. There are other ways to make enemies."

"Enemies who try to kill you or your sister?" He laughed, soft and sarcastic, like his leftovers were a sad excuse for lunch. "I lead a pretty boring life."

Famous last words. "I'm only trying to say you need to be careful. Take a minute to think about whether you might've ticked anyone off lately."

"I tick people off weekly. Most of us cope without resorting to murder."

Alex finally followed Nick into the kitchen area. She

couldn't let him walk away from the subject. "Will it kill you to let me help you? Humor me for a minute."

"This is always how it's going to be with you, isn't it? You could never let me be. You always have to be right."

"I'm not trying to be right—"

"You're not listening to me, either." He practically threw his plate into the microwave and jammed the buttons to reheat it.

"And you're listening to me?" Too late, she realized the challenge rising in her tone was a mistake.

Nick slowly wheeled on her. "I hear you. You're pushing, pushing, pushing all over again. I don't have any enemies. No nemeses, no archrivals, no leftovers from a shady past. Don't have them now, never have. I'm not the kind of person who makes enemies. Clear enough?"

"Nick—"

"You can stop hounding me."

Seriously? She was trying to save his life here. "Fine." She held up both hands in the universal I'm-backing-off gesture. "Your funeral. Literally. I'll see myself out."

At the door, Alex took a split second to glance back. The microwave had beeped to announce its cycle was complete, but Nick stood at the counter, both fists pressed against the glimmering granite.

If he wanted to stand there clenching his fists instead of protecting himself, she couldn't change that. Maybe that was what she'd done wrong all those years ago. Not just pushed him, but pushed to change him. As if she'd ever wanted that. She only wanted him to be who he said he wanted to be.

And once again, he refused. He wouldn't listen, just shut down, and she was walking away from him, from hope for them. Because that was what he wanted.

Had there really been a moment there where she was thinking about the past—where *he* was savoring a memory? Yeah, right. Their memories should stay where they were—

in the soon-to-be forgotten past. Assuming Nick lived long enough to forget her.

Alex yanked open the door, the October afternoon heat assaulting her instantly. In a situation like this, you couldn't help someone against his will.

S he was dreaming. She knew it. She knew the spot, she
knew the bushes where the killer hid, she even knew
the slice of sidewalk visible from here. But something
was different.

It was lighter than last time. Still not full dawn, but close
enough to make a difference in the shadows and the lights.
Alex's view jostled, almost as if the killer was bouncing on
his heels.

A silver Mazda rolled through the parking lot and
pulled into a spot. The killer craned his neck to watch.

Nick—Nick?—*Nick* climbed out of his car, rubbing his
eyes like he'd been awakened too early. He grabbed a grocery
bag from the car and started toward his apartment.

The killer hung back, but soon fell in step behind him.
Without a hoodie to obscure his features, Nick was
unmistakable.

Alex screamed for him to stop, fought against every footstep, but the killer kept walking. Just under the building bridge, like before, the killer moved in. He grabbed Nick from behind.

Not Nick. Not Nick. Not Nick.

This time the killer was more prepared, or more sure of himself. Alex could feel the grip of a handle in his hand. Her stomach pitched like she was on a roller coaster. Then the weapon plunged into Nick's back, below his ribs. Despite Alex fighting with all she had to stop this, change this, a few quick jabs left Nick rasping for breath on the sidewalk.

Alex caught a glimpse of Nick's face, the surprise and betrayal in his wide eyes. She strained every muscle to make the killer go back, help him, but the killer walked away, his footsteps echoing against Nick's labored gasps as they grew farther and farther apart.

Alex sat up in bed and checked the clock. 7:02. The dreams never let her sleep that late. She whipped around to check the window. Already more light than in her dream. Too late, too late, too late.

She'd accepted the dreams, that she couldn't change them. Up until now, all she could do was solve the murders. Could the dreams have changed so much that now they were forcing her to watch what she could've stopped? For all she knew, they were they happening real time. Taunting her by making her watch the murder while she slept instead of trying to stop it.

She shoved that thought aside. Didn't matter. She had to get there. She jumped into her slacks and blouse set out for the day—never knew when you'd get called in, so it paid to be prepared. Once again, she found herself racing downtown nearly as fast as her heart raced in her chest.

It was 7:15 when she pulled onto the right street, almost full light.

Worry twisted in her gut. Was she too late?

She rolled through the underpass, scanning the sidewalk on the other side of the street. No cops. No blood. No body.

No Nick.

Alex cruised the complex's crowded parking lot before she found a vacant spot on the street. She had to be sure he wasn't crumpled behind a parked car or hadn't been dragged off. Anything.

The sidewalk was empty. Still no Nick. If the dream had come true this morning, there would still be *some* sort of evidence here. She paced back and forth over the small amount of the real estate they'd covered in her dream. She wasn't too late. If it was happening this morning, she could still stop it.

Suddenly, something didn't feel right. The sixth-suspicion-sense muscles in her body clenched, though it took a second to pinpoint exactly why.

Footsteps. Footsteps approaching from behind.

She was having a hard time believing the dreams now, but could they have let her down that much? Luring her into a trap?

A frosty drop of fear plummeted through her, and the condensation cloud of her breaths came faster.

Alex was about to jog back to her car when a hand landed on her shoulder. She grabbed the hand's wrist and whirled around, half a second from laying this guy out.

Nick. Not hurt, not bleeding, standing there, trying to pull free of *her* grasp. Like she was the one who'd grabbed him.

Well, she *had* grabbed him. She released his wrist and fell back a step. "Morning."

"What are you doing here?"

"I—I'm only—I was worried about you."

One of his eyebrows inched upward. "Worried about me."

"No offense—" She moved back half a step.

"I'm not offended. Just . . . surprised. That you care."

Care? No, that wasn't what she meant. Or was it?

Maybe so. She was here. That said something.

"I'm not trying to say—" Nick paused, then pushed forward. "I guess it just stopped feeling like you cared a long time ago, you know?"

Wait, wait, wait. He was the one who dumped her—the one who said he didn't want to get married. And *she* didn't care? "What do you mean, it stopped feeling like I cared? Of course I cared."

Nick's gaze snuck away, like the quiet street demanded his attention. No, like he couldn't stand to look at a liar.

"Maybe we remember things really differently, but I always cared." Alex paused, and he still didn't raise his gaze. "It might not have seemed that way, but I swear to you, I did."

"Okay, maybe you cared—but it seemed like you never heard me, just trampled right over me, over everything I said."

"I never did that."

Annoyance crept into his tone. "How about when I wanted you to stop pressuring me?"

Alex barely managed to fight back the retort: *you mean let you be lazy?* Snapping at him wouldn't get them anywhere. How were they having a conversation instead of an argument about this seven years too late? Apparently she wasn't the only one who'd carried this around for too long. "I was—I was only—did you ever say that to me? In those words?"

"I don't know." Nick shrugged to match his answer. "I shouldn't have had to."

Alex dropped her volume to the same murmur. "Can't read your mind—but that doesn't mean I didn't care. I always thought *you* stopped caring."

He pondered that a long time. Too long, it seemed. Alex tried to fill the silence. "I guess sometimes I rush too much, and . . . maybe don't think enough." Even as she said it, she realized how much that had changed since their relationship ended—since the dreams began. She'd learned to watch more, observe, analyze, slow down before she pushed ahead blindly. Was that enough to make a difference to him? "I didn't mean to make you feel like I didn't care," she concluded. "And I've grown up a lot since then. I've had to. Guess we both have."

Nick still didn't look at her, but he nodded slightly. "I'd better get to work."

Alex stepped aside to let him past, though the sidewalk was wide enough for them both. He was a few feet away when she turned and called after him. "Candyce *was* driving your car that morning, wasn't she?"

He glanced back. "Yeah. We traded for the week so she could pick something up at IKEA in Charlotte. Her car's too small."

She managed to not point out again how much that made him seem like the intended target, and Nick ambled away.

Alex pivoted to do the same but hesitated before crossing the street. She scanned the evergreen boxwoods lining the parking lot Nick had disappeared into. Either the dream was still coming, or she'd actually prevented a murder.

She inhaled, savoring the potential victory. She'd take it.

If this was how the dreams were changing, she'd definitely take it.

Her triumph and conviction lasted right up until the dream started again the next morning. As much as she wanted to bound out of bed once she saw that same brick warehouse, she had to watch and see if anything changed. If *she'd* changed anything.

Nick walked down the street. The killer followed. He attacked, stabbed, ran, and Nick lay on the sidewalk, dying. She recognized the betrayal on his face from more than the last dream—it was the same expression he'd had when she shouted back things aimed to cut him, hurt him as much as he'd hurt her.

Alex tore herself from her dream with a sharp breath, as if watching Nick die caused her physical pain, like she was the one gasping for air, stabbed and bleeding. She whirled around to check the clock—6:32. Still dark outside. Still time to make it to Nick.

She grabbed her khaki slacks from the chair by her bed. Would she run to him every morning? Would that be their new morning routine? *Hey there, Nick, are you dead yet? No? Have a great day.* Her dreams had taken her right over the edge.

She wasn't sure she cared. Grateful the dreams had put her in the habit of showering at night, she fumbled over the buttons of her burgundy blouse and raced out the door.

It was still dark—darkish—when she pulled onto his street. In fact, it was perfect. If she had to, she could do this every day. No matter what problems they'd had, she couldn't stand by and let Nick be cut down.

Or maybe she did still care about him "that way."

There were no parking spots on the street this time—and no one lurking in the boxwoods—so Alex rounded the block and pulled into the apartment building's cramped lot. The same one Candyce and Nick used in the dream. Alex kept well away from that silver Mazda but found a place she could still see the sidewalk amid the shrubbery.

If his car was here, he was safe for this morning. Or at least the whole sequence of events hadn't started yet.

With the radio on low, she beat out an impatient rhythm on the steering wheel. The minutes crawled by even slower than the sun crept over the red brick warehouse and the ugly glass-clad skyscraper to the east. A train chugged by.

A southbound flock of geese honked overhead. The fog burned away.

Alex waited until after 7:30. The sun was up, the sky much lighter than in her dream. Crisis averted.

Right?

She had to be sure. The street had been clear when she'd driven by, and she hadn't seen Nick or anyone resembling the killer, but what if the dream wasn't quite right on all the details?

Alex shook her head at herself as she climbed from the car. How many times would these dreams make her doubt her sanity before she lost it altogether?

She'd made her peace with the dreams, but she hadn't bargained on having them change. Now her peace was shattered like the thinnest ice.

Trying to keep out of sight as much as possible, Alex crept to the pavement that led from the parking lot to the sidewalk. She peered around the corner—again, no cops, no blood, no body.

He was safe.

Alex turned back to get in her car and get a jump on her day's work. As soon as she touched her door handle, she heard Nick's voice. "Lex?"

And she was caught. She pivoted to him, but the look on his face—somewhere between intrigued and hurt—cut off her defenses.

"Why are you pushing this so hard?" he asked.

Did he have to use that word? She wasn't trying to pressure him, not this time. She needed to be there. Didn't he understand?

Alex almost laughed at herself. Nick wasn't the only one expecting telepathy. But she actually did have some sort of clairvoyance. That was exactly why she was here.

And it was driving her nuts.

Nick's expression shifted into concern. "What's the matter?"

For the first time in at least six years, Alex let herself really focus on him, on his eyes, the deep, glowing amber that drove other people jealous. She'd turned to those eyes countless times for reassurance, for help, for peace.

Exactly what she needed. She'd carried this burden alone, barely alluding to the truth only to the most prying people for the last six years. She'd lived thirty-seven murders—thirty-eight, if you counted Nick's—through the eyes of the killers.

"Would you believe me if I told you something that makes me sound crazy?"

"Detective Alexandra Steen, crazy? Having a hard time picturing that."

Alex dropped her gaze, acknowledging his point with a silent chuckle. How many times had she questioned why the dreams would afflict someone whose best quality was her pragmatism? She waved him away. "Never mind."

"No, wait." He took her elbow before she could escape to her car. "Listen, I—the other day, after you left my apartment, I realized . . . you *have* changed. I thought you weren't listening, but you weren't shouting back at me like you would have before. You're trying to analyze this, do it right, and I want to help." He waited until she dared to meet his gaze. "You can tell me."

Alex swallowed, staring at his bronzed hand, drawing in that little bit of warmth and strength. It'd been way too long since she'd had that silent support.

But she'd never told anyone about the dreams. Would Nick really be the first? She tried to swallow again, but her mouth was dry. "I . . . I had a dream."

She dared to check Nick's reaction. He managed to school his features from uncertain to understanding in record time. "I'm guessing it wasn't the same as Dr. King's."

"No." Alex drew a bracing breath. Was she ready for this?

She was ready to share the burden, to not be the only one who knew about the dreams, to have someone believe her. But could Nick be that person? Or would she dump her burden on him only to never see him again?

Nick slid his hand down from her elbow to take hold of her fingers, adding his other hand to hers, too. Alex met his gaze again, and there was the acceptance she'd once felt from him so unconditionally. The rest didn't matter now; she needed to take this leap to trust him. To find peace again. To save him. "I dream about murders before they happen. I saw someone attack Candyce, and now he's after you."

He didn't pull away, but his eyes widened. He watched her in silence. "You're not joking."

She shook her head.

"How many times?"

"Total? Few dozen. About you two? Every day this week."

Nick looked away, but not disbelieving—more like he needed a minute to process.

A minute? Years of murderous nightmares and Alex was still trying to get a handle on it.

"So how does this work?" he asked at last, a single note of skepticism in his voice. "You dream about murders, see who did it, and then arrest them?"

She couldn't meet his disbelief. She focused on her car door. "No, I only see the murder itself, through the killer's eyes. I still have to figure everything out."

"And I'm assuming you've had your head checked."

Alex huffed out a laugh in a cloud. The department psychologist usually didn't get involved unless there'd been true trauma, not just another murder crime scene or "disturbing dream." The one time she'd actually had to talk to the guy, he'd written it all off as déjà vu.

"And you're not joking . . . or lying."

Nick made the accusation in a light tone, but the seriousness jolted her. If there was one thing Nick could

267

never stand, it was a liar. His father had lied to his whole family about even the most trivial things, and Alex had made extra sure to be scrupulously honest with Nick. She held his gaze steady. "You know I would *never* lie to you."

He stood there thinking another minute. "You're serious." It wasn't a question.

"Dead."

He flashed a smile at the awful gallows-humor pun. "You're sure I'm in danger."

"I am."

Alex held her breath while Nick thought it through yet again. It didn't matter how long he thought about it—she'd spent hours herself—nothing about it would make sense. She'd barely come to accept it and understand the rules and use the dreams as best she could.

"There might be someone." Nick offered the idea like a life preserver.

But what would he suggest? A doctor? A therapist? Dorothea Dix?

"I'd almost forgotten, but the guy just came into the office again last week."

She tried to hammer the pieces together, but she didn't have enough context to make them fit anywhere in the conversation. "What guy? Start over."

"Sorry. A couple months back, we had to let one of our key employees go. He got pretty bitter about it online. To the point where we had to threaten to sue."

Oh—oh. Someone who would want to hurt him.

He was accepting her dreams. He was trying to help. Surprise blanked out her mind for a split second. Of all the responses in the world, acceptance wasn't one she'd actually imagined. Hoped for, but not dared to visualize. Something in her mind seemed to settle back into place, as if the time away from him or the disruption of the dreams had broken a piece inside of her and that little bit of validation finally fixed it.

"Any credence to his complaints?" she asked, leaning against her car door.

Nick pondered that. "Well, we did fire him, and he'd helped develop several of our products, but the things he was saying . . . we were unethical, immoral, blocking him from the unemployment he was entitled to—as if he wasn't fired for misconduct. Candyce said we had a case for defamation and wrote up a cease-and-desist a week or two ago."

So Candyce had gone on to law school like she'd always planned. Something about that was gratifying. But Alex needed to focus on the case. "Sounds like he was angry. Can you imagine him turning violent?"

Nick bit his lip like he was trying to hold back the truth. "Wish I could say no, but honestly, part of the reason we let him go is because his drinking's gotten out of control, so I don't know. He was raving when he came into the office last week. We nearly had to call the police—you guys."

Alex suppressed a grim nod. Alcohol and indignation definitely made a volatile cocktail.

They finally had a suspect. They still didn't know when he'd strike, but they knew what was coming. And maybe—maybe—Nick would be willing to work with her to fight back.

"Are your dreams always right?" he asked.

She met his gaze, like that would brace him for the answer. "Always."

He shuddered, and Alex raised an eyebrow in silent question.

"You're telling me I could die any day," he said.

She studied him, the way his jaw seemed to settle into a set of acceptance. The reality was really setting in. "I don't mean to pressure you," she said, "but we have to do something."

He didn't argue, but he didn't agree either.

"I can't let you live in fear. I think we need to fight back."

Once again, she didn't breathe as she waited for his reaction. "Okay," he said at last.

Quenching relief flooded into her chest so quickly she almost wanted to fling her arms around him—but she didn't. Instead, she said, "We need a plan."

Nick nodded, squeezed her hands, and walked around to climb in the passenger seat of her car.

Alex tried not to marvel at how long it'd been since they'd been on the same team—instead, she reminded herself that they *were* on the same team now, and that was all that mattered to keep Nick alive.

She hoped.

After a stressful morning in court on the Cook case, Alex was finally able to call Officer Harrison at the recess for lunch. She paced the waxed concrete floor, high heels clicking over the exposed aggregate. Even the '80s styling grated on her nerves today. She hated to have a potential murderer arrested on a simple assault, but she needed this guy off the street before he could hurt Nick.

When Harrison answered, Alex cut directly to the point. "Nick Carpenter thought of someone who might try to hurt him."

"Him?" Harrison asked. "Not his sister?"

Crap. But it wasn't that much of a leap to think she might be in danger because of him, even if you hadn't seen the dream. "Possible that they were attacking her to get back at him."

Harrison contemplated that one a moment. "Okay, you got a name?"

"Geoff Bryant. Used to work for Nick—until Nick fired him."

"Well, there's your motive," Harrison muttered. "Got an address?"

Nick had already texted her the photo and address from Carexa's personnel files. "I'll pass it on."

"Okay. Any other information?"

Alex flipped through her memory of her conversation with Nick this morning. "He's got a drinking problem, so be careful. Probably doesn't have much of a criminal record, but that may've changed recently."

"Great. Thanks for the lead." His tone didn't leave any room for an invitation to help work on the case. Granted, she had to be back in the courtroom in twenty minutes, but she could help after she was done testifying. Whenever that was.

Not good enough. "I want to work with you."

"You are. But this isn't a homicide."

Sergeant Oscarson's hard-nosed reputation preceded him throughout the department. He definitely wouldn't appreciate her devoting more time to this case—and obviously she couldn't play hooky from court.

"We'll keep you in the loop," Harrison promised, "and see if we can track Bryant down today."

"Great." Before she ended the call, Alex scrambled to find some reason or excuse to stay on this case. But the only compelling reason was the one she didn't dare say out loud.

The afternoon crawled by with an excessively detailed cross-examination that kept Alex on her toes. By the time court adjourned for the day, she was mentally spent from watching her every word, walking a mental tightrope—but she had to see if they'd started questioning Bryant yet.

Alex wasn't even to the parking garage when Harrison answered. "Detective Steen." He didn't sound pleased.

Then neither was she. "Harrison."

"We went to the address you sent us, but no one was home. Neighbors said his wife left him a few weeks ago, and they haven't seen him in a couple days. Weren't sure where he might drink or stay. Checked bars in the area. They knew him but hadn't seen him lately either. Haven't dug up any family in the area. Brick wall."

Wow. They'd done a decent job in a few hours—but that was definitely not what she wanted to hear.

"We also talked to a couple people who said it's been months since he was laid off. Why wait this long if the motive's revenge?"

"To serve it cold," Alex murmured. "Plus, this week he came into the office raving."

"We'll try to follow up," Harrison said. But they both recognized the empty promise. Harrison shifted gears. "Sergeant Oscarson called today. Making sure we weren't taking you from your homicide duties."

Alex swallowed a groan. If Oscarson'd gotten his back up, she needed to watch her step during work hours. Harrison's case seemed to be dead-ending already. "No worries there," she said. "Sounds like you've run down your leads."

Harrison agreed and ended the call, leaving Alex frustrated as ever.

She had to save Nick. This went beyond her normal homicide duties, even beyond the drive the dreams gave her. Because she did still care about him. She needed him.

They didn't have time to wait around for Bryant to stagger home. That dream would come true one of these mornings. But if he'd already run, they might never find him in time to stop him.

Then again, Alex knew *where* to find him. She just had to figure out when.

An evening of investigation was just as unsuccessful as

the uniformed officers' had been. Early the next morning, Alex glanced over at Nick, in her passenger seat again, waiting. The dream had been the same that morning, but for now, he was alive and breathing next to her, and they were waiting for a killer to take his place in the shrubs. Nick eyed the bushes uncertainly.

The terrain was familiar, but staking out his own neighborhood could only be new territory for him. It was above and beyond her normal duties, too. And she had to tell him that, what this meant to her—what *he'd* meant to her, even if he still didn't want her. The words weighed on her tongue, bitter and sweet.

"Is this what you do with every dream?" Nick broke the taut silence.

"First time," she murmured, fixed on the street. "Never had enough details to stop them before."

He rested a reassuring hand on her shoulder. "Tough to watch, huh."

Alex patted his hand. She couldn't quite bring herself to admit that it was, but for someone who wanted to be out there proactively protecting people? "Tough" was the understatement of the year.

Every dream up to now, she hadn't made it in time to wait for the killer to strike, only to try to bring some semblance of justice. But nothing she did would ever give those parents and spouses and children their loved ones back.

This time, she was doing exactly that. She shrugged deeper into her jacket, almost wishing she had Nick's hoodie. Almost eerie—the darkest before the dawn. They were waiting for someone who wanted to kill Nick. She was here, but there were no real guarantees he'd be safe. For all she knew, their plan was part of the set-up of the dream that she wasn't privy to. They could be making the dream come true.

She could be sending Nick to his death.

Her heart dipped at the thought, but that was all. It

should've been scary, or at least unnerving. But she wasn't doing this alone. Simply sitting in silence together was comforting. Peaceful. She'd missed this, the reassurance, the centering, the peace—him.

"Thanks for trying to save my life," Nick said. "You didn't have to—"

"Of course I did." Alex looked to him, to those eyes that somehow understood even the craziest thing she'd ever told anyone. "I . . . I've missed you."

The modest side of his smile flashed across his face. "I've missed you, too."

She studied his expression. Worry grated at her nerves. If they were unwittingly making the dream come true, this might be her last chance to tell him all the things jostling in her mind. "I'm sorry—I'm sorry I pushed you so much that I pushed you away."

Nick turned to gaze out the windshield. "I'm sorry I let you."

"Why?" she barely dared to breathe. "Why didn't you want to get married?"

He gaped at her. "You were the one who said you didn't want to get married."

It was Alex's turn to stare out at the street. Hadn't he said that? She sifted through the sharp shards of the argument in her memories. She was pushy. She was controlling. Every time she brought it up, he didn't want to talk about marriage. But had he ever actually said he didn't want to get married? Had *she* been the one to say it? So angry and hurt that she'd imploded the relationship? And she'd spent years blaming him?

She couldn't remember what she'd said anymore. But the words seemed to echo back to her, this time in her voice.

Nick continued. "Just because I'm not doing something as fast as you want doesn't mean I'm doing nothing."

Was that how she'd treated him?

Of course it was. Wasn't she surprised to hear he'd

actually gotten off his butt and set up a successful business instead of worrying and wishing? She never doubted his ability to do it, but . . . part of her believed if he was ever going to pursue his grandiose plans with the way he always obsessed over the nitpicky details instead of taking action, someone else would have to kick and drag him into it. Probably her.

But only because she wanted him to fulfill those dreams, too. Because she'd loved him.

And part of her still did.

"And—" Nick began, but cut himself off.

"And just because I press doesn't mean I don't care."

He licked his lips and fell silent again. "I was going to say sometimes I still regret letting you go. Making you go. When I did want to move forward."

She whirled on him. "You did? But—I thought—you said—" Or had he?

"I think we both said some things—a lot of things—we didn't mean that day. I was always so scared I couldn't do it, couldn't be married. I couldn't repeat my father's mistakes. I had to be absolutely sure. To be comfortable."

To feel safe. The implicit message echoed in the car. That was all either of them had wanted—what they'd found with each other—what they'd lost. Then Alex had lost it all over again when the dreams started.

She'd begun to find that again, and now she was risking it all—that peace, that centering, even Nick himself—to try to make him safe for good.

Before Alex could put that into words, movement on the sidewalk across the street caught her attention. Black jacket. Jeans. Athletic build.

She checked with Nick. His lips compressed, taut and grim, and he nodded. It was Bryant. It was their guy.

Bryant glanced around. Alex froze, even her heartbeat suspended for a long second. But he didn't notice them parked a few cars down across the street. No other pedestrians—no witnesses—roamed the sidewalk, so he took his place among the boxwoods.

Silence coated the inside of the car like a thick coat of ice. They waited long enough that it wouldn't seem suspicious before she started the engine. Nick covered his face with one hand on his forehead like he had a headache. Alex was careful to not look at Bryant as they pulled past, though she did watch in the side mirror once he was in sight. No movement.

Good.

They rounded the block and pulled into the lot where they'd met an hour ago. The bag with a prescription for Candyce waited on the front seat. Making the dream come true right down to the details.

Except the final ones, she hoped. Her heart seemed to be coated with fine frost, as if it would crack if she dared to use it.

Alex pulled in behind his car and looked to Nick. There was a very real chance this was the last time they'd see each other. The last time he'd see anyone. Anything could happen once he left the car.

Were they playing into the dream or changing it? She couldn't breathe.

Nick leaned across the center console and planted a kiss on her forehead. "Thank you," he said. "No matter what happens."

She wasn't a mind reader, but the subtext in his eyes was hard to miss. All the things that'd stood between them all these years suddenly weren't half the problem they'd seemed. They could work together, even respect one another. There might be hope for them—as long as they survived the next ten minutes.

Too many words hung unsaid in the car, choking out the air until Nick opened his door. Of course, the minute he was behind the wheel of his car, Alex thought of all the things she should've said—she'd be there for him, she wouldn't push him like that again, she still cared.

She loved him.

Instead, she sat in silence as Nick pulled away, headed to his parking lot.

To make her nightmare come true.

Although she still couldn't help feeling like part of her mind was spinning out of her reach, something about this felt good. Felt right. She was finally taking control of the dreams and the power they should've given her from the beginning. She could—she *would*—stop a killer before he claimed his victim.

Alex followed Nick onto the road, but he was already down the block. He passed over the train tracks just before his parking lot—and just before the red railroad crossing signal lights began flashing.

No, no, no. This little side street had no barrier gates, but the train was only a few yards from the crossing. Even her lights and sirens wouldn't do her any good.

Alex stomped on the gas, though she knew she couldn't make it. She needed Nick to wait for her. She fumbled for her phone to call and tell him, but her frenzied fingers only flipped the phone onto the floor of the passenger side. She watched, helpless, while Nick turned into his parking lot. Then the train charged past, cutting off her view.

She slammed on the brakes, stopping short of the danger zone. Her heart hammered louder than the cars clattering over the tracks. How long could this train be?

Alex leaned down, straining her seatbelt and her arm to reach her phone where it had slid, the farthest corner of the floorboard. Would he notice she wasn't there? He wasn't supposed to look back; he was supposed to trust her and her plan.

She had to call him. She had to warn him.

Before she reached her phone, the train's last car passed. She could still make it. Alex stomped on the gas and shot down the street to save Nick, like she had the past three mornings. Only this time, the threat was certain.

She slowed down to whip into the parking lot—but a car pulled up the wrong direction in the narrow entrance, blocking her out. Her blood froze. With the traffic coming the other direction, this car would be waiting a while.

"No, no, no." Alex slapped the steering wheel and jammed the accelerator. Alternatives, alternatives—a couple small streets on the right, and then this street dead ended at Duke Street—a one-way that'd take her farther from the scene.

One thought sliced through all the others. Nick would die, and it was her fault. She'd pressured him into this.

Snapshots of the dream flashed before her gaze. Walking up behind Nick. Her throat contracted.

Was that happening now?

She scanned the street again—then she saw it. A maintenance path through the apartment complex. Her car wouldn't fit down there, but she certainly would.

Alex swerved across the street between two cars coming the other way, pulling backward into a handicap spot. She vaulted out of the car and flat-out ran past the building and down the maintenance path.

And slammed into wrought iron bars. A fence. Her pulse screamed a protest in her ears. Of course there was a fence. All vertical bars, it was unclimbable. No gate, no nothing to get through to the private patio area beyond.

The dream cut in on her mind again. Through Bryant's eyes, she followed Nick down the sidewalk. Her arms—but not her arms, out of her control—wrapped around Nick's neck.

No. She couldn't let that happen. Her heart throbbed in her throat as she raced back to her car, and then past. She'd have to cut through the parking lot on foot.

Alex rounded the building and hit the parking lot pavement at a dead sprint. Just past the rental office, a car backed out in front of her. No time to stop. It barely clipped her hip, bumping her a foot to her left. Hot pain flashed up her side. She smacked the trunk, and the driver stopped abruptly.

She could almost feel Nick's weight against her—no, against Bryant, pulling him tight. The knife handle in her grip.

Alex raced on. Why did this seem like such a small lot when you needed a spot, but when you needed to get across, it was huge?

Her thighs screamed and the cold air stabbed into her lungs. She tried to shove away the images from the dream, the killer, the stabbing, the bloody knife. It was happening now. She was too late.

Every breath showed up in a cloud as she plowed right through. She didn't need air, didn't heed her muscles' protests, didn't stop. She had to save Nick. Nothing else mattered.

She felt the knife handle shudder as the blade jabbed into his back. She almost had to check to see if her hands were wet with his blood.

Even if she wasn't the one doing the stabbing, his blood would be on her hands.

Finally, she reached the other end of the parking lot and the path to the sidewalk. The path Nick must've just taken. The path that was supposed to lead to his death.

She banked the turn, arms and legs still pumping. There, in the shadows under the building: Nick. The killer—Bryant. Bryant didn't have him yet.

She wasn't too late.

He grabbed Nick around the throat.

"Stop!" Alex screamed, breathless. "Police!"

Bryant startled and checked over his shoulder. She barely had time to slow and draw before she reached them. "Hands up!"

"I wasn't—I wasn't—" Bryant tried.

"Hands up! Police!" She was almost shaking from running and terror, and she wouldn't feel safe until she had him disarmed and cuffed. He could still strike.

It didn't matter how hard she was breathing, she couldn't seem to get enough oxygen. Because Bryant still had Nick. "Hands! Up!"

Slowly, Bryant raised his hands, letting Nick go. Something glinted in Bryant's right hand, and he cast the briefest glance at Nick.

Her cop-instinct muscles clenched. "Drop your weapon!" Alex barked between gasps. "Drop it now!"

The knife clattered to the sidewalk, and Nick kicked it out of Bryant's easy reach.

"On the ground!" Alex ordered. With her breath and pulse gradually coming under control, she could use the scary-authoritative policewoman voice she'd cultivated much more effectively. "Get on the ground!"

Bryant dropped to his knees, coming to accept that it was over. Alex grabbed his shoulder with her free hand and shoved him forward, tacitly reiterating her command. "Face down on the ground!"

Still stunned that his plans had gone wrong, and possibly too drunk to wonder why, Bryant finally complied. Alex planted a knee on his spine and wrenched his wrists behind his back to slap on the cuffs. "You're under arrest," she huffed.

Nick helped Alex to her feet, and she called in the report. Within minutes, backup rushed over with lights and sirens blaring. Alex stood back, still gulping down air, as the officers loaded Bryant into a squad car, collected his weapon and bustled him off to jail.

There were still statements to be taken—leaving out the pesky detail of her prophetic dream, of course—clean-up to be done, paperwork, evidence, more, but it was over. The hard part was over.

She'd done it. She'd stopped a murder.

Not just anyone's murder. Nick's. In the middle of the bustle, his arms wrapped around her shoulders, and she turned to him.

The dreams were right: there was no such thing as a coincidence. They'd drawn her back to Nick, brought them together again, saved his life. Alex still didn't understand all their purposes, but she knew this: the dreams wanted her to be with Nick.

And so did she.

"You really hustled to get here," he observed.

"Oh, no." She laughed between the last residual gasps. "Took me seven years."

A smile dawned on his face. "Thank you for pushing."

Alex looked into his eyes and pulled in a deep breath, the first she'd been able to take without the cold air cutting her lungs like glass shards. Because Nick was here. Nick was okay. And they might be, too.

She took another breath. This time, the cool air seemed to fill her with calm. Nick's presence was once again bringing her the peace she desperately needed—from the dreams, from her job, from risking his life.

"Thank you for being there for me," she managed. "For centering me."

"I'm sorry I was an idiot—I should've known you didn't mean what you said back then. You were just being you— passionately you—and that's something I've always loved."

Alex waited for the shock to hit. A week ago, reconciling with Nick would have been inconceivable. But instead, the quiet peace still filled her like gentle sunshine.

"I'm sorry I ever said those things," she said. "I wasn't thinking—but I am now."

"Can . . ." Nick hesitated, searching her eyes. She didn't dare press him. "Can we try again?"

"I'd like that. We can go as slow as you need."

"Or as fast as you want." Nick leaned down and kissed her, and Alex had a whole new reason to be breathless.

About Jordan McCollum

PHOTO BY JAREN WILKEY

An award-winning author, **Jordan McCollum** can't resist a story where good defeats evil and true love conquers all. In her day job, she coerces people to do things they don't want to, elicits information and generally manipulates the people she loves most—she's a mom.

Jordan holds a degree in American Studies and Linguistics from Brigham Young University. When she catches a spare minute, her hobbies include reading, knitting and music. She lives with her husband and four children in Utah.

You can catch up with her online at JordanMcCollum.com and join her newsletter to find out when her next book will be out!

The Ghost of Millhouse Mansion

by Elana Johnson

Other works by Elana Johnson

Elevated

Something About Love

Possession Series
Possession
Surrender
Abandon
Resist
Regret

Elemental Series
Elemental Rush
Elemental Hunger
Elemental Release

One

Naomi unlocked her office and stepped back into the central heat, sighing, though she loved using her lunch hour to bike the trail along the river. The October air held the crispness of late fall, and after twenty miles with the wind in her face her nose surely shone like Rudolph's. Because of its high elevation, winter would settle in Silver Hills soon, though there were still two weeks until Halloween.

She kicked off her riding shoes and cranked the radio. She shimmied back into her pencil skirt and settled at her desk. With her calendar already open, it only took one glance to confirm what she already knew: Her next client wouldn't arrive for another hour.

A simple renovation job on a childhood toy. Marion was supposed to be bringing it with her. Naomi made enough in the town of Silver Hills to get by restoring toys, clocks, and other antiques. She managed to get a job doing a kitchen renovation, or redecorating a master suite, or redesigning someone's basement every month. She loved the projects the townspeople brought her, loved restoring old homes as new families moved in, loved working with people, textiles, art, space.

But what she really wanted was a crowning jewel in her interior design career.

She wanted the Millhouse mansion.

One of the oldest buildings in Silver Hills, the house sat outside of town, past the old church and the original courthouse—a two-story, pink brick building Naomi adored.

Naomi drove out to the mansion at least once a week, just to look at the bones of the place. She itched to get inside and assess the condition of the hardwood floors, discover if the kitchen had running water as the rumors went. She fantasized over what fixtures she'd find, if the parlor had a mantle over a gorgeous fireplace.

She'd been waiting for years for the owner of the Millhouse mansion to get his act together and restore what was sure to be the most beautiful building within two hundred miles.

But Colt Jennings didn't seem to care about the old house. He lived part time in a cottage— which Naomi had restored— next to the original school building. If he knew she'd chosen the craftsman countertops and dark maples in his study, he'd never said anything.

Not that she had any reason to speak with Colt Jennings. The man ran an outdoor guide company, leading fishermen through the fifty square miles of backcountry surrounding Silver Hills as they caught trout. He only lived inside city limits during the winter, and Naomi hadn't seen him around for months.

She ventured out to his property whenever she felt like it, with its massive mansion, run-down outbuildings, and abandoned gold mine. Well, not entirely abandoned. The legends floating around told of seventeen spirits confined to the property—the mansion, the outbuildings, as far north as the river as it ran out of the old mine—after a ceiling collapse killed the men in 1861.

After that collapse, most of the miners had moved on to more fertile rivers to hunt their treasure. A few families had stayed, and the Jennings were the ones who bought up the Millhouse mansion along with the gold mine.

As far as Naomi knew, they'd lived there for generations. Colt's mother had died in the house, and the stories said that was the day he left for good.

Naomi didn't know as much about that as she did the history of Silver Hills. She'd grown up here and gone away to college to study interior design while Ramona Jennings was dying. Colt, on the other hand, had been shipped off to boarding school early, only returning to watch his mother die.

Naomi glanced at the clock, wondering if she had time to drive out to the mansion before her next appointment. She didn't. Disappointed, but determined not to let Colt's obvious apathy toward antiques get to her, she leaped from her desk and started hanging Halloween decorations around her office.

A particularly gyration-worthy song came on her radio, and Naomi clapped and scream-sang along with the lyrics as she did a little jig to the rhythm. She had some moves left from the high school dance team, but her knee-length pencil skirt prevented her from completing a proper high kick.

So did the low laughter coming from behind her.

Horrified into a halt, Naomi stood stock still, listening to be sure there was indeed someone there. There was, with a very deep chuckle.

A man, then.

Perfect, Naomi thought. Finding a worthy date in Silver Hills had been challenging. Naomi had considered moving to Denver or its suburbs many times to increase the pond size.

But the houses there didn't have the character of Silver Hills, and her own mother was nearing the end of her life. So Naomi stayed.

Scrambling now, she reached for the remote and lowered the volume on the radio before turning around.

Her heart dropped to her knees. She was pretty sure her mouth followed suit, because none other than Colt Jennings stood in the doorway to her office, wearing a form-fitting black leather jacket and a very Cheshire-cat-like smile. Naomi momentarily lost her train of thought just looking at him.

He could've looked happy, had the emotion reached his eyes; they were dark like coal and glittering like the stars at midnight. Naomi sucked in a breath to keep from asphyxiating on the spot.

"Hey," he said. "I hope I'm not interrupting." His tone suggested that he didn't really care if he was or not.

"Of—of course not." Naomi tried to set the remote back on her desk but ended up throwing it toward him. Her face burned, and she ran her hands through her hair in an attempt to put herself back together.

His almost-black hair called to her—*come touch me, too.* She clenched her fingers into fists. "What can I do for you?"

Had he come to ask her to renovate his house? Her heart picked up speed, and not just from the stubble along his strong jaw and the careful, powerful way he crossed his arms across his chest.

Just looking at him sent shivers into places where such things should not exist. She wrapped her own arms around herself, hoping to hold everything together.

"My aunt has some toy she wanted you to look at." He hooked his thumb over his shoulder, indicating the lobby behind her.

"Oh," Naomi said, slipping behind her desk to slide her feet into her heels. "I was expecting Marion. Was she not able to come?"

"She asked me to, because the item is at my place." He covered his mouth and coughed.

Naomi frowned. "It's a rocking horse, right?"

"I think so," Colt said. "She said it's at the house and that I needed to let you in to look at it."

Naomi froze, her mouth gaping again. "Your house?"

"The Millhouse mansion," he clarified, his eyes turning stormy. "Can you come out and look at it?"

Colt wondered if this woman understood English for how hard she was trying to figure out what he'd said. Naomi Harding was the type of woman Colt normally gravitated toward. Tall, beautiful, put together with matching jewelry and detailed makeup. Heels, and pencil skirts, and dark, shiny hair. Colt liked it all.

But he'd learned his lesson: Women like Naomi weren't genuine. Colt knew from more experiences than he cared to recall.

Beneath the layers of designer clothes, the false eyelashes, the strappy heels, he'd find a woman who wasn't really worth knowing. She'd probably break up with him through a blasted text message, like the last woman who'd worn a ruffly blouse like hers.

Women like Naomi only made him want to rush outside, get on his bike, and *ride*. But Aunt Marion was a force to be reckoned with, and she wanted that blasted horse tended to. Said she and Colt's mother used to ride it for hours as their daddy played the fiddle and sang.

Now that Colt's brother Rick had gotten himself hitched, Aunt Marion was convinced a grandniece or nephew would be along any minute. And they'd need a rocking horse, which meant Colt needed to get the "best antiques restoration expert" out to the mansion, like, yesterday.

"So can you go?" he asked again, his head pounding. He'd just gotten over a cold, but it felt like he was coming down with something new. "Aunt Marion said she had an appointment." He glanced around at the half-decorated office, wondering if he'd gotten the time wrong.

"She did—she does," Naomi said, finally moving out from behind her desk. With the heels, she stood nearly as tall as him. Fine, he still had a good six inches on her, which he used to look down at her.

"You're going like that?" He let his eyes travel the length of her body, appreciating the curves her clothes accentuated. He'd look, and nothing more, even though his fingers tingled with anticipation of what the creamy skin along her collar might feel like.

"Should I go in something else?" she asked, giving him the same once-over she'd received.

A flush rose in his neck, and he couldn't believe she'd affected him like that. Her careful appraisal made his heart swell. He shut down the warmth invading his body—he wasn't the Grinch, and he wasn't interested in learning to use his heart for anything beyond staying alive.

"It's kind of a rough place," he said. "But whatever. If you break a leg because of that heel, don't blame me." He turned and headed for the door.

Her clicking shoes followed him. "You have home owner's insurance, don't you?"

"I guess," he said.

"Maybe I should put on my riding shoes."

"Riding shoes?"

"I bike at lunch," she said.

"You bike at lunch?" Why couldn't he say anything that wasn't a question? He'd never gone stupid like this before. Maybe his senses had been scrambled by the subtle coconut smell of her skin.

"They're specialized shoes," she said, glancing first at her feet and back into her office. "No, I'll wear these." She headed out to the sidewalk, leaving Colt staring at her swishing hips, wondering how heels could be better than specialized biking shoes. They at least had a non-slip sole.

He shook his head and joined her outside. As he zipped his leather jacket to his throat, he cursed the winters on top of this mountain. He missed the milder climate of Texas, though he had no desire to return.

Colt slid onto his motorcycle while Naomi watched, her lips drawn into a pout. "You know where the mansion is, right?" he asked. "You want to follow me?"

She cocked one hip. If she started tapping her toe, she'd have the sexy schoolteacher act down pat. "I know where it is," she said. "I'll see you there." She got into a sensible sedan and started the ignition.

Colt didn't wait for her. He could only ride his bike for a few months out of the year, and by the looks of the clouds coming over the mountain, he'd be lucky to make it home tonight before the sky opened.

He took the dirt roads out to his family's house—*his* house, now that Rick had gotten married and moved to the city—at breakneck speed, the thrum of the machine beneath him a welcome distraction from Naomi's curves and his worsening headache.

He arrived first, a cloud of dust in his wake. He fished in his pocket for an aspirin and dry-swallowed it. After dropping his helmet onto his handlebars, he headed into a house he hadn't been in for years. His mother had expressly asked him not to sell it, but he had no desire to live in it. Too many rooms, with too many memories—things he'd rather forget.

Stepping through the double-wide front doors was like stepping back in time. The foyer stretched two stories tall, with an open living room on the left and the door to his father's private study on the right.

Colt took a deep breath, getting an under note of his father's tobacco and a hint of the spiced candle his mother burned to cover the smell of smoke. That about summed up their relationship—ever at odds with each other.

Rick had taken the brunt of it, especially after Colt broke Scott Foster's nose and got himself sent to boarding school in Connecticut. At least in the dorm room he'd shared he didn't have to listen to his father's drunken rages, his mother's crying, or his brother's condolences. At least on the Eastern Seaboard, no one knew how screwed up he was. So messed up that he'd often seen apparitions wandering in his backyard.

He'd never told anyone, and he never planned to. Just the same, he glanced around, taking in the inches of dust and the stillness in the air. While he sometimes brought tour groups out to the property, he never allowed them inside the house. He showed them the outbuildings, the old livery stable, the blacksmithing room in the dilapidated shed, the outhouse. But they did not so much as step foot on the porch.

He drove them out to the mine, but again, he'd put up a fence and didn't allow anyone to cross it. He'd seen the forms of men out there too, their faces shining with hope but their eyes dead with the hours they spent underground panning for something they couldn't even see.

The stream ran through the far edge of his property, moving underground a hundred yards later, where a big strike in 1861 had caused hundreds to flock to this small offshoot of the South Platte River.

Too bad no one told them these mountains were prone to earthquakes. Seventeen men had been inside the mine when it collapsed, and Colt knew them all. The old newspapers were down at City Hall, and he'd memorized them by the time he was ten years old.

He didn't see anyone now, though. Couldn't feel anything either. Maybe he'd been away long enough to convince the dead miners there was nothing worth hanging around for.

The crunch of tires announced Naomi's arrival. She carried a clipboard as she toddled on her heels, which brought Colt more joy than it should. Watching a woman mince her way through gravel shouldn't excite him, and yet it did. She brushed a stray lock of hair out of her eyes as she joined him just inside the door.

Her sharp intake of breath sent his pulse pounding. Had she seen someone? He searched for the source of her gasp but saw nothing and no one. He finally focused on her. She held her hand to her heart, her fingers bunching the fabric, dangerously lowering her neckline.

She swept her eyes across the formal living room, down the wide hall, and to the door of the study. She crouched in her pencil skirt and brushed her fingers through the grime on the floor. She released her breath in a satisfying whoosh. "Pine." She glanced up at him, and he had never seen anyone so beautiful.

"Are they the original floors?"

Heck if he knew. He shrugged, and she straightened. "How can you not know?"

"Why do you care?" he challenged.

"I restore more than toys, Mister Jennings." She pinned him with a fierce glare that only made him want to step closer and kiss her. "And I'd do anything to restore the Millhouse mansion."

Two

Naomi couldn't believe she'd been so bold. Couldn't believe she was standing toe-to-toe with Colt Jennings. Okay, slightly less than toe-to-toe, as the man stood at least six and a half feet tall. And he was definitely more than just the guy who owned the Millhouse mansion. He was . . . *tempting.*

You need to get him to hire you, she thought. *Not stand here thinking about how to get him to ask you out.*

"Anything?" he asked, shifting his weight closer to her. The heat from his body bled into her personal space, and she didn't exactly hate it.

"Anything," she replied evenly. "Have you ever considered restoring it?" She stepped away from him to get some air that wasn't filled with the scent of motor oil and driftwood, both of which were suddenly somehow the most alluring scents on the planet.

"I mean, look at that chandelier. It must be a period piece. I've never seen anything like it." She gazed at the yellowed glass above her. Perhaps it used oil, as there was some evidence of the burn. "May I?" She gestured down the hall, barely able to stop herself from running from room to room until she'd seen everything.

"Be my guest." He frowned as she moved away, her shoes making soft clacks in the dust.

She prayed she wouldn't fall, but she was glad she hadn't changed into her riding shoes. They cost four times what these heels did, and she'd look even more ridiculous parading through his house on the uneven soles. Not to mention they clashed with her skirt.

Off the hall she found a gorgeous, if run-down, powder room and a large library that leeched her breath away. Shelves—built-in shelves!—stretched to the ceiling, with tall windows between them. So much dirt stuck to them, hardly any light entered, but Naomi could still imagine the grandeur of this room. Upon closer inspection, she realized the skies outside had turned gray, further muting the light coming into the library.

A fireplace sat opposite the windows, and Naomi ran her fingers across the mantle, collecting a fair bit of dust. She didn't care. This place had history. Character. Charm. The sound of roaring flames, snapping, crackling, popping, entered her head. She sighed from the warmth of the fire, wishing she'd been here to see this house when it was really alive.

Warmth flowed over her skin, and when she glanced down, she saw a fire burning in the hearth. Startled, she fell back a step, a scream catching in her throat when she saw a man sitting in the chair positioned to the right of the fireplace. He wore a heavy coat over a pair of trousers. He didn't have much hair on his head but sported a stylish handlebar mustache.

As her mind whirled and her heart hammered, she stared, gradually realizing the man wasn't corporeal. He looked aged, yellowed, like newspaper gone soft. Still, he raised his weary eyes to her, opened his mouth in a silent greeting, and vanished.

"I didn't spend much time in here," Colt said.

Naomi spun to find him just inches behind her. Had he seen the man sitting in the chair? Felt the fire burning? She rubbed her arms as if cold, the gray stone of the fireplace now radiating a chill. Had she seen anything at all?

"Not much for book learning," he added. "You?"

Her eyes darted back to the chair. Empty. "Yes," she finally said. "I graduated in interior design and earned a certificate in antique restoration a year later."

"Fancy." He seemed to roll his eyes as he looked at the painting hanging above the fireplace. "My father. He wanted me to be a doctor, like he was." He pinned her with his midnight eyes. "That's why I hated school. Didn't want to be a doctor."

Naomi wondered what a patient might feel under the care of his large hands. She shook her head as he started to leave, dislodging the thought and reminding herself that she needed to work toward getting him to hire her. "Wait," she said. "Did you—I mean . . ." She didn't know how to ask him about the man she'd seen.

"Did I what?" He closed the distance between them again, his gaze intense and utterly captivating.

"I thought I saw something," she whispered, like if she kept her voice down it wouldn't be true. Like the ghosties hiding in the library wouldn't know she'd seen them.

Fear raced through Colt's eyes, but he blinked and it fled. "It's an old house," he said. "And there's a lot to see. Come on. The kitchen was my mother's favorite room. Always trying to feed people."

Naomi followed him, her steps less sure. She was reminded of a story about this house she'd learned as a child.

A smallpox epidemic had struck the town early in its life. It almost wiped out the entire population of Silver Hills.

A woman named Belle worked at the dance hall, and she'd brought the sick and dying miners out to the abandoned mansion to help them back to full health. Under her care, most of them healed quickly, but she'd fallen ill herself.

The legends said Belle had wandered into the mountains and found an old woman, who was able to restore her health. Belle returned to the mansion, but when the townsfolk went searching for her to thank her for saving their husbands, they found the house empty. No one ever saw her again—until years later, a veiled woman was seen weeping at the graves in the cemetery.

Witnesses swore it was Belle, but no one could find her. Some said she'd been wandering in the mountains all those years. Some said she never existed at all. Some believed she'd simply moved somewhere else after her healing. No matter what, the people of Silver Hills honored her by naming the mansion at the mine after her, one Belle Millhouse. The name stuck, even after a wealthy doctor purchased the house and moved in.

Naomi recalled the story, wondering if Belle was a ghost. Perhaps she was still in the house, nursing those who needed it. Naomi shook her head. That wasn't right. No one had lived in the Millhouse mansion for years. And Colt's mother had died here, not been saved by some long-lost ghost.

I thought I saw something paraded through Colt's mind. What had she seen? When? Where? And more importantly, who?

Colt had been admiring her enthusiasm and childlike awe at inspecting the house. He remembered being awed with it as well, but he'd been eight and Rick had been eleven, and they'd located every nook and cranny where they could hide from their nanny. Rick used to sneak butterscotch discs from his father's study and hide them in the alcove in the attic. That was their secret meeting place when their dad hit the bottle too hard.

Colt hated the library, as that was his father's pride and joy. He'd entertained more politicians next to that fireplace than Colt could name. But somehow, he sensed that Naomi had seen someone he knew. He wondered why. On her deathbed, his mother still wouldn't admit to seeing anything unusual in the house, but Colt had seen the transparent men since he was a small child. In fact, he couldn't remember a time when they weren't there.

And no one else had ever been able to see them. Not Rick. Not Aunt Marion. Colt hadn't been brave enough to ask anyone else, and he felt the same cowardice now as he pointed out the blown glass lamps in the dining room, the black marble countertops, and the handcrafted alder cupboards his mother had ordered from Holland. She'd found the Dutch wooden shoes endearing and wanted the same type of wood in her kitchen.

Her pocketbook was twice as deep as her wish list, so she usually got what she wanted. Now that Colt owned half of what his mother had once, he realized his wish list couldn't be bought with money.

He'd tried. He owned three motorcycles, and he still couldn't go fast enough to outrun the crazy. He cut a glance at Naomi, who was running her hand lovingly along a cabinet door. If she'd seen someone, maybe he could talk to her about it. Maybe Colt could finally let his demons out and not be judged, ridiculed, or afraid he'd be caged in a padded room.

"Does the house have running water?" Her voice

brought him out of the fantasyland where she saw the same ghosts he did and they laughed about it over cocktails.

"Last I knew," he answered, moving out of the kitchen and into the informal family room. He heard the sound of running water behind him, spurting as the air in the line cleared. Naomi made a sound of approval, and he turned to find her writing something on her clipboard.

"Are you taking notes?" he asked.

"Yes," she said without looking up. "If I'm going to restore this place, I need—"

"Slow down, sweetheart. Who said you were going to restore this place?"

She raised her eyes slowly to his, and he realized he shouldn't have used such a sexist endearment. At least not with her. "Oh, you'll hire me, Mister Jennings," she said. "After you see what I can do for your rocking horse, you'll be begging me to spruce this place up."

"You should call me Colt," he said. "Mister Jennings was my father, and I hated the man."

She blinked, shock bringing a beautiful blush to her fair skin. "I'm sorry." She moved into the family room with him. "Why did you hate him? Is that why you don't want to restore the mansion?"

Colt hadn't meant to say it. Didn't know how to explain. "I don't have much fondness for the place, that's all." He turned to the wall where his mother had hung pictures of him and Rick, dating as far back as babyhood.

"Don't you think it deserves to be preserved?" She trailed along behind him as he moved down the lengthy wall of photos. "I mean, this place is a landmark. It's like the courthouse, or the first school, the saloon, the depot."

Silver Hills had more than its fair share of historic buildings, all decorated for the tourists and groups that came through town. Main Street itself had over forty buildings, some from Silver Hills and some from the surrounding areas. His favorite was the general store, where he imagined he and

Rick could've bought penny candy and peppermint sticks before wasting an afternoon in the tall grass behind the house.

Along with the tourists came the outdoor enthusiasts. Colt led them on fishing expeditions for the best trout fishing this side of the Mississippi. This late in the season, though, he'd have to rely on his savings and inherited fortune to keep warm this winter.

A bank of thunder shook the house, startling him and causing Naomi to stumble in her heels. He reached out and steadied her, a rush of fire shooting up his arm and into his chest. Their eyes locked as the air around them crackled with heat and electricity.

The room darkened, and Colt heard the wind battering the walls, rumbling the glass and causing mayhem with his plans to get home before the storm hit.

Naomi gently extracted her elbow from his grip and moved to the bank of windows in the kitchen. "It looks bad," she said. "We should get back into town."

Another bolt of lightning—the electricity Colt had thought came from contact with Naomi—lit the house, a crash of thunder following almost immediately.

"I don't think we're going anywhere," he said.

Three

"What do you mean?" Naomi hated that her voice had the ring of hysteria in it. "It's just rain."

Colt peered up through the window. "I don't think so, sweetheart."

"Would you stop with the—the *endearments*?" she sneered. "I have a name."

He gave her a half grin, which made her stomach do things it hadn't done in a long time. Maybe she didn't mind being called *sweetheart* when it was his voice talking.

"It looks like—"

The angry pelting of hail hitting the roof drowned out the rest of his sentence.

"Yep. Hail," he practically yelled. "We'll need to hunker down here until it passes."

Naomi couldn't believe it was hailing. That she was here in the Millhouse mansion while it hailed. She'd never had such good luck.

"You want to find that horse?" Colt asked.

Of course, the company's attitude could be improved upon. The way his hair had been trimmed into a half-hawk, with a gorgeous wave along the top and shaved sides, certainly didn't need improvement. And it must take a heck of a lot of muscles to lead fishermen through the wilderness, because dang. Colt's biceps strained against the sleeves of his jacket, which was practically begging to be taken off.

As if reading her mind, he shed his leather jacket and draped it over a settee in the family room. "Place holds its heat upstairs. That's where the rocking horse is." The white shirt he wore seemed a bit see-through, but she didn't want to stare too hard to make sure.

Naomi hadn't worn a jacket, so she let him lead the way toward the grand staircase across from the entrance to the library. She gripped the handrail for support, noting that it wobbled under her weight. Once she reached the top of the stairs, she made a note on her clipboard that the railing would need to be replaced.

Colt flipped a switch, because the hallway before them lay in darkness. Nothing happened. A shiver ran through Naomi, and goose bumps erupted along her arms and neck. She felt like she was being watched, but as she turned in a slow circle, she saw no one but Colt. He wasn't watching her but casting his eyes around as well, as if he felt what she did.

"Do you feel that?" she asked. Almost a tangible sensation, but not quite. Someone was definitely in the hallway with them. She slipped her arm through Colt's, gripping his forearm with both her hands.

"I feel it," he whispered. He dipped his head closer to her ear. "What did you see in the library?"

"A man," Naomi admitted. "He was wearing a coat and he had a mustache. He was sitting in the chair in front of the fire."

The frantic plinking of hail on the roof filled the silence between them.

"You think I'm crazy, don't you?" she whispered, finally daring to look at him. But he didn't look dubious. Instead, he studied her with fascination, the fire in his eyes hard to decipher. Could've been attraction, but could've also as easily been confusion. Maybe both.

"I don't think you're crazy," he finally said. He opened his mouth to continue, but the lights blazed on, cutting him off. He exhaled sharply—more relieved than he should've been.

Naomi didn't know what to make of his behavior. How could he believe she'd seen someone sitting in the chair downstairs? But the sincerity in his words rang true. She felt certain he'd been about to say something important, and now the moment was lost.

He moved down the hall, but she kept her arm in his. He didn't seem to mind, and she was secretly glad. With him, she'd be safe.

Embarrassment crept through Naomi. She couldn't believe she'd told Colt she'd seen a man in the library. A ghost. Ridiculous!

Colt's hand slid down her arm, and his fingers twined themselves between hers. "The man you saw is Jacob Lawson. He died in the mine collapse in 1861. His son was inside, panning with him."

Naomi's blood ran cold. "You know who he is?"

"He was the only one wearing a coat at the time of the collapse." His tone hid more secrets, but Naomi couldn't get past the fact that he believed her.

"So you believe me?" For some reason, it mattered to her.

"I've seen them all." He stopped outside a closed door and squared his shoulders. "I see them every time I'm here. I know all their names, because I've studied the archives."

The way he looked at her with such need, such openness, made her believe him. She nodded. "Okay, so we're not crazy if we can see the same things."

305

He gave a short laugh that sounded like a bark. "Oh, we're crazy all right."

The feeling of being watched returned, and Naomi turned around. She screamed as she came face-to-face with a woman.

Colt pulled Naomi into his chest, pressing her back against him as he quickly placed his hand over her mouth. "Shh," he whispered in her ear, his lips accidentally brushing her lobe. Something strange burned within his core, something very much like the desire to kiss her ear for real.

"What do you see?" he murmured instead.

"A woman." The words barely escaped between his fingers. "She's wearing a long dress, and her hair is in two braids. She's staring right at me."

A woman? Colt had never seen a ghostly woman on his property. He didn't know what to do or say next.

"She's leaving," Naomi said, her head turning slightly to the left. She relaxed in his arms, but he didn't let go. "Um, Colt? I think she wants us to go with her."

He slid his hand into hers, ignoring the swoop in his stomach. He was too old and too jaded for a stupid swooping stomach. For crying out loud. He'd sworn off women in Texas, and he certainly wasn't going to get involved with someone he could've grown up with. Someone who hadn't escaped Silver Hills when she'd had the chance.

"Lead on," he whispered.

"You can't see her?" The way Naomi wobbled on her heels as she moved down the hall proved her panic.

"I've never seen a woman out here, no." He set his jaw when she paused outside the last door on the right. This room was over the family room and had been his as a child.

"She went in there."

"This is my bedroom." He couldn't bring himself to open the door. He knew what he'd see—he'd been in here after his mother had died and knew it hadn't changed. Her last breath had contained the words "Forgive me."

He hadn't known what she needed to be forgiven for. It was his father who had been cruel. Colt had no happy memories of his dad. He hadn't missed him while he was at boarding school, and he hadn't come home for his funeral when he finally drank himself to death. If anything, Colt needed his mother's forgiveness for adding to her troubles.

"Should we go in?" Naomi asked.

Colt answered by turning the knob and letting the door drift open. His bed lay rumpled, exactly as he'd left it the day he'd walked out the front door. Five years of harsh summer winds driving dust through cracks and the bright sun fading colors greeted him.

"She's standing at the window." Naomi clung to him, pressing her leg against his. He didn't mind, and though the situation was anything but erotic, he still felt every inch of her next to him.

"She's gone." Her breath whooshed out in relief, and Colt's muscles relaxed too.

"Did you recognize her?" he asked.

"I know some history," Naomi said. "But not enough to recognize spirits wandering through a house I've dreamed about exploring."

Colt wondered if that included his bedroom. She disentangled herself from him and went to the window. He joined her, more than curious about this woman and the ghost she'd seen. *Why* could she see them, especially when no one else ever had?

"I used to love climbing out this window," he said. "See the perfectly flat piece of roof there?" He pointed to his left. "That's the overhang on the back patio. I'd sit there for hours when my parents fought. Sometimes I'd sleep out there when I didn't want to be caged by walls."

She slipped her hand into his and squeezed. When she let go, Colt felt every empty space between his fingers.

"Do you have history books here?" she asked. "Maybe in the library? Maybe we can find her and figure out what she wants."

Colt took a few more moments to gaze over the landscape, his heart skipping every third beat. He swallowed, his stomach warring with the aspirin he'd taken. Maybe he should've had something to eat with it, or at least a drink of water.

He scanned the land out the window, his brain bouncing from one side of his skull to the other. His eyes drifted closed as the vertigo intensified and then faded. He gripped the windowsill as he reopened his eyes, grateful things had solidified into their proper places.

The hail had turned to slushy rain, but he could still see the barn in the distance, the stables, the storage sheds. Closer to the house, his mother had kept a flower garden, now overrun with weeds and prairie grass. What could the ghostly woman have been looking at?

"Colt?" Naomi prompted from the doorway, and he turned.

He didn't glance left or right as he left his bedroom. He didn't want to restore this house, because then he'd be expected to live in it. And he could never do that.

Four

olt looked as white as a ghost himself as he kept pace next to Naomi. She was grateful he hadn't run off and left her to navigate the hall and stairs in her rickety heels. If she was being truthful, she was grateful he'd seen similar things. And thrilled to be holding his hand, even if it was only for a crisis situation.

She'd forgotten the safety and comfort in the human touch. Naomi hadn't had much luck in the dating department, and most of her interactions were with her senile mother. She also had a neighbor, Edith, who called Naomi and asked her to stop and get eggs or milk on her way home from work. Naomi would then stay for dinner and have a real conversation that didn't include the words "paint stripper" or "blow out that wall to make more space."

She fantasized about what it would be like to come home to this house, completely redone from top to bottom, where Colt would be making coffee in the kitchen. He'd plant a kiss on her temple, and they'd take their dinner in the family room, in the spot where the sun lingered longest.

The idyllic images faded as she stepped into the library. Colt turned rigid, one step wooden and the next fluid. "Hey, Jacob." He nodded toward the windows, where Naomi discovered the mustached man, wearing his coat.

The apparition didn't speak but simply walked through the glass and disappeared into the storm. Naomi moved to the windows to take in the same view as Jacob. The library faced east, the view overlooking the city of Silver Hills. She could see the farms spread out, the three-story library, and the long row of historical buildings on Main Street.

From this vantage point on the hill, she could see everyone and everything. She wondered what Jacob had been looking at, thinking about, as he stood here.

"Are they all here?" she asked. "All the victims of the mine collapse?"

"Yes," Colt answered simply. "But there was no record of a woman."

"What about Belle Millhouse?" Naomi asked, her mind leaping to the story she'd been thinking about the first time she'd seen Jacob. "The stories say she brought all those sick men here to nurse them back to health."

She turned to find Colt bent over an open book.

He slowly raised his gaze to hers. "She did," he said, his voice flecked with the sound of a sore throat. "Even though she didn't own this place. No one did. She was the maid for the family that bought the house a few years later." He flipped several pages in the book as he yawned. "Come look."

She crossed the room to his side, slipping out of her shoes to alleviate the pinch in her pinky toes.

"Her mother had trained her in healing with herbs," Colt said. "She brought the men out here to prevent the spread of the disease." He pointed at a picture.

"That's her," Naomi said. "That's the woman I saw."

Colt cleared his throat. "When the house was purchased, the new owner brought out the preacher and hired four women to scrub the place from top to bottom. Belle was one of them."

"It could use that again," Naomi commented, her eyebrows rising in a suggestive stance.

Colt's eyes fell closed for a long moment, and he swayed on his feet. She braced herself against him. "Are you all right?"

"Yeah, fine," he said, but he still looked a little woozy. "I've been getting over a cold."

"It seems like you're just starting," she said.

He glanced at her, his eyes deep and mesmerizing, yet also glazed with pain. His eyelids fell half-closed for one heartbeat, two. He swayed to a symphony only he could hear.

His eyes came fully open as he reached for her and caught empty air. "You're really pretty," he said, his mouth curving into a smile.

While Naomi thought Colt was the embodiment of male perfection, she'd hardly known him long enough for him to blurt such things. She slid her leg away from where she'd been supporting him, realizing too late that she shouldn't.

His knees buckled, and he fell to the floor, his eyes rolling back into his head as he lost consciousness.

"Colt!" Naomi knelt next to him as a blast of cold air filled the cavernous library, like someone had opened a window. She checked over her shoulder, and sure enough, every window along the east wall stood open, the wind and rain pelting the bookshelves.

The wood will get ruined! she thought, aware of how ridiculous that was. It was a house, and Colt was a person. Still, she jumped to her feet and ran across the room, grateful she'd shed her heels. She wrestled with the window for a long minute before aged, warped hands covered hers and pulled the pane into position.

The ghost of Jacob worked with the ghost of Belle as they systematically latched all the windows into place. Naomi stood paralyzed, unsure of what to do next. When Belle finished the last window and turned to her, Naomi sprang into action.

"He fainted," she said, hurrying back to Colt's side. "What should I do?" His face was pale, and his lips had turned an unsettling shade of gray. He hadn't seemed that sick. A cough. A sniffle. A sore throat, maybe. Had he mentioned having a headache? Naomi couldn't remember, and her medical training only extended to putting a Band-Aid on a paper cut.

Warmth radiated from the fireplace, a welcome addition to the library. Naomi glanced up to find Jacob sitting in the same chair she'd seen him in earlier. He wore the same clothes, the same somber expression on his face.

"How can I help Colt?" she asked.

Jacob looked over her shoulder, and when Naomi turned, she found Belle standing there. She walked away, pausing at the door to the library in a silent invitation for Naomi to follow her. Before she did, she grabbed a throw off the back of the unoccupied chair, beat it against the floor to remove as much dust as possible, and gently tucked it around Colt. He hadn't seen Jacob the first time, and she didn't know if he could feel the warmth from the fire or not.

Belle had moved into the kitchen, and she pointed at one of the alder cupboards. Naomi opened it and found jars of all sizes, some with powders in them, some housings pastes, some holding liquids. None of them bore a label.

"Which one?" Naomi searched Belle's expression for answers, but the ghost remained mute. Naomi thought she must be nightmaring. After all, she'd never imagined ghosts when she fantasized about finally stepping foot into the Millhouse mansion. She'd only thought of paint colors, fabric swatches, and preserving the original floors, mantles, windows.

A loud thud behind her sent her heart into overdrive, causing her hand to catch on one of the bottles and send it crashing to the countertop. The earthy-sweet smell of herbs and dirt reached her nose. After the ear-splitting crash faded into silence, Naomi listened but heard nothing but the strumming of her heart.

She didn't know what to do. Had Colt regained consciousness and fallen again? Maybe someone had knocked on the door. Naomi's mind ran wild with possibilities. As she stood trying to make sense of it all, Belle reached down and began tracing her finger through the spilled paste on the counter.

P-E-P-P-E-R-M-I-N-T.

Belle looked at Naomi meaningfully, but one more glance into the cupboard confirmed that Naomi would never find the peppermint. Another sound from the library drew her attention, and she flew back that way, praying she'd find Colt alive.

Colt hit his knee for a second time on the blasted armchair. Why couldn't he lift his leg high enough? Why was the library so stuffy? Who had lit that oppressive fire?

"Naomi?" he called, his voice a mere shell. His heart raced but seemed to be skipping as many beats as it took. He needed a drink of water, badly.

"Colt!" Naomi dropped to her knees in front of him and smoothed his hair off his forehead. It felt like a natural thing for her to do, but the current that buzzed through him suggested that he'd prefer her to be more than a simple nursemaid. "Are you all right?"

He still couldn't quite see clearly. The room seemed to be layered behind a pale green film. As Belle and Jacob crowded behind Naomi, a bolt of anger shot through him.

He hated this house, hated this library. Hated the spirits that wandered his property.

For a few moments upstairs, he'd considered hiring Naomi to renovate the house. Turn it back into the historic charmer it could be. Maybe he'd even move back into the house—maybe with Naomi. His thoughts had scared him, and he'd dismissed them almost as quickly as they'd come. If he did restore the house, he'd donate it to the county as a historic landmark. He could never live here again, even with a beautiful woman by his side.

"I think so," he said, leaning his head against the dirt-encrusted upholstery. He closed his eyes, experiencing Naomi through his other senses. Her tropical scent lingered so close; her fingertips brushed his hair, his jawline, his hand. He opened his fingers, and she settled hers in the empty spaces.

"I don't feel very well." He hated feeling weak and disliked even more that she'd witnessed it.

"I got that part." Her soft voice came so near that he opened his eyes to find her face mere breaths from his. "I don't think you have a cold."

He certainly didn't feel cold with her so close. Something drip, drip, dripped through him, adding strength to his feeble places with every passing moment. "Do you think I'm contagious?"

She shook her head, her eyes dropping to his mouth. He was thinking about kissing her too. It wouldn't be wise, he knew. He barely knew Naomi, though her good reputation had preceded her. Yet he felt drawn to her the same way he'd always been captivated by the gold mine on the hill. He stayed away from the mine, just like he'd abandoned the house. He should keep his distance from Naomi too.

He absolutely shouldn't be leaning in, the anticipation of kissing her overwhelming his good sense. His lips brushed against hers, a mere touch. She sighed, and that simple release sent his desire soaring. He slid his hands along her shoulders, up her neck and into her hair as his mouth found hers and held on.

She melted into his embrace, and he didn't care what was wise and what wasn't, what was contagious and what wasn't, or if she would judge him for seeing ghosts. He simply lived in that moment, unhurried and unaccustomed to feeling something warm for a woman.

Naomi pulled away too soon. He opened his eyes to find her head ducked and her fingers fiddling with a ruffle on her blouse.

"Wow," he said, to get her to look at him.

She smiled, a lovely curving of lips that clearly revealed more than she intended. He saw a flash of appreciation in her eyes before she straightened and went to stand at the windows. He stood, expecting his legs to be unsteady, but was surprised to find them strong. He joined her and watched the sleet slice through the sky.

"Looks like we might have to stay the night," he commented, watching her out of the corner of his eye. She stiffened—the response he'd expected—then slipped her hand into his.

"There are lots of bedrooms, right?" she asked.

"More than anyone would ever need." He squeezed her fingers. "I'm thinking maybe you should restore this place. Make it a landmark historical piece."

Her eyes widened, and she searched his for the hint of a lie. "Are you serious?"

"Deadly."

"You're certainly that." She gave him an impish grin. "Are you feeling all right?" She glanced toward the bookcase, where he'd fallen.

"Much better." Colt couldn't remember the last time he'd fainted, and while he did feel better, stronger, something inside still wasn't right.

Naomi's lips flattened, but she accepted his answer. She pulled out her cell. "I need to call my neighbor if I'm not going to come home. I was supposed to stop by tonight with chicken soup."

"You cook?" His stomach roared at the very idea of food.

"I'll look in your cupboards," she said as she dialed and moved away from him. She left him alone in the library, and Colt couldn't stand it. He followed her out, but instead of going into the kitchen where he could hear her murmurs, he turned and entered his father's study.

His mother hadn't touched this room either. She had a sick way of leaving things the way they'd last been. Colt didn't understand it. She hadn't loved his father, and if it were his choice, Colt would've thrown everything out and filled the room with greenery.

He couldn't help wondering what Naomi would do to a room like this one. Heavy burgundy drapes obscured the view. A large, black desk hulked in the center of the room, with an equally giant chair behind it. The desk held medical papers, a decanter of brandy—his father's favorite liquor—and random office supplies. Bits of newspaper clippings sat pinned together, and the bookshelves behind the desk were littered with town memorabilia, hospital journals, small bottles with colored liquids, and medical textbooks.

Colt found it ironic that his father saved people's lives as a profession, but he'd killed himself with alcohol.

Jacob entered the room and sat down in Colt's father's chair, Jacob's eyes forlorn and focused on Colt. He had never thought to ask them why they were still here, or if there was something he could do to send them to their restful afterlife. But when Naomi had mentioned figuring out what the spirits wanted, Colt had felt warm. He knew he needed to solve something for them.

"What do you want?" he asked Jacob, who continued to stare at him. Finally, as though the words Colt had spoken needed to sink through dozens of layers before they reached Jacob's ears, the ghost rifled through the papers on the desk.

Colt heard soft footsteps running toward him. "Colt!" Naomi burst into the study. "I think you'd better come here."

He grabbed the paper Jacob had indicated but didn't take the time to examine it before joining her in the foyer.

Five

Naomi had confirmed with her neighbor, Edith, that she was okay, that she'd gone out on a job and the weather had prevented her from returning. Edith had agreed to call Naomi's mother that night, and Naomi had gone into the kitchen to see if there was more than bottled medicines in the cupboards.

"Look," she said, pointing at the counter where the poultice had splattered. The stuff still smelled like moss, with a bit of black licorice, and still had the word *peppermint* carved into it. But now, another herbal mixture had been spread across the marble. This one was almost black, viscous like tar, and smelled just as bad.

Someone had swiped their fingers through it in an angry slash that spoke a warning to Naomi.

Colt studied the counter while she explained to him that Belle had brought her out here and indicated that she needed to find peppermint to wake him. "But you woke on your own. And this wasn't here," she said, her voice straying into her upper octave. "What do you think it means?"

He ran his hand through the top of his half-hawk, reminding Naomi of how soft and thick his hair was. "I don't know."

They both glanced around; Naomi expected to see another apparition that would lead them down a yellow brick road to a fantastical land. Nobody was there. A smudge of black caught her attention.

"Colt, look." Her lungs didn't expand properly as she stepped to the wall holding all the photos of Colt's family. A black thumbprint rested beneath a picture of an elderly man. Another beside a picture of a mother and father with two young boys. A third mark completely obscured the face of a third picture—obviously a man from the visible tie and jacket in the photo.

Colt removed the three pictures from the wall. He studied them while a storm rolled across his face. Naomi found this version of Colt terrifying, as well as desirable. She wanted to be the one to calm him, to soothe him back into the Colt who wore a casual smile and radiated a surprising gentleness.

"Who is that?" she asked.

He pinned her with a dark look. "My father."

Colt stared into his father's face, the one of him as a young doctor—Colt's age now. Both he and Rick had already been born. A three-year-old Rick sat on his mother's right knee, a one-year-old Colt on her left. His father towered above them all, just as he had in real life. His mother, Rick, and Colt all smiled at the camera. His father did not, his hand on his wife's shoulder in a possessive grip.

"This is me with my brother and parents." He pointed at his toddler self. "I was cute, right?"

A slow blush entered her face as she took the picture from him. "The cutest," she confirmed. "Where's Rick now?"

"He lives in Denver," Colt said. "Owns a sports bar. His wife's an attorney." He didn't like the big city life, though it had some advantages over living in a town where everyone knew everything about you.

In the next image, his father glared out of the photo, his glasses perfectly positioned on his face. "This was when he graduated from medical school," Colt said. "He married my mother the next day, and they moved into this house. Both Rick and I were born here. Dad had a private practice in town, and he worked the emergency room at the hospital on the weekends."

Naomi took the picture from him, examining it. For what, he didn't know. He gripped the last photo, the one that had been completely marred with the black substance. Any appetite he'd had had been quelled by the foul-smelling poultice. He'd hated those things when his mother tried to use them on him, and the years hadn't improved their stench.

"This one was when he retired. The mayor threw him a party, and Dad insisted he get his picture taken. He bought his own frame and put it on the wall where he wanted. Mother hated it, because his eyes were too glassy. It was too easy for everyone to know he was a drunk." Colt gave a short, barking laugh. "But everyone figured that out when he died from alcohol poisoning only a week later."

He passed the photo to her. "Still, Mother never took it down."

"Why not?"

Colt shrugged. "She was a superstitious woman. Thought he'd know and never leave her alone."

Naomi met his eyes, a new hope shining in hers. "Could she see the—you know, the things we can see?"

"No," he said. "I asked her when I was twelve. She said to stop making things up and go do my chores."

Naomi frowned. "Could she have been lying?"

Colt considered it. He'd never thought of his mother as a liar. She'd been the one to send him away to boarding school. She wrote every week, apologizing for making him leave but insisting it was the only way to keep him safe. Colt hadn't had to wonder who she was protecting him from.

And in truth, Colt had been relieved. He didn't like living in such close quarters with ghosts. Feeding the chickens and mucking out the horse stalls meant he had to work away from the house, and the spirits would often follow him out there.

A crash brought Colt out of his musings. He joined Naomi as they hurried down the hall and into the study. The glass decanter now lay on its side, the copper-colored liquid dripping like blood onto the pine floor.

Drip, drip, drip.

Colt stared at the liquid, the paper Jacob had indicated crumpling as he fisted it.

Drip, drip, drip.

Naomi pressed closer, her shock seeping into him as she wrapped her hands around his forearm. He liked it when she did that—it made him feel like he could protect her. At the same time, she possessed an inner strength all her own. She spoke with ghosts, followed them, and wanted to help them find their rest. In a lot of ways, she'd already helped him by admitting that she could see the same apparitions he could.

"What do the ghosts look like to you?" she asked, her voice shattering the silence. He startled as she moved into the room and reset the bottle. She took some papers from the desk and used them like towels to soak up the brandy.

"They look like people," he said.

"Transparent?"

"No," he said. "Like you or me. In full color."

She frowned, keeping her eyes on the yellow floor that

had been brightened by the spill. "They don't look like that to me."

"They don't?" Something cold and charged moved through him.

"No." She stood and faced him. "They look transparent, warped, yellowed with age." She took a step closer as tears formed in her eyes and her lower lip trembled. He reached out to cup her face in his hand. She pressed her cheek against his palm, a single tear warming his skin.

"They look like you do, Colt."

Colt pressed his forehead to hers, and he felt so real. But he wasn't. She'd first noticed something off about him when he removed his leather jacket. The shirt underneath should've been more corporeal, but she'd been so distracted by his muscles, she hadn't connected the dots. And now, standing with the faint light from the windows in the formal living room coming in behind him, she realized she could see right through him.

Colt Jennings was a ghost. Which meant he was dead.

How can he be dead? she wondered. She hadn't heard anything around town, and as newsworthy as his death would be, everyone would know.

She seized on an idea, pulled away from him, and yanked her phone out of her pocket. She hastily looked for the number of the hospital and dialed while he stood there watching her.

"Information desk, please," she said when the operator answered. She waited through four agonizingly long rings. "This is Naomi Harding. I'm wondering if Colt Jennings is there," she said, raising her eyes to meet his.

That beautiful storm crossed his face before he turned away.

"Oh, hello Miss Harding. It's Olivia."

"Hey, Liv. Can you tell me if Colt has been admitted there?" For the first time ever, Naomi was glad she'd grown up in Silver Hills and knew a lot of its residents.

A pause came through the line. "Yes, Colt was brought in late last night. He's in—oh, he's in the ICU."

The phone slipped from Naomi's grip. "You're in the hospital," she said. As she stared into his starry eyes, an ache blossomed in her chest. Of course she would fall for a guy who was one hundred percent unavailable.

She didn't understand how he could be standing there in front of her. How he could've waltzed into her office and laughed at her dancing. Ridden his motorcycle out to the mansion, or fainted, or done anything he'd been doing. She only knew that he was there, in front of her, squeezing her fingers like he was alive, and well, and interested in her. Leave it to her to always attract the weirdos.

"What am I doing here, then?" he asked.

"Unfinished business?" she suggested.

He glanced at her mouth, quickly lifting his eyes back to hers. He brought a paper between them. "Jacob indicated this."

"Let's have a look," Naomi said, her voice only shaking slightly.

Colt didn't know what to think, or feel, or do. She'd just told him he was in the hospital. He wondered if anyone had called Rick. He wondered how it was possible to feel hungry if he wasn't corporeal. How could he be standing here in the foyer of the mansion, holding her hand? Nothing made sense.

Naomi gently extracted her hand from his and took the paper he was practically strangling. Frustration pooled inside him, a feeling he wasn't used to. He feigned confidence whenever he didn't feel that way. But this—this situation was something foreign.

Her eyes flicked from left to right, right to left, as she read. "It's a journal entry," she said slowly. "Your father's." She glanced over her shoulder in the direction of the kitchen. "Maybe that's why the photos of him were marked." She held out the paper. "You need to read this."

Colt ripped the page from her hand, still wondering how such a thing was even possible. He felt the paper in his hand, smelled the smooth coconut of Naomi's hair, had tasted the sweetness of her lips. He couldn't be one of the apparitions he'd grown up with.

Could he?

He stepped away from Naomi so she wouldn't see him smash something with his bare hands. After climbing to the second floor, he took the long journey through the halls to the back staircase that led to the attic. The air grew colder and damper, but Colt pressed on until he had arrived in the secret alcove he and Rick had used as boys. No butterscotch wrappers remained, but this was a safe place.

He took a deep breath of the humid air, steeling himself to read the letter. He could barely stand to see his father's slanted handwriting. The cursive was shaky and hard to read.

I hope one day my family will find a way to forgive me. I'm not a perfect person, and I've made a lot of mistakes. I want my sons to know that I love them, that I have always protected them. No one knows that I can see the seventeen miners who died over a hundred years ago. They talk to me in my nightmares and follow me around the house when I'm home.

In order to keep them away from my family, I've been trying to locate their remains and give them a proper send-off. I've been able to complete this task for sixteen of the miners. The last, a Jacob Lawson, I have never been able to find what he lacks. I'm leaving this record so my wife and sons will know why I spent so much time locked in my study, why I buried myself in my work, and why I had to drink when I came home at night.

I'm telling them this in the hopes that they can stop hating me, and move on. If possible, I hope one of them will succeed with Jacob where I failed.

Another spirit, Belle Millhouse, has been lingering these past few days. I haven't quite figured out her story yet, but she nursed those with smallpox, and she seems concerned for Jacob. Perhaps once he is gone, she will be able to find rest also.

All my love to my wife and sons,
Augustus Jennings

Colt stared at the words, not quite believing them. He'd never mentioned the spirits to his father. And the man had died before Colt returned from boarding school. Colt hadn't tried to see the miners, and he hadn't noticed that they were almost all gone. He'd stayed with his mother through the last hours of her life, buried her next to his dad in the family cemetery on the hill, and left.

A sharp tug pulled at Colt's heart, and it felt a lot like forgiveness. Or at least understanding. His father had endured the same visions, probably the same fear, the same confusion, about seeing the dead miners.

He folded the letter carefully and tucked it into his

326

pocket. Rick would want to see it. Colt didn't know if it would change how his brother felt about his father, but it had shifted something inside Colt.

A scream echoed from downstairs, followed by the terrifying sound of glass shattering.

In less than a second, Colt was on his feet and sprinting down the narrow steps to the second floor.

His fingers tingled as he ducked his head into the study.

Empty.

Library.

Empty.

Once down the hall, he saw Naomi's bare feet and legs sticking out from behind the kitchen counter. He found her lying in various puddles of greens, browns, and yellows. The poultices and pastes mixed with her blood. Shards of glass lay scattered everywhere.

Colt knelt next to her, feeling nothing as his knees came down on sharp edges. He swiped her hair off her forehead to find a long gash just above her hairline. Her eyes fluttered, open and closed. "Colt . . ."

"Stay with me, sweetheart," he said, the endearment much more genuine this time. His hands came away slick with herbs and blood. "Don't go to sleep, okay? Stay awake."

"She . . . wants the . . . peppermint." Naomi managed to raise one hand, her finger pointed over his shoulder. "I think they . . . need it to . . . find rest."

He turned to find Belle Millhouse standing over him, a bottle raised over her head. She flung it at the ground, where the clear liquid contents splashed his pants as well as Naomi's chest and face. The glass sluiced through him without damage, but Naomi's arms didn't fare so well.

He slowly straightened and held up his hands. "Okay, the peppermint."

Belle gestured angrily toward the cupboard. Colt cast another look at Naomi, whose eyes had closed. He detected the faint rise and fall of her chest as he stepped to the cabinet.

He had no idea what peppermint looked like, and none of the bottles bore labels.

He began by uncapping the first bottle and smelling. *Definitely not peppermint.* He tried another. This yellow liquid smelled like lemons. A third bottle got taken down. This one seemed to have bits of twigs mixed in with what smelled like grass.

Bottle after bottle came out of the cupboard; Colt smelled each one. None of them were remotely close to peppermint. He turned back to Belle. "There's no peppermint here."

That was clearly not the answer she wanted. She dove to the floor and selected a particularly large piece of glass. Before he could fathom what she was doing, she pressed it against Naomi's neck.

Colt held up his hands. "Okay, okay. I'll keep looking."

Belle bared her teeth, and Colt headed to the only other room where he'd seen bottles of liquids. His father's study. He noticed that the scent of tobacco had faded considerably. Or maybe his nose was full of so many smells, he couldn't separate them.

Colt went to the shelves behind the desk, noting that it had started snowing, casting the dusk into a pearly gray. The first decanter he pulled down smelled like alcohol. So did the next. And the next. Each had something floating near the bottom, but none gave him the impression of peppermint.

He picked up the last bottle, a mere speck wafting around in the clear liquid. Maybe a fiber of clothing or a fingernail. A chill coiled through Colt as a line from his father's journal did.

I've been trying to locate their remains and give them a proper send-off.

No sooner had Colt uncapped the stopper than did he inhale a lungful of clearly peppermint air. He held it like it was precious as he went back to the kitchen.

"I found it."

Belle stood, the glass shard dropping from her fingers as she reached for the bottle. Gone was her demonic snarl, vanished were her flat eyes without differentiation from iris to pupil. Jacob appeared beside her, and she handed the bottle to him. He swirled the contents, smelled the liquid, and shrugged.

Colt suddenly understood. These spirits couldn't detect scent. Since he wasn't quite dead yet, he supposed he still could. Just like he could still feel hunger, still taste, still feel.

Even as he thought it, he realized he didn't feel hungry anymore. No emptiness in his stomach, no growling. Nothing.

His condition must be getting worse. Maybe he would die. Would he be destined to wander the mountain at Millhouse mansion like Belle and Jacob?

Jacob stepped up to him, tears glistening in his eyes. He raised the bottle as if saying farewell and faded from sight. Colt felt certain it would be the last time he saw him. He looked around for Belle, but she had already gone too.

He hurried to Naomi's side, relieved when her shallow breathing disturbed a lock of her hair. Still, she wasn't going to survive long in her condition. He slid his hands under her body, noting that he could no longer feel her warmth or the texture of her clothes.

Neither one of them was going to make it.

Still, he had to try. He fished her keys from her purse and strode down the hall to the wide front doors. Snow and wind greeted him on the porch, but he felt neither their sting nor their chill.

He laid Naomi in the backseat of her car, got in the driver's seat, and drove like he'd never driven before.

Seven

Naomi woke in the hospital, the sterile warmth the first thing she noticed. Second was the scent of antiseptic. For a moment, she thought she'd gone to her mother's nursing home. But there were too many beeping machines in this place.

She struggled to open her eyes, squinting into very bright lights. A woman sat in the chair beside her, her knitting needles flying as she hummed to herself.

"Edith," Naomi croaked, her throat cracking. She needed a drink like a fish needed water.

The elderly woman abandoned her knitting and put both hands over Naomi's. "Hello, dear."

"What happened?" Naomi tried to make sense of the cloudy images in her head, but she didn't recognize anything.

"You were injured out at the Millhouse mansion." Edith showered her with grandmotherly love, her hands like weathered paper against Naomi's. "Something didn't feel right, so I contacted the police after you called. I can't believe you went out there alone, dear."

Naomi frowned. "I wasn't alone. I was with . . ." But no name came to mind. Wispy images of a rugged face, a warm mouth, a kind voice. There, then gone. A yellowed coat floated by, then the flat eyes of a woman who wore two long braids in her hair.

Then more pain in her skull than Naomi had borne before. She screamed, distinctly remembering doing that at the Millhouse mansion. The name running through her head was *Colt! Colt! Colt!*

Colt paced outside a patient's room, wondering how long until he could go in. Fine, paced was a strong term, as he was in a wheelchair, one leg broken above the knee, one below. His brother pushed him back and forth, back and forth, at Colt's insistence.

"Who is she?" Rick asked, and Colt wished he could provide an answer. He didn't know Naomi Harding beyond the fact that she restored antiques and decorated homes. He hadn't been in Silver Hills for months, yet this room number had been in his head when he'd awakened in the hospital last night.

He'd been reckless, stupid, on his motorcycle. Three broken fingers, two ribs, and both legs. The helmet had saved his limited brain function and his good looks, as Rick had been joking for two days. Colt was glad someone could. He'd woken after only a day of unconsciousness, a sign the doctor seemed to think indicated Colt would make a full recovery.

But he was going insane. He had a picture of a woman in his head, a room number, and the inexplicable urge to make sure she was okay.

Finally, the door opened, and the nurse exited. "You can go in now. She's awake, but barely. And she's been medicated, so she'll be going to sleep soon."

Colt nodded, already wheeling himself into the room despite his injured fingers.

"I got it," Rick said, a touch of impatience in his voice.

Colt was grateful he was there, but he didn't care if Rick was put out over this impromptu visit. He had to see her, this Naomi Harding.

Even seated in his wheelchair, he was tall enough to see over the railings on the hospital bed. "Hey," he said, surprised at the softness in his voice. The gentleness. The inkling of love.

"Colt." She said his name like he was her savior, her breath of fresh air after a long time underwater.

He brushed her hair away from her forehead to find the gash he knew was there. How he knew was a mystery to him. He just did. The wound had been stitched together, but not covered. He blinked, saw a ghostly woman—*Belle*—with the glass shard pressed against Naomi's throat.

He sucked in a breath when an angry welt on her neck matched what he'd just remembered.

"You're in full color now," she said, her voice little more than a rasp. Her eyes drank him in, glowing with a muted light because of the meds she'd been given.

Memories flooded Colt's mind with her words. Taking her out to the mansion to look at a rocking horse. Finding out she could see ghosts, too. Telling her about his father and brother. Kissing her. Freeing Jacob and hopefully Belle. Saving the woman he was pretty sure he was falling in love with as she bled out in his arms.

"You're really pretty," he said, this time saying it because he felt it, not because he was in intense pain and about to pass out.

Beside him, Rick chuckled. "Smooth line, brother."

"You saved me," she said. "Thank you."

Colt didn't know what she could remember and what she couldn't. He pressed his lips to her temple, wishing he could tell her everything now. But her eyelids drooped, and with Rick so close, now wasn't a good time.

"I think you saved me," he said. And she had. She'd given him a glimpse of what a real life could be. Not the half-life he lived camping next to rivers and streams during the summer and hiding in his prison of a house in the winter. With her, he wouldn't be alone to obsess over why he was crazy, why his dad had hated him, and why his mother never disturbed anything in the mansion.

He lifted Naomi's fingers to his lips and kissed them.

"Do I still get the job?" she asked as she smiled at him.

Colt laughed, the sound fixing him. Healing him more than he ever thought was needed. "Yes, sweetheart. You got the job. I want the whole house restored, from top to bottom."

Her head tilted to the side as her eyes drifted all the way closed. "Can I live there with you?" she whispered.

"I wish you would," he said.

About Elana Johnson

Elana Johnson's work, including *Possession, Surrender, Abandon,* and *Regret,* published by Simon Pulse (Simon & Schuster), is available now everywhere books are sold. Her popular ebook, *From the Query to the Call,* is also available for download, as well as a *Possession* short story, *Resist.*

Her self-published novels include two YA contemporary novels-in-verse, *Elevated* and *Something About Love,* as well as a YA/NA futuristic fantasy series, which includes *Elemental Rush, Elemental Hunger,* and *Elemental Release.* Her next two novels, a YA time travel thriller and an adult contemporary romance, will be released in 2016 from two different publishers. She is represented by Marisa Corvisiero of the Corvisiero Literary Agency.

School teacher by day, Query Ninja by night, you can find her online at her personal blog, Facebook, or Twitter. She also co-founded the Query Tracker blog and WriteOnCon, and contributes to the League of Extraordinary Writers. She lives in Utah with her husband and two children.

Visit Elana online:

Website/blog: ElanaJohnson.blogspot.com
Twitter: @elanaj
Facebook: Author Elana Johnson
Tumblr: ElanaJohnson.tumblr.com
Wattpad: Wattpad.com/user/elanajohnson
League of Extraordinary Writers:
 LeagueWriters.blogspot.com
WriteOnCon: WriteOnCon.com

Dear Timeless Romance Anthology Reader,

Thank you for reading *All Hallows' Eve.* We hoped you loved the romance novellas! Heather B. Moore, Annette Lyon, and Sarah M. Eden have been indie publishing this series since 2012 through the Mirror Press imprint. For each anthology, we carefully select three guest authors. Our goal is to offer a way for our readers to discover new, favorite authors by reading these romance novellas written exclusively for our anthologies . . . all in one great collection.

If you enjoyed this anthology, please consider leaving a review online at Goodreads, Amazon, Barnes & Noble or any other store. Reviews and word-of-mouth is what helps us continue this fun project. For updates and notifications of sales and giveaways, please sign up for our newsletter at: TimelessRomanceAnthologies.blogspot.com

Also, if you're interested in become a regular reviewer of the anthologies and would like access to advance copies, please email Heather Moore: heather@hbmoore.com

Thank you!
The Timeless Romance Authors

Made in the USA
Coppell, TX
02 September 2020

35448681R10193